One moment Patrick had been standing there, his arms relaxed at his sides; the next flung backwards into the pine needles like a rag doll.

No amount of training could have prepared me for what happened next. I supposed I stopped running as I approached Patrick, fearful of what I might see. I fell and there was soil and dead leaves in my mouth, but I still saw the man walk up to Patrick and shoot him again from point blank range.

"Have fun, soldier," he said, and then smoke or darkness swallowed him up.

Also by Margaret Duffy
Published by Fawcett Books:

A MURDER OF CROWS

DEATH OF A RAVEN

Margaret Duffy

FAWCETT CREST • NEW YORK

A Fawcett Crest Book
Published by Ballantine Books
Copyright © 1988 by Margaret Duffy

Library of Congress Catalog Card Number: 88-30168

ISBN 0-449-21741-8

This edition published by arrangement with St. Martin's Press, Inc.

Manufactured in the United States of America

First Ballantine Books Edition: February 1990

With many thanks to Alastair for permission
to quote from
Wizards of the East.

PRELUDE

"Ah, but in such matters it is only the first step that is difficult."
(Madame du Deffand: to Cardinal de Polignac, when the Cardinal told her that St. Denis, after being decapitated, had picked up his head and carried it two leagues.)

Tonight we would be doing it for Siegfried—or so I hoped. My partner in our joint enterprise was still downstairs gloomily reading *Defence Weekly*.

It was not that he lacked enthusiasm for our project, merely the result of a week spent at Army Staff College and on the final morning, today, being required to take part in a three mile march at the double carrying full pack and rifle. On previous occasions special provision had been made for him to prove his undoubted fitness on an exercise bicycle, but this time apparently not. Typically, it seemed that I was the only one angry about it.

Siegfried, the name deliberately chosen for its lighthearted daftness in order to prevent us becoming obsessed, was the baby we had been attempting to bring into existence for nearly six months. Trying in an ordinary casual sort of way, that is; so far there had been no moves to resort to more scientific methods. Patrick has spent far too much of his life inside medical establishments since the Falklands War and I saw no reason why he should further submit himself.

Gossip columnists had enjoyed a week's easy copy when we had remarried. Womens' magazines had cooed over the prospect of Ingrid Langley, romantic novelist, actually falling in love again with the man she had divorced four years previously after ten years together. The gutter press wondered if it was a sympathy move on my part, taking pity on a wounded soldier who had crawled, cold and crippled, to my doorstep. But, Patrick didn't crawl to anyone.

I had come to bed at a little after nine-thirty to rough out a plot for a new novel, *Two for Joy. One for Sorrow* had been published late the previous September. It was now March and I had a new agent to run my writing affairs. Patrick had applied his military acumen to the world of publishing and so far emerged triumphant from all skirmishes. His first success had been to arrange the television dramatisation of an earlier novel, *Barefoot upon Thorns*, and filming was now underway on Dartmoor and in the South Hams of Devon.

I don't usually write in bed. My desk is in the spare bedroom, cool and serene, tucked under the thatch at the eastern end of the cottage. It suits me well. If my working environment is too cosy I tend to doze and daydream.

About Siegfried mostly . . . During our first ten years together Patrick had wanted children desperately, or more particularly a son. But why a man normally so articulate on every other matter had kept his longings to himself still puzzles me. I'm not attaching blame. I'd been equally quiet about my own aversion to starting a family. We simply hadn't discussed it. So the successful novelist had carried on taking the pill without telling him. Our first real bust-up occurred when he found an opened packet in my handbag. From then on our relationship had deteriorated and Patrick spent longer and longer periods away from home, ostensibly with his unit. There had been one last visit, one last blazing row, and I had thrown him out of my cottage—yes, *my* cottage—into the rain.

When it came to his second proposal I had had four years to do some serious thinking. Actually, for perhaps three years and eleven months I barely progressed beyond a kind of vague self-congratulatory haze: I had rid myself of him, there was a widening readership eager for my novels, good reviews, pats on the back from my editor and agent. And during these years I had married Peter, a friend of Patrick's.

Then, just before our first anniversary, Peter was killed.

Strangely, deeply though I mourned Peter, I suddenly saw the appalling way I had treated Patrick. Instead of fond memories of Peter, all I could think of was the night I had thrown Patrick out of my house, screamed obscenities at him, smashed his classical guitar during that last terrible row.

Fate, his stubborn love for me, perhaps even sub-conscious signals of mine asking for his forgiveness, brought him back to me. He was so weak after recent hospital treatment for injuries received in the hills above Port Stanley that he fainted at my feet.

When he proposed to me a few weeks later, I had already decided what my answer would be. I say "proposed" but in truth the first thing he offered me was a job. He wanted me to be his working partner and the job was a very special one, spy hunting for MI5.

I already knew the army thought highly of him. It was one of the reasons he had been in command of a small undercover unit living in sheep pens during the South Atlantic conflict. And secretly, deep down, I too had always yearned to live a soldier's life: mud, sweat, blood, tears and all. Perhaps I was mad. Now that was offered to me, and although Patrick has been invalided out of activities officially regarded as the real rough stuff our life together since has sometimes convinced me that I most certainly was mad to accept.

"Time for Siegfried," I said when the man in my life

appeared round the door in his bathrobe. Not film star looks by any means. No, not pretty, just sexy.

He groaned. "Every morning up at five, tea and a crust. Lectures until noon, soup and a crust. PT and more lectures in the afternoon, tea and two crusts. Lights out at eight."

"With cocoa and a crust?"

"If we were lucky."

"The calendar," I reminded him ruthlessly.

He sank on to the bed. "You'd have thought we were conscripts by the way we were treated."

"You'll feel much better when you've had a shower and shave."

For answer he subsided like a crash-landed hot air balloon and appeared to go to sleep. I nudged him with one foot and then again, harder. He really was asleep, breathing deeply and evenly.

"You're a fine inspiration to a writer," I complained, and then smiled to myself, remembering my as yet unwritten novel, *A Man Called Celeste*. In nearly every way Martin Celeste *was* Patrick, or at least the Patrick who had sailed to the South Atlantic.

I looked at him as he sprawled rather gracefully beside me on the bed. Dressed, there is only one indication of the appalling injuries he had sustained, a slight limp when he is tired. Certainly his gait is somewhat unique, developing over the months as he became stronger into a slightly sinister lope. But not sufficiently outlandish to make it obvious that below the right knee he has an artificial leg.

Martin Celeste too was tall, had grey eyes and was always thin, whatever he ate. His greying black wavy hair usually, like Patrick's, badly needed a trim. But Celeste hadn't fought in the South Atlantic so that was where the similarity ended. Because of his Falklands injuries Patrick looks older than his thirty-nine years. Until he grins and then there is the boy I first fell in love with when we were both at school.

I gathered together the notes I had just made, promising

myself that I would find the first rough draft of *A Man called Celeste* and take another look at it. It would be a very long novel, perhaps the work of many years.

My hesitation was because I knew that *Celeste* would be quite different from all the others I had written: less cosy, more true to life. At this stage in my writing career I might be taking a risk. Perhaps I was drifting into a new style already, I thought, my gaze on a passage of my notes that I realised I had been reading over and over until I knew it by heart. It would have to be censored. My work was not yet associated with passages of quite such explicit love-making. I leaned back, closed my eyes and re-composed the episode in my head, only to finish up with something even more torrid.

"That's porn," I muttered.

"What is?" asked Patrick sleepily.

"I'll show you," I said, and undid his bath robe.

CHAPTER 1

Colonel Richard Daws, veteran of Malaya and Northern Ireland, came into his office, apologised for keeping me waiting, tossed a file into an already opened lower drawer of a filing cabinet and slammed it shut with one foot.

"Filthy morning," he growled, glaring briefly at the rain sluiced windows.

I produced my gift, a *mille-feuille* from Harrods' patisserie, definitely his favourite. It was our little conspiracy, the occasional sneaking of cakes past his secretary. She disapproved, saying that the fresh cream was bad for him. This was probably true but so was being alone in the world, I reasoned, and no longer having a wife to indulge him now and then in his love of cream cakes.

We both enjoyed the ritual that a pastry of such flawless lineage demanded. The Colonel took two cups and saucers, kept wrapped in a clean tea towel, from a drawer of his desk—bone china, Wedgwood Black Astbury, not the usual Poole Pottery for every day—and poured us both coffee from a jug on a hotplate. Whatever the china, his coffee was always superb.

"Are you working?" he asked, deftly and unselfconsciously coping with a cloud of pastry crumbs.

"*Two for Joy*'s on the drawing board," I told him. "And the shooting-script of *Barefoot Upon Thorns* has been sort of referred back to original author. The director isn't happy with it and thinks I ought to have been allowed to write it in the first place. All in all I'm fairly busy.''

"Thomas Fuller," mused Daws. " 'They love dancing well that dance barefoot upon thorns.' Is that right?''

I smiled at him and his blue eyes twinkled back. Really he was far too nice to remain a widower. Every time I met him I put all my single friends' names through my mental computer hoping to find just the right partner for him, and always drew a blank. They simply weren't good enough.

"Did you ask because you have a job for us?" I enquired, knowing that by doing so I would lose the pleasant social Daws in exchange for Daws of the steely stare, upholder of the realm.

"Canada," he replied, wiping his fingers on his handkerchief. "Full team.''

"Tell me about it," I requested, wondering why it wasn't a job for MI6. That is the security service responsible for gathering intelligence overseas, MI5 looks after domestic counter-intelligence. D12 is a small unit under Daws' command that deals with foreign efforts to interfere with MI5's work.

"Hear about the British engineer—Andrew Quade—killed in New Brunswick last week?"

I could hardly believe my ears. Ever since Peter, a Plymouth policeman, was killed by gunmen there has been a series of strange coincidences to remind me of him, almost as if he is haunting me.

"Of course I have," I said. "He was a friend of Peter's, and of Patrick's once. I spent most of last weekend in Launceston trying to comfort his wife."

Daws never wastes time on conventional reactions. And perhaps it was not such a coincidence after all. Because of the nature of his job Peter had known hundreds of people in Plymouth and the surrounding countryside. He and several others, including Andy Quade, had been involved in a joint

Services and Police boys' club project. Now they were both dead.

I said, "A few years ago, when Andy left the Navy, Peter talked him into trying for the police, but he was getting on a bit by then and they weren't too happy about the Chinese laundryman episode."

"What was that about?" Daws asked in off-hand fashion. But his eyes glowed. He loves being given snippets of lurid military gossip.

"A laundryman on the *Caprice* where Andy was serving went berserk with a knife and sliced a young AB to ribbons. Andy shot him without being ordered to."

"And the police turned him down!" The Colonel's eyes almost disappeared as he screwed up his face in amazement.

"The police do mistrust *Boy's Own* heroism," I said. He must be all too aware of police sensitivity to firearms but the attitude of every military man I have ever met is "Go and sort the bastards out" when it comes to real trouble. Their training makes it a natural reaction.

Daws, meanwhile rummaged amongst the paperwork on his normally tidy desk and disinterred a flimsy sheet of paper, its muddy colour identifying it as a Ministry of Defence internal memo.

"As I expect you're already aware from his wife there were no other vehicles involved," he said. "The police in Port Charles think that Quade may have swerved to avoid hitting a deer . . . or that he had been drinking and misjudged the bend. We'll never know of course, the car was burned out."

I tried to quell the remorseless mental images of a man trapped and burning to death. "Rubbish on both counts," I told him. "Knowing Andy I'd put money on him hitting the animal deliberately and then cutting it up for someone's freezer. As for drinking . . . well, he didn't."

"Didn't drink!" Daws exploded.

"Just fruit juice."

"An ex-Fleet Chief who didn't drink!" Clearly, Daws thought I was having him on.

I shook my head. "He caught hepatitis in Hong Kong shortly after he joined the Navy and was very ill. A Surgeon Commander read the Riot Act over him—stay on the wagon and your liver might see you through. What on earth has Andy's death to do with D12?"

He looked at me over the tops of his glasses and I knew that we were about to enter that part of my life governed by the Official Secrets Act. He said, "Quade was employed by DARE—Devonport Admiralty Research Executive. Heard of it?"

"Vaguely," I replied. "Don't they have an office over a building society branch in Royal Parade, Plymouth?"

"The entire premises are theirs—the building society just uses the ground floor."

"So DARE have moved out of Devonport?"

"Not entirely. They keep a drawing office at their old place near the Naval dockyard opposite Albert Gate. All above board—they work on unrestricted stuff there in case anyone's nosey."

"Let me get this straight," I said. "Andy was working on something sensitive and there are suspicious circumstances surrounding his death."

"You've just confirmed that there are," Daws said, a rare smile twitching the corners of his moustache. "All right—no secrets. Christopher Fraser, the managing director of DARE, received what he regarded as a crank letter just before the team of which Quade was a member went out to Canada to work on a design contract. He took it to the police when he heard about Quade and it was given to me."

"Question," I said. "Don't people usually destroy crank letters on receipt?"

Daws sighed.

"I'm sorry," I said.

"You misunderstand," he assured me, fixing me with the

famous steely gaze. "The thought came into my own mind
the moment you began to speak. A writer's intellect can be
very stimulating."

Patrick insists that when I am very, very pleased my reaction is the same as that of my cat Pirate and I sit with eyes
half closed, silently purring. Pleasure notwithstanding this
was a bouquet indeed from the Colonel, a man slow both to
damn and praise. Much more importantly, it was one of the
first indications he had given me as to my personal usefulness
other than merely being Patrick's wife and occasional cover.

"The letter's down in analysis now," Daws was saying.
"Nothing much to go on—the usual blackmail kind of thing—
words cut from newspapers and magazines and pasted onto
a sheet of A4 typing paper. If I remember correctly it ran:
'Withdraw from the project now and everyone will stay alive.'
Pretty childish really. A skull and crossbones had been drawn
at the bottom."

"Surely he couldn't renege on the contract?"

"Of course not. Besides, DARE needs this kind of pres-
tige business. It's precisely what Fraser's been working towards for years, a toe-hold in the international field."

"I suppose he might have thought the letter was from a
disappointed rival."

"It's possible," Daws conceded.

"Is all this to do with the Canadian Frigate programme?"
I asked, adding when he looked surprised, "I do read all
those defence publications that Patrick brings home."

The Colonel poured out more coffee for us both. "DARE
are designing the controls system. It's a bit hush-hush in
more ways than one—all supposed to be the product solely
of Canada, but they haven't built a warship for over twenty
years and now haven't the technology."

"Political dynamite?"

He frowned. "Not in a way I would have thought likely
to result in death threats. And the frigates are needed—badly.
Everyone over there, and that includes members of the gen-

eral public, are fed up with their Armed Forces being regarded as something of a joke. I should imagine that if there's
political dynamite it's on this side of the Atlantic. DARE are
doing a lot of work for Trident.''

Curiouser and curiouser. I said, ''So you want me to go
out there and collect material for a novel while Patrick and
Terry lurk in the undergrowth?''

''You remember when you went to stay the weekend with
Lady Ann, ostensibly as my sister-in-law, because she
thought one of the staff was watching every move she and
her husband made?''

How could I forget? Lady Ann's husband was quite a senior man in MI5 and thought his dear lady was imagining
things in her old age. Treasured memories of those few days
included Patrick, helped by Terry, the third member of our
team, trying to look professional while disguised as a fencing
contractor, and taking nearly the whole of the Saturday to
put in three posts. And then, looking very much unlike a
fencing contractor, somehow being outside the drawing room
door through which the miscreant, who proved to be no more
than a common or garden jewel thief, was just about to bolt.

''Like that,'' Daws said. ''I've been asked to provide some
operatives to help protect the team. I thought a man and a
woman arriving together would look more normal. The Major mustn't use his real name though because you're sufficiently famous for it also to be known who your husband is.
People might put two and two together.''

I meekly agreed, thinking about a certain fencing contractor climbing through my bedroom window, then forced
myself to concentrate on what Daws was saying.

''It's being arranged. Very easily as it happens. The company actually building the controls system, Nasonworth
Electronics of Montreal, has an Englishman, David Hartland, as one of its directors. Hartland has a weekend home
in Port Charles and has made it available to the DARE people
since Quade's death so they can all be together under one

roof and kept under the eye of the Royal Canadian Mounted Police. Everyone's taking the threat very seriously now.''

Daws leaned forward and spoke more quietly. ''It's entirely my idea that you're going. I have my reasons for you there. Above all remember that David Hartland does not know that you're involved in the security services. He's been told that you know there's some kind of trouble—no more. He won't question that and you've nothing to fear from him. In a way he's our man in Montreal.''

I opened my mouth to speak but he forestalled me.

''On the surface it might look as though this is MI6's problem but I've stuck my neck out because I've a feeling that it might be more important to some people to smash DARE than to slow down the Canadian Frigate Programme.''

''What cover will we be using?''

''A replacement for Quade must be sent.''

''A consulting engineer only skin deep?''

Daws realised that he was still holding the memo and placed it back on his desk with a deliberateness that reminded me of someone laying a wreath. ''The Major's not too happy about it.''

I got the impression that Patrick had said no but somehow without actually defying orders.

''I see his point,'' Daws continued slowly. ''He knows absolutely nothing about electrical engineering and even if the DARE people help him out he will still have to attend meetings with the shipbuilders and Nasonworth.''

''Terry has an HND in something to do with electronics.''

''No,'' Daws said without hesitation. ''That won't do at all. I want the Major himself within the household so he can keep a close watch on internal security. From what Hartland tells me his entire grounds are crawling with RCMP personnel so it would be a good idea for Meadows to live rough nearby and do his own surveillance. It'll keep a check on their standards too.''

The old school, I sighed inwardly. Absolutely out of the

question to have an officer with snow inside his collar while his underling basked in the warmth indoors.

After another short silence Daws cleared his throat and said, "Seen him lately?"

I came out of my reverie with a jolt that left a nasty resonance, a bit like the aftermath of hearing a horse kick a piano. "You mean you don't know where he is?"

"Er—no."

I forced myself to think clearly. "I last saw Patrick the weekend he came back from his yearly assessment. Friday the 14th of last month."

The Colonel's gaze went to his calendar on the wall but I already knew the date, the 23rd of April, a Wednesday.

"And he hasn't contacted you at all since then?"

"He went back to work on the Monday," I told him. "That would be the 17th."

"Oh, I know about that," Daws said before I could continue. "He spent two weeks doing what everyone assumes he gets paid for—organising the PM's security on all visits outside London." Uncharacteristically, Daws chuckled. The *mille-feuille* seemed to have worked wonders. "Prevented a student from throwing an egg in Coventry and then managed to catch the PM when she tripped at Heathrow three days later."

I had already guessed what Patrick had been up to for at least part of the time. By now I was used to him being forbidden to contact me whilst thus engaged on his official duties and had to content myself with an occasional glimpse of him on the television news. Always not far from the lady's elbow he often could not avoid being in camera shot, to everyone but his family yet another ceaselessly watchful security man.

I said, "He phoned me the day Andy was killed, last Wednesday, and asked me to contact Andy's wife. I tried to but she was staying with her mother. I only managed to get hold of her on Friday morning and spent Saturday afternoon and Sunday with her. I assumed Patrick was doing something for you.''

A beautiful long case clock in one corner of the room ticked off a few more seconds into eternity.

Daws turned his attention to the computer terminal at his elbow. ''I gave him and Meadows their orders late on the Wednesday you say he phoned you.'' He spent the next minute or so punching buttons on the keyboard and reading the information that appeared on the screen.

It didn't need an ability to read sideways for me to come to the conclusion that the computer didn't know where he was either.

''So you've heard nothing from him since last week?''

''No.''

''Did you make any comment about his assessment?''

''Too tired,'' I replied. Then in response to the knife edge stare, added, ''They made him do the route march with full pack. It was a new medic, I understand.''

''Majors don't necessarily have to obey medics,'' Daws grated.

''He wouldn't make a fuss—not in front of the others. Anyway, I got the impression he did it to find out if he could.''

At this Daws relaxed slightly. Damn you, I thought, so long as any blame can't be laid at the Army's door you're not too concerned.

''If anything,'' Daws mused, using the keyboard to recall some information, ''he was found to be more fit than on the previous assessment a year ago. Would you say he was worried about it?''

People who perform fifty press-ups before breakfast every day *are* generally worried about their fitness. ''Not really,'' I lied. ''But we do seem to be skating around defining whether we're talking about physical or mental fitness here.''

Eyes narrowed, Daws said, ''I'd be very interested to hear any comments you have to make about either category.''

''Fitness isn't just to do with recovering mobility after

being blown up,'' I said. ''It's learning to live with the thought that you're never going to be quite the same again, and accepting it. Before he was injured Patrick had a very high opinion of himself. Recovering his self-confidence to a reasonable degree has been the real achievement.''

No, I wasn't selling my husband down the river. This was my very own spy probe into the normally impenetrable Whitehall. I wasn't about to mention Patrick's recurring nightmare of being fired, huge crowds shouting ''Cripple!'' at him.

''I can't give you the results of the psychological tests,'' Daws said, realising what I wanted.

''I'm not asking you to,'' I replied. ''But if he's never given so much as a hint of how he's regarded—''

''Can you contact him?'' Daws interrupted.

This was a leading question. To admit that there was a phone number or address the existence of which MI5 was kept in ignorance was tantamount to treason.

We stared at each other stonily and I won.

'' 'Flippant','' the Colonel said with a grimace. '' 'Flippant, sarcastic, has sometimes quite the wrong attitude for a man of his rank, and as far as an enemy is concerned is utterly lethal with both brain and hands.' Will that do?''

For some reason tears pricked at my eyelids. ''I'll ask around,'' I promised.

I spent the rest of the day at the secret London address, a building that from the outside purported to be no more than the rather shabby offices of an export company, and then caught a late afternoon train back to Devon. During a snatched lunch I had rung Terry Meadows' number but there had been no answer.

I was sure that behind the urbane exterior Daws had been seething. He can tolerate his staff being flippant, sarcastic and even faintly murderous during a full moon, but for them to wriggle out of the system altogether was inconceivable, unmentionable and, to use his own words, wouldn't do at all.

CHAPTER 2

It was snowing hard at Halifax, Nova Scotia. As the de Havilland DASH 7 thrashed up though the murky sky, chunks of ice were hurled from the propellers and clanged into the sides of the fuselage. Only those inured to such seemingly pioneering flying ignored the noise, ostentatiously dozing or stagily thumbing through the handout magazines. Together with the nervous old ladies, I jumped at every bang.

I had found it convenient to fly from Prestwick. A visit to an old friend who lives at Bridge of Weir, Renfrewshire, had been planned for some time and as Daws has always impressed on me that one of my chief assets to him is my independent way of life, my invisibility as he calls it, which means that he doesn't have to find excuses for me to be in various places, it seemed a good idea to keep my appointment then fly on from there.

The flight from Halifax to Port Charles was short, only taking forty-five minutes, and when we landed snow had reluctantly given way to driving rain. But my spirits were well and truly raised by now, partly due to a last minute phone call from the Colonel. The missing link had reported in, he had said cryptically. Don't forget to bring me back a lobster. The eastern shores of Canada are rich in all kinds of sea food.

It was raining too hard to see if I recognised any of the people peering through the windows of the arrival lounge. I declined one of the umbrellas being handed out by a stewardess and ran across the tarmac, collecting a few odd looks from the other passengers.

Inside, a few minutes later, disappointed to see no welcoming party, I was hefting my case from the carousel when I noticed a woman, well dressed and pretty in a fragile way, come through the main entrance and gaze searchingly at the new arrivals. Our eyes met.

"Miss Langley?"

I told her I was.

"I'm Emma Hartland." Rather awkwardly she held out a hand.

I said, "I'm never sure whether women shake hands either," and we did, laughing, the ice broken.

"David's in Montreal," Emma said on the way to the car, having apologised that they no longer had a chauffeur to carry my case.

"Will he come home on Friday?"

"Thursday probably. If he can. He's quite worried about these DARE people."

"It's very kind of you to make your house available like this."

She unlocked the car, a gleaming monster in silvery grey of a breed as yet unknown to me. "David believes in flying the flag," she replied.

Flying the flag seemed to be a general custom in Canada, I discovered as we travelled west. Each and every building, including petrol stations, seemed to have a flag pole with the familiar scarlet maple leaf on a white background whipping in the stiff sea breeze. There were quite a few Union Jacks as well but of course New Brunswick is part of Loyalist Canada where refugees patriotic to the Crown fled after the American War of Independence. They were rewarded with vast tracts of land by George III.

The unique environment hit you right between the eyes. The good, the bad, the beautiful. Countless trees, a thousand lakes—so many that I knew most did not have names—a hideous scar in the landscape with an oil refinery steaming and festering in its centre, a pulp mill pouring filth into a river, and cormorants diving for fish in the stinking yellow water. Over all of this a serene sunset, the sky a delicate pink fading to turquoise.

I dragged my gaze away from notices proclaiming Beverage Rooms, Fried Clams and Super Mufflers, realising that Emma was speaking to me.

She smiled at my apology. "Your friend Robin has taken the day off to be at home when you arrive."

"How good of him," I murmured. Robin! Ye gods, was that what he was calling himself?

"Although, strictly speaking," Emma went on, "he wouldn't have gone in today. They told him at the hospital to take things easy this week."

I actually felt the blood drain from my face.

"You didn't know?"

I shook my head speechlessly.

"Nothing serious," she continued, concentrating on a road junction. "He had a touch of fever last week—something to do with an old injury. David thought it best that he receive proper attention so he was packed off to hospital for a few days."

A week! Patrick had been in Canada a week! I pulled myself together and thanked her, realising how much this would have cost with no NHS, and she smiled again.

"He really was quite poorly. David's such a big softie—he can't bear people feeling ill." Then on the next breath she added, "I really wasn't sure whether I ought to call you Mrs. Gillard—David said you were married to an army officer by the name of Patrick Gillard, and he was very highly thought of."

I took my time over answering. "It's a question of security. Langley was my maiden name and the book world refers to me as that so perhaps it's easier to stick to that when you introduce me to others. My mother was convinced when she called me Ingrid that it was a name that couldn't be shortened. Time has proved her right.''

"I loathe pet names," said Emma. "No one ever calls my husband anything but David in my presence. Dave and Davy sound so trivial and commonplace.''

I turned to look out of the window in case she saw and misunderstood my smile. No one, to my knowledge, has ever attempted to call Patrick Paddy in my presence.

The largest built-up area in Canada, Port Charles lay like pieces of a torn up patchwork quilt over the low hills that overlooked the Bay of Fundy. The colour came from the houses, nearly all clad in wood and painted in bright but tasteful shades of blue, pink, yellow and green. There was none of the stone and brick monotony found in Britain, and every house seemed to be different from its neighbour and be situated in an acre or two of land with native trees, cedar and spruce, left to grow undisturbed to provide privacy. Thus the effect, despite the oil refinery and pulp mill, was quite pleasant.

We crossed the city centre, in the fading light a confusion of shopping malls, hotels and office blocks, and four miles further on drove into a suburb Emma informed me was called Moss Vale. Even inside the car I could sense the opulent hush pervading the tree-lined streets.

The Hartland's Maritime home, Ravenscliff, was set high on a hillside facing the sea. Set into the hillside would be a more accurate description. As we approached and entered the driveway, I could see that sheer cliffs of reddish coloured stone formed a backdrop to the garden, magnificent pines growing at their foot.

As we covered the half mile or so of driveway Emma explained that the house was usually only occupied by herself and her husband during the weekends in the spring and summer. They used their flat in Montreal, only a short distance from his office, during the week and spent most holidays either on their cruiser moored on the Saint John river or flew home where they had a cottage in Norfolk. Their son, Mark, studied architecture in Toronto and lived at his flat during term time. During the vacations he usually stayed with friends and they didn't see much of him.

"I never know when he's coming home," Emma finished by saying. "I'm not sure whether he likes to surprise us or simply can't be bothered to pick up the phone."

The garden was quite superb. As we swept up to the front of the house I beheld seemingly acres of velvety lawns, neatly raked gravel paths and banks of different shrubs, some still encased in their winter protective covering of sacking and plastic. Scarlet tulips blazed from flowerbeds. And, built on to a wall, a heated greenhouse, surely the ultimate luxury in this part of the world.

The house itself was a surprise. I had expected Ravenscliff to be built of brick and stone but it was the usual wooden construction, painted white. On the western side of the building was a verandah, or deck as I already knew Canadians called them, complete with a red cedar swinging garden seat and barbecue. To the east of the house, but not connected to it was a row of garages and a stable block.

Robin, I reminded myself as we went indoors. Robin, Robin, Robin.

Nevertheless, when we came upon Robin warming himself in front of an ornate woodburning stove in the open plan living room, I was struck dumb, only vaguely aware of Emma excusing herself saying she would ask the cook to make tea.

There was no doubt about it, Robin looked decidely wan.

"You've lost weight," I said when, just good friends, he kissed my cheek.

He grinned. "The eagle-eyed writer." Then he motioned me to silence with a finger to his lips, took his wallet from the inside pocket of his jacket, found a scrap of paper and wrote with the pen he found on an antique writing desk in one corner of the room.

Mystified, I took the message from him. Every room, every nook and cranny, every tree in the garden, he had written, even the greenhouse and stables, were bugged. We would have to remain just good friends publicly and also in private.

It was shattering. I threw the note into the woodburner while the news sunk in. It would mean that unless the pair of us went right off the property nothing could be discussed, no councils of war held, no hint could be given that I knew Robin very well indeed. I couldn't even ask him if he knew the reason for the microphones as we weren't supposed to know of their existence, or for that matter about any theories he might have concerning Hartland's apparent paranoia.

For a moment disappointment and anger almost took hold of me. Instead of a few weeks cover job spent in socialising and unhurried preparation of *Two for Joy*, I was now landed with twenty-four-hour days of concentration when one slip of the tongue might ruin everything.

Robin was smiling at me, obviously aware of everything that was going on inside my head.

"Are you obeying orders and taking the rest of the week off?" I enquired.

"No. There's no need. I'm fine now."

My resentment and anger began to turn into panic. Robin and I were part of a team and the teamwork depended heavily on close communication. How, if any real communication was barred, were we going to do the job? And first and foremost I am a writer by profession. My training for Department 12, mostly of the self-defence variety, had not turned me into a super-spy.

Robin, damn him, was smiling at me again. "Headache?" he asked.

I sank into a chair. "It was a very early start," I replied, taking the cue. "The Gas Board started digging up the road outside at four am."

Robin sat down too. "Great here, isn't it?" he said.

"Bright as ninepence houses surrounded by a muddle of pick-ups and Skiddoos . . . all mixed up with garden gnomes, plastic Snow Whites and hand-painted statues of the Virgin Mary."

"Fibre glass garden wells," I added. "And wooden butterflies on the outside walls like those flights of plaster ducks you used to see at home. What on earth are super mufflers?"

"Silencers," he told me. "Cars, exhaust pipes for the use of."

We were both laughing when Emma returned. She asked Robin to put some more wood on the stove and the conversation turned to general matters until the tea arrived. Then, when a tray had been set before her on a low table by a middle-aged woman who was introduced to us as Dot, short for Doris, Emma commenced gently to question me.

"This Colonel . . . Daws, is it? He's not really MI6 at all, is he?"

"Search me," I said. "As far as I'm concerned he's just a rather charming army officer who asked me if I fancied working on my novel in Canada to keep a few British engineers company."

"Surely he didn't just phone you up out of the blue."

"No, I met him at a Mess dinner."

"Daws only surfaces at occasions like Mess dinners," Robin said. "The rest of the time he can be run to earth pruning his roses and writing irate letters to *The Times*."

But Emma seemed to think there had been a breach of security. "Didn't you find it a rather strange request?"

I sipped my tea, taking my time. "No, why should I? Patrick probably mentioned to him that I was looking for a bolt hole."

She gave me a cool look, then an enigmatic smile. "I'd forgotten about the Major for a moment. David told me that he packed a lot of hardware and could be found close to the Prime Minister when she was being shown around sewage farms."

I filed away this small insight into David Hartland, raising my eyebrows at Robin and making sure that she saw me. "And other such establishments," I murmured. "He does love places where he can take his green wellies." I buried my nose in my cup, hearing Robin's soft chuckle. The green wellies were an in-joke between us.

"I'll carry on riding shotgun tomorrow," Robin said to Emma.

"Only if you're sure you're fit," she replied. Then, turning to me she said, "The DARE team have all been travelling to work together under police escort while Robin was ill. As you can imagine this tends to draw attention to them even more."

As she was speaking cars were scrunching to a standstill on the gravelled drive outside the window, one a taxi, the other a vehicle I knew to be a Plymouth Caravelle, a large American saloon car seating six. Down the drive, a police car tooted a horn in farewell and reversed out of sight.

"It's David!" exclaimed Emma. "Oh, God—and his assistants." With that she fled from the room, presumably to warn Dot about extra mouths to feed.

Robin drew me to the window. "That's Hartland," he told me, indicating the man paying off the taxi "The guy driving the Plymouth is Drew McAlister—he's the senior consultant heading the DARE bunch out here. The woman's Margaret Howard, his personal assistant. The tall untidy-looking bloke is Paul Rogers, he's the same rank as Quade was. The other two standing together like Tweedledum and Tweedledee are Nelson Redding and Earl Lawrence. As Emma said, they're Hartland's boys from Nasonworth."

"Redding is the senior man," I guessed.

"That's right—he's project leader."

"Do any of them know who you really are?" I knew that the question was quite safe, Hartland had been informed that I was aware there was a security situation.

"They know I'm a minder but not my real name. Not even

Hartland knows that. It was his own request so he doesn't have to worry about having a lapse of memory and ruining everything.''

''How does it feel to be a Robin?''

''Haven't you seen a North American robin?''

I reminded him that I had only arrived an hour previously.

''Well, they're big, bolshie and aggressive.''

''Just like you,'' I sighed despairingly.

CHAPTER 3

A few minutes later I came to the conclusion that this was a description that could equally apply to David Hartland. He was certainly big, both tall and broad-shouldered, a man who would dominate both at work and in his own home. Entering his domain he was full of bonhomie, the perfect host, seeking me out as he came through the door while explaining to his wife that he had brought work to last him the week home to Port Charles as the threats to those now under his care worried him and he wanted to be on the spot. I noticed that neither Redding nor Lawrence appeared entranced at the prospect of him breathing down their necks for four days.

Wincing, I retrieved my hand from Hartland's grasp and wondered why he had not phoned to let Emma know he was bringing extra people home for dinner. Perhaps, like his son, he enjoyed surprising her.

"Good flight?"

I made a suitable reply and then he took me by the arm and introduced me to the rest of the company, beginning with McAlister. Drew was warmly polite but obviously under stress, his assistant merely polite, pricing my clothes. Redding and Lawrence were still sulking. The untidy and youthful Paul Rogers proved to be the most interesting, shy and impatient to tell me about a book he was writing, the authentic author's gleam in his eyes promising well.

Just then Emma took me upstairs to show me my room or

rather boudoir, the only word that could justly describe a creation of palest pink filmy draped nets and, encircled by Chinese rugs, a vast four poster waterbed. But it seemed unlikely, due to the listening devices, that I would be making waves on it with my working partner. Still, Patrick *is* prone to seasickness.

"Lovely flowers," I commented upon noticing an arrangement of cream carnations.

"Home grown," Emma said. "They were old Bill's pride and joy."

"Your gardener?" I enquired, picturing a sudden demise and schooling my expression accordingly.

Emma pulled a face. "Retired to his daughter's home in Vancouver. It was all rather sudden, and as far as I'm concerned his successor can go right back where he found him."

I showered and changed, selecting after some hesitation a Laura Ashley pink and black cotton skirt with black blouse and matching padded waistcoat, an outfit on a similar level of formality as the one Emma was wearing and assuming, wrongly as it happened, that the men would remain in their dark suits. When I went downstairs everyone, Emma included, was sporting denim in various shades.

Robin, now openly armed but with a tin of Moosehead beer in one hand, said, "It's nearly midnight by your body clock."

"Just watch out I don't turn into a pumpkin," I retorted, and then smiled in superior fashion when he slopped his beer from laughing.

Paul's book, I discovered when I spoke to him, was not a treatise on marine controls systems, a discipline upon which he was an expert, but a who-dunn-it set on a passenger liner, with a body in every locker. I braced myself for him to ask me to have a quiet word in the ear of my publisher but the request did not materialise.

"I'm not expecting miracles," he concluded with a shy smile. "Writing's really relaxation for me. It's also taught me to look at people and places in an entirely different way. I find myself filing away people's mannerisms to use at a later date.''

"Sometimes they recognise themselves if you're not careful,'' I remarked dryly, recollecting losing a few friends when my first novel was published. ''You have to mix them up a bit.''

"Really strong characters have to be used just as they are though, don't they?'' he demurred. ''I made Andy the detective in my story, but I hardly feel that I can carry on using him now.''

"You must,'' I said. ''He'd have wanted you to. People like Andy deserve to live on in other ways besides their friends' memories.'' Then I added, ''Tell me about him.''

Paul understood that I was unable to mention the word death. He shrugged sadly. ''What is there to tell? We said cheerio to him at work because he was going out to Quispamsis for the evening and an hour later he was dead.''

"D'you think . . . ?'' I began.

"No one knows,'' he said gently. ''I don't think that he was the sort of guy to drive stupidly and lose control of a car. But you have to remember that we hadn't been out here long, and it was a strange car, and driving on the other side of the road . . .'' Paul shrugged again.

At this moment Robin presented himself and offered to escort me into dinner.

"I'm sure they don't go in for all that formal codswallop out here,'' I told him but the fool stood there fluttering his eyelashes, an arm crooked for me to take.

"Talking of interesting characters . . .'' Paul said musingly to no one in particular. ''Have you met Freddie, the new gardener?''

"Sort of,'' said Robin.

"How can you sort of meet someone?'' I asked scathingly.

"You can with this bloke. He came at me a bit on the fast

side with a pair of sheers and then laughed like hell when I decided to go in the opposite direction.''

''Unique sense of humour,'' I agreed. ''Emma said she couldn't wait to get rid of him.''

Paul said, ''Bill told me that he came from a hostel for destitute men.''

''Poor chap.''

''And is rather strange.''

''Sounds as if he has every right to be.''

''Don't go too close to him,'' Robin warned. Then, in response to my glare, continued. ''He chews whole cloves of garlic like peanuts and avidly reads filthy magazines. I'm not sure which represents the more serious threat to you.''

From the way his eyes glittered, I knew I was being well and truly teased.

After dinner, a delicious meal that reflected none of the headlong panic I was convinced had arisen in the kitchen after the sudden influx of extra people, I sat talking for a long time to Drew McAlister. Drew was as much a Scot as his name suggested, as was his assistant, Margaret Howard. I forced myself to keep an open mind concerning their exact relationship for in truth they were a very attractive couple; he in his late forties, grey-haired and slim, and she a real red head, the sort that must have caused battle royal in the glens as men fought for possession of her ancestors. My caution paid off for later in the evening Drew mentioned with the smile of a man in love that his wife would soon be joining him for a short holiday.

According to McAlister, Paul was the real brains behind the project. He himself was only present to make sure that the young man got up in the mornings and didn't write too much of his beloved novel during working hours. I asked him, all innocence, if the Royal Navy also enjoyed the benefits of DARE's control system but he merely smiled and changed the subject. In other words, don't ask that kind of question. I could hardly tell him that I had signed the Official Secrets Act.

I went back to talk to Paul who was on his own having failed to draw the Nasonworth trio—Hartland, and his two assistants—away from their obsession with anti-icing supply reduction valves. Chatting to him I couldn't help but wonder why Emma had apparently deserted the gathering, and also why her husband seemed totally to have ignored her since his explanatory statement upon entering the house. And, glancing at him surreptitiously now and again, it seemed to me that he had quite the wrong kind of aura for a man who had been described as a big softie.

Robin joined us shortly afterwards, bringing me a cup of coffee, having complied with Hartland's request to provide everyone with the drink of their choice.

"He hauled me over the coals about the non-appearance of the second minder," he said, obviously, and cleverly I thought, working on the precept that we ought to say some of the things our host would expect of us otherwise he would begin to be suspicious.

"I thought the idea was that he would live rough," I said.

"That's what I told Hartland but he seems to think that the Mounties would have detected him by now. He thinks Daws has sold him short."

"Perhaps Freddie's a Mountie," I suggested and for the second time in one evening was the cause of spilled beer, by Paul this time.

"Blasphemy," Robin hissed with a worried look at the two Canadians, thus making Paul laugh even louder. "No, Mounties are only allowed to disguise themselves as trees and moose and things like that. Not as more than slightly disgusting gardeners. Dot reckons he stole a pair of her knickers off the washing line."

"Woolly ones," said Paul succinctly. "I'm not surprised—there's not much in the way of heating in his room.

You can sometimes see him in the greenhouse after dark. I reckon he goes in there to get warm.''

"Are you having me on?'' I demanded to know.

"Scout's honour,'' Paul insisted.

"Do they feed him?''

"Well, Dot doesn't—not after he stole her knickers.''

I thought of the lobster we had eaten for dinner, and the *filet de boeuf en croûte* that had been left over, and then of the conservatory on the south side of the house filled with a stupendous collection of cymbidium orchids positively glowing with health in eighty-five degrees Fahrenheit.

"He's OK,'' said Robin, knowing all about my agonising over lost kittens and worms drowning in puddles.

"I know you better than you think,'' I said, not caring if Hartland heard me now, never mind played his tapes back before he went to bed. "*And* when you're lying through your teeth.''

Robin looked startled. "That imagination of yours.''

"What's imagination to do with it?'' I stormed. "You both think it's funny don't you? Someone who's not quite all there sitting in the greenhouse trying to keep warm and going hungry.''

"Honestly—'' Robin started to say but I cut him dead.

"No one's going to starve while I'm around.''

I stood up and everyone looked at me. "Goodnight,'' I said brightly.

"Goodnight,'' they all chorused and went on with their conversations.

A small pang of alarm made me hesitate. "Is it safe?''

"It?''

"*He*, then,'' I said heavily. Why are men so damned difficult sometimes?

"Perfectly.''

"Surely . . .'' Paul began.

"Perfectly safe,'' Robin assured him. "That's if she

doesn't get frostbite—it's colder out there than she'd ever imagine.''

I heard this remark as I left the room. And also his soft laugh.

He was right of course. Even though the first of May was only three days hence I could see that the whole garden was sparkling with frost when I peeped around the curtains of a window in the hall.

I went out through the kitchen door, purloining the cold remains of the beef and some cheese on the way but forgetting a coat. By the time I had gone ten yards my teeth were chattering.

From the hall window I had seen that the greenhouse lights were switched on but they were not bright enough to guide me across the garden. I had to rely on an almost full moon for that and only had one bad moment when I tripped over a rock lying in the middle of the path, stubbing my toe. It seemed a strange time of the year to rebuild a rockery.

It was paralysingly cold.

I couldn't see anyone in the greenhouse but snicked up the latch of the door and slid it open, desperately in need of heat myself by now. A wonderful scent of warm, damp earth and growing things wafted into my nostrils and I took several deep appreciative breaths. There were ferns and yet more orchids, gloxinias in pots, Bill's carnations growing in the borders and rows and rows of baby polyanthus in pots on the slatted wooden staging.

I sniffed the air again, detecting a hint of garlic. Then I saw the source of it, sitting on the staging looking at me through a fern, knees under his chin, grinning like an oversized goblin. It was enough to make anyone's hair stand on end and, such was the shock, I think mine did.

''Sugar for the horse, sugar for the horse,'' cackled Freddie.

I dumped down the food and bolted. No, Freddie wasn't safe. One hand had moved in the most lewd gesture I had ever seen.

CHAPTER 4

On the Wednesday of that week, after Robin had convinced me that driving on the right side of the road and staying alive could be achieved by the majority of British drivers, I hired a car. Or rather I rented one, as the man in the garage described the transaction. With difficulty I persuaded him that the vehicle I required did not necessarily have to be large enough to play a game of baseball in, and emerged cautiously from the forecourt with a product of the land of the rising sun.

Emma had offered to lend me the family pick-up that was used to take gear to their boat but I declined without offending her. Never borrow cars, Daws always stressed. Now, with Andy's death still haunting me I was going to do as I was told.

I made myself go to Quispamsis. Right away, not giving the coward within time to make excuses for not doing so. Until I had shared a little in Andy's last moments, seen the road as he himself had seen it seconds before he died, stood at the spot where it had happened, he would remain only a shadowy figure in my memory, merely a man with whom Peter had worked to help found a boys' club.

Not for one moment had I imagined that the site of the accident would be easy to find, cherishing the thought, the nearer I got to Quispamsis, that looking for it was entirely my own idea so no one would blame me if I failed after a short search and my nerve deserted me. Then, quite suddenly, I came upon it.

The blazing car had started a small fire—small by Canadian standards, that is—a narrow band of forest destroyed some fifty yards long. The point of impact had been a large spruce, now dying from a shattered trunk and looking as though it was keeping vigil, slightly bowed.

I stepped from the car into an uncanny silence, the only faint sounds the breeze occasionally whispering through the peeling bark of the birches and, in the far distance, a bird singing the same sad four notes. It reminded me of the responses to a litany.

Grass had begun to grow again on the scorched earth but was not yet tall enough to conceal twisted scraps of metal that had dropped from the burned-out vehicle when it had been removed. Then—Oh, God!—I saw a blackened shoe. I bent down to touch it but found myself unable to do so.

Standing quite still I thought of Carol, Andy's wife, eight months pregnant with their first child, her condition preventing her from flying over for the funeral. Andy's remains had been cremated after a short service at the Anglican Church in Port Charles and his ashes sent back to England. I could think of nothing more ghastly than to wave goodbye to your husband, and then a short time later receive all that was left of him contained in a small urn.

A brightly coloured woodpecker startled me by flapping noisily into the dying spruce above me. It drummed into the blackened bark searching for insects. I thought of Andy, a strong presence that you couldn't ignore, a force to be reckoned with. In appearance he had strongly resembled Patrick but his black hair had been straight not curling and this, coupled with a rather solemn manner, had caused Peter to nickname him ''The Raven.''

I sat in the car for a while, thinking of nothing at all, numbed. Then I drove back into Port Charles. When I arrived at the city boundary it was still only two in the afternoon so I went into a Tim Horton's doughnut café and drank coffee. I wasn't hungry.

"Have a nice day," chirped the girl behind the counter as I left.

Hartland brought Redding and Lawrence home for dinner again that evening and judging from her frosty manner towards him, again without giving Emma prior warning. I fully sympathised. She seemed to be taking her task of watching over the frigate programme personnel very seriously.

I sat next to Earl Lawrence at dinner. It was difficult not to take an immediate and strong dislike to him for he held in lively contempt anything or anyone who wasn't Canadian. He appeared to regard the DARE team as little more than office juniors to do his bidding. I gathered from his conversation that he had little time for his boss: Redding, either.

"Awful about Quade," I remarked, aware that he didn't possess the kind of intelligence to suspect me of setting a trap for him.

"Yeah," he replied slowly. "But we all have to go sooner or later."

"He was a good driver," I persevered. "Didn't drink either."

"The suspension's not so good on Yank cars as you guys are used to at home."

I recovered from the remark so amazingly free from malice. "Is that a fact?"

"Yeah," he said again. "Some are risky on our roads. When folks buy them they usually get the suspension stripped out and replaced with something a lot stiffer. Hit a bump in the damn things and you're off the road before you know where you are."

"D'you think that's what might have happened to Andy?"

His mouth reassumed its usual sour twist. "Lady, I've no idea what happened to him. Why don't you hold a séance and find out?"

I'm thicker skinned than he could possibly know. "I'm surprised no one's mentioned murder," I murmured.

"Why should they?"

"You're aware of the threats that have been made. And you know as well as I do that he wasn't the kind of man to die driving himself into a tree."

"He was like a big kid," Lawrence said. "And talking of big kids . . ."

I followed his gaze to the open door and the man just entering the room. Several impressions crowded into my mind: Emma's cheeks assuming a faintly pink tinge, Hartland frowning and, if anything, going a shade paler, Robin smiling behind his hand, the anticipatory gleam in Paul's eyes. This person was, apparently, some kind of catalyst.

"Lee!" cried Emma. "I'm so glad you could make it after all."

"Leander Hurley," whispered Robin in my ear. "Liaison Officer, Canadian Navy. According to McAlister, he *is* the Canadian Navy."

I had already worked out for myself that nothing in North America is on a small scale but this did not prepare me for Hurley's six foot six or thereabouts, bright red curly hair and blazing blue eyes. Most certainly, I immediately decided, the Vikings *had* discovered the New World.

"I hope you didn't bring Freddie beer again," Emma said primly after he had apologised for becoming fogbound during a sea trial in the Bay of Fundy.

"What else has the poor guy to enjoy?" Hurley said in a tone that, for him, was probably a whisper. He then eyed the assembled gathering and I quailed in anticipation of another hand crusher. But when he picked me out he strode over to bestow upon my fingers a quaintly old-fashioned kiss. Definitely a man to be watched in every sense, I thought, smiling back.

"A real live English author," he said, giving me a calculating stare. Later I discovered that he looked at everyone

like that at the first meeting. There was no real brainwork
behind it. It was a bit like the beam from an unmanned
lighthouse.

Wishing that he would let go of my hand and aware of a
tiny frown between Emma's immaculately plucked eyebrows, I said, "Surely there are plenty of writers in Vancouver."

Hurley looked at Robin and then back to me again.

"Am I right?" I asked, taking back my hand.

"Surely you are ma'am," he replied, and from his wary
manner I knew he thought we had been gossiping about him.

"I've been listening to the radio," I told him. "People
tell me I have a good ear for remembering accents."

He gave a satisfied nod. "Then where would you place
our Freddie?"

"He talks like a parrot from a deplorable background," I
said, and everyone laughed.

"Pieces of eight! Pieces of eight!" mimicked Robin but
went quiet when I gave him a look.

Detecting continuing undercurrents I answered Hurley's
questions about my writing and then, after dinner, he joined
Robin and me in one corner of the lounge. Unlike the Nasonworth contingent he was not interested in talking shop
and I began to wonder if Emma or her husband had dropped
a hint to him that Robin was not the engineer he was pretending to be. In a way Hurley *was* like a child, eager for
knowledge. He laughed easily, which is not to say that he
laughed at anything and everything, but he explored for humour and, finding it, injected a little more of his own. No
one, I mused wryly, could be more of a contrast to Earl
Lawrence. There did not seem to be one iota of spite in him,
but something about him did make me wonder if he was
putting on an act.

I went to bed early, thinking about the presence of listening devices in every room and the more I thought about it
the angrier I became. On the first night, undressing, I had

wondered how sensitive they were and whether one could suffer from indigestion without losing one's social reputation in New Brunswick. Then other aspects of this quite unwarranted snooping had occurred to me.

On that night I had switched on the bedside clock radio and found CBC's classical music station. When the door of my room had opened and closed soundlessly at a little after midnight I had not been alarmed, and had merely turned up the volume slightly. Conversation in the circumstances had been impossible and I had been helpless with laughter initially at my visitor's contrite expression after the fright I had had. During the first movement of a symphony and after I had forgiven him, he had made love to me with breathtaking urgency. We had not dared speak. So there had been only Beethoven and that sweet, sweet strength.

I felt the business of the security surveillance within Ravenscliff, while not directly related to my brief, to be sufficiently interesting to be worth investigating. I had already drawn a diagram of the house, both upper and lower floors, marking exactly where everyone slept. It had not seemed necessary to make a separate drawing of the basement, or rumpus room as it was called, and I had merely noted that McAlister and Paul were bunking down in a partitioned corner of it, the one nearest another woodburner. Redding and Lawrence, of course, went back to their hotel and on the Friday afternoon of that and every subsequent week, flew back to Montreal for the weekend. As it happened, after an incident on the first Thursday after I arrived, the invitations to dinner ceased altogether.

It had become fairly obvious that Lawrence thought the armed protection of the DARE team a waste of time. Whether he was the type of man to relish argument or whether the tension of being shepherded around by an armed guard became too much for him was difficult to decide. When he began to bait Robin I found myself unable to interest myself in his reasons, only condemn his stupidity.

To be fair, everyone had been drinking steadily, before dinner, during and afterwards. One could not fault David Hartland's generosity with alcohol and I was beginning to wonder if it was his practical solution to the increasing tension within his household. With or without this purpose in mind he was pouring rye for himself and his colleagues and had left a bottle of Scotch within range of the Britishers. The trio from DARE were becoming more indiscreet by the minute; Robin and I frankly agog.

McAlister, his accent mellowed until he sounded like a television advertisement for the golden product of the glens, said, "We could always stick a harpoon on the front end and then they could sell it as a whaling ship."

Paul Rogers, recounting a meeting he had attended that day to Margaret Howard, "So I said to this guy, if you don't build in any safeguards and then shove twenty-five thousand horse power down one prop shaft instead of two then you're going to bend the bloody thing."

Ouch, I thought, that was a dig at Nasonworth whose fame in the engineering world up until these heady days of frigates had depended on the production of flight simulators.

"The difference," Robin observed thoughtfully, "between pranging the boat on the jetty and a screen lighting up with pretty coloured words—'Oops, try again.' "

McAlister and Rogers cried with laughter at this point and even Margaret smiled widely, stirring things even more by directing her gaze straight at Hartland.

"Big joke," growled Lawrence.

"Speaking personally," said McAlister, "I'm just voicing an idea that came to me since a conversation with one of your senior consultants yesterday."

"Along the lines of what?" enquired Hartland smoothly.

"That they ought to be submarines."

Redding was in the process of taking a mouthful of whisky

and almost choked. "Rubbish!" he exclaimed when he could speak.

"The whole idea of frigates calling the tune is obsolete," McAlister continued. "We found that out in the South Atlantic."

"Britain isn't scrapping her frigates," Redding pointed out.

"We've got nukes."

On reflection I'm sure that McAlister hadn't intended to sound so smug. But he was still talking.

"It's political. I know it's political—you know it's political. The all Canadian dream: a maple leaf on everything. Even on the bog paper, which comes from China."

Here, unfortunately, Hartland remembered that he was British and chuckled. Robin, disastrously, got a fit of the giggles. This does not happen very often and I continue to pray that he will soon grow out of it. Worse, the drink activated his imagination, normally strictly dormant.

"And the hoard brooded," he intoned. " 'Verily we need advice,' they murmured. 'Let us seek wise council from the wizards across the eastern sea,' they muttered. 'Verily *they* would not have got into this turmoil,' they cried. 'All will soon be perfect!' they bellowed. And all were suffused with a great euphoria.

"So they mounted the great silver bird—the great bird that flattens the buttocks, confuses the thoughts and dulls the spirits. And thus they came upon the abode of the wizards, a tall white spire that pierced the very clouds. And the wizards were indeed strange beings."

He seemed to have run out of ideas so I took over. "Those who lived below the clouds were rough ogres, steeped in black arts, committing few of their secrets to parchment, telling those who lived above the clouds nothing. Those who lived above the clouds were even stranger, writing and speaking a profusion of curious tongues, committing their multitude of thoughts to monsters with many baleful green eyes.

"And those in the middle," said McAlister, "who lived in the clouds were strangest of all for they worked in a perpetual fog, huddled together for comfort and protection and holding hands. And their feet were permanently cold."

Robin had collected his thoughts. " 'Help us! Help us! For we have travelled far and are in great turmoil,' cried the horde, but the tower remained silent. 'Help us! Help us! For we have travelled far, are in great turmoil and these sacks of gold are very heavy,' cried the horde. Trumpets sounded. 'Welcome,' boomed the tower and the horde passed into the hands of the wizards of the east."

The minder then became quite helpless, apparently oblivious to a member of his audience approaching with singular lack of humour.

"Call yourself a bloody bodyguard!" Lawrence shouted. "You're so inept it makes me nervous to be in the same room with you."

Robin, suddenly sober, looked up at him derisively.

"If an armed man came through that door you'd wet yourself," Lawrence went on, if anything shouting more loudly.

"Cool it!" Redding ordered sharply. "You've had too much rye."

"If you'd like to go out and then come in again," Robin offered helpfully, "I'll be quite happy to blow your ears off."

Only he did not say ears.

I put out a hand to place it restrainingly on Robin's shoulder but his acute hearing had already alerted him to something. The door opened precipitately and in burst a young man.

"Hi, everyone!" yelled Mark Hartland.

The bullet missed him but only, I discovered later, because Mark is a seasoned squash player and dived sideways when he saw a stranger pointing a gun. A split second later Robin was sitting on him on the floor.

Emma was the first to recover from the shock. "How many

times do I have to tell you to ring and let us know you're coming?'' she shrieked.

"It was meant to be a surprise," said Mark, rubbing a shoulder. He grinned up at Robin. "Show me how to do that—eh?''

Further surprises followed in the shape of three burly members of the RCMP, armed and bearing a vociferously complaining Freddie whom they had come upon heading in furtive fashion towards the house.

The explanations were somewhat lengthy.

CHAPTER 5

Redding and Lawrence left immediately, receiving from Hartland a curt nod indicating that he would smooth things out. I was rather relieved about this for Robin was still clearly in a mood to vent on Lawrence his glorious displeasure.

While Hartland spoke, proving to all of us that he was a master of diplomacy, and Freddie stood placidly in a Mountie's strong grip smiling gently at the bottle of Scotch, I suddenly wished that a secret camera was filming the proceedings and that Daws could one day view his team in action.

Greatly daring, and still not altogether sober, Robin pushed the Scotch nearer to Freddie. With all outsider attention still on Hartland there was no one to notice the look of horror flit across expressive features that denoted his displeasure at being expected to drink out of the bottle. Robin fetched a clean glass. Then, Hartland busy explaining that the prisoner was a member of his staff, the gentleman in question slithered through his captor's hands like a freshly landed fish and poured himself a consoling drink.

With three days' growth of beard, grimy hands, fingernails packed with dirt, Patrick sat on the floor cross-legged and sipped his whisky. He has always had a theory that ordinary people notice nothing and was about to prove that the average policeman is no exception. Beneath the grime, filthy jeans and equally dirty tee-shirt, was the *soigné* army officer who

DEATH OF A RAVEN

had accompanied me to many parties and was always one of those to sit on the floor when there were not enough chairs. I felt like cheering.

This joy of joys, alas, soon came to an end. Hartland roughly told him to finish his drink and leave and was so infuriated by the leer "Freddie" then bestowed on me that he ordered out the Mounties as well, telling them that he no longer required them to provide outside surveillance.

"That was a mistake," Robin said, coldly angry, to Hartland a few minutes later. The three of us were the last to leave the room.

"I'll thank you to leave all exterior security to me," Hartland snapped, and walked out.

"Still thirsting for blood?" I enquired.

"These mikes . . ." said Robin pensively, and from his expression it seemed to me that he was not so much thirsting for blood as already wallowing knee deep in the stuff.

"What mikes?" I said, giving him a chance to undo the damage.

There was a short but violent inner skirmish between his self-control and professionalism on the one hand, and anger and tiredness on the other.

"The ones you were asking me about—for your dictating machine."

"I'm with you now," I told him, feeling quite shaky.

"I've got a catalogue. I'll let you have it tomorrow." He plodded from the room.

This exchange had been a demonstration of the real hazard of Patrick's disobeying orders. Terry might be younger and able to soak up the immense amount of information that I was sure McAlister had been cramming into him, but he could not cope with prolonged tension in a situation where his considerable courage and flair in an active rôle was not called into play. The day after day tedium of being cooped up with increasingly bad-tempered people who looked to him to protect them virtually twenty-four hours a day could not be permitted to go on much longer.

I had no doubt that Patrick had reasons for placing himself outside the Hartland household. Equally certain was that he had been on the same mission as the men from the RCMP, to discover why a shot had been fired, and it had suited his purpose to be brought indoors by them. Now you know as much as I do, I thought, and you'll have to break your own cover. I did not even contemplate that he would do something as simple as knock on the front door and say who he was. The situation was too eccentric for that.

I went upstairs wondering what Terry had been about to tell me concerning the bugging devices.

The next morning there was a hint of spring in the air and everyone was in good spirits, Terry included. I made a point of giving him a bright smile to tell him that I had no intention of reporting his lapse to a higher authority. He grinned back. He always knows what I mean.

The question uppermost in my mind had been answered. Asleep, the night before, I had suddenly become aware of someone in my room. Again, I had not been alarmed. Intruders with malice in their hearts do not normally sit on the end of their intended victim's bed ravenously devouring what I discovered to be half a cold roast chicken. So I had merely smiled into the pillow and, later, taken him into my arms. He had washed and shaved and, with the radio switched on, both of us buried beneath the luxurious comforter, we had slowly and languidly made love.

Afterwards, replete in all senses, he must have thought it all out. In a while he had slid out of bed, put on the light and begun to crawl around on the floor. Then I heard him huffing and puffing as he wriggled beneath the bed.

A hand and arm bearing aloft what looked like a hearing aid battery with two short pieces of wire had come into my line of vision.

"Is that a declaration of war?" I had asked.

The head had reappeared wearing a ferocious squint and then gone away again.

"You look a right lunatic crawling around with nothing on."

My nail file had been acquired and utilised to unscrew the minute device and perform untold havoc on its insides. Then he had replaced it from whence it had come.

"If anyone investigates, it will merely look as though it's failed."

"You haven't answered my question."

Shivering, he had come back into bed. "Terry has a theory that Hartland had them put in to check on Emma's night time activities."

I had already discovered, by a little sleuthing of my own, that Emma slept alone and her husband had a study cum bedsitter in what had originally been servants' quarters over the garages. Also that Leander Hurley had returned to Ravenscliff on the night of the Wednesday after I had arrived, climbed the tree outside Emma's bedroom window and stayed until about five the next morning. Her room was next to mine and presumably Emma didn't care if I knew for she had made a lot of noise during what must have been fairly wild lovemaking.

"Hartland's impotent," Patrick had said.

"How d'you know?"

"Terry told me."

"So how does Terry know?"

"Emma told him—in bed."

Which was why my smile to Terry had been a bright one but the eyebrows raised.

As far as I was concerned the mood of slight elation departed with the DARE team, escorted by Terry, on their way to work. I found myself shivering upon perceiving the look Terry received from his commander, the message not losing anything in the distance separating them across the expanse of lawn. However provoked, the look said, you do not drink too much and let off reckless shots indoors. I doubted if it was the last that Terry would hear of it. Patrick had angrily brushed aside my explanation of how obnoxious Lawrence had been.

I strolled in the garden and pondered on what we were about to do. On the surface of it what Patrick had planned was preposterous, melodramatic and even dangerous. But in order to get skeletons from cupboards, he had pointed out, you sometimes have to dynamite off the padlocks.

The man that everyone but Terry and I knew as Freddie gazed across at me and, holding a rake, went into a robotic dance routine. This, I realised, was for Hartland's benefit. He was the last to leave and approaching Emma's car, keys ready in one hand to unlock the door. Hartland stopped in his tracks. Everyone always does. Patrick is a horribly realistic robot.

"Get on with your work!" he shouted, and bad-temperedly stabbed the key in the lock.

Then, the most odd feeling came over me. As in a dream I saw Hartland get in the car and drive away, spraying Freddie with gravel as he speeded past. I saw the expression on my own husband's face after this had transpired and did not recognise him, only viewed someone less than quite sane.

The sensation of uneasiness persisted. I walked away from him, no longer feeling the sun's warmth even though it was now full in my face. Since arriving in Canada I had experienced a feeling of general malaise and had put it down to jet lag. Now I was not so sure. If I was being reduced to a trembling ninny when witnessing my husband in one of his more bizarre rôles, it suggested that I was losing my nerve. Even worse, I could no longer face him being near to me while playing the part of Freddie—and the plan he had put forward meant that Freddie and I would get very close indeed.

I sat on a stone garden seat and, appalled with myself,

continued to tremble. In rare moments of real illness and emotional upset I seem to be a spectator of my own weaknesses. So here was a woman getting on for forty who had been entrusted with a little make-believe, the outcome of which would make her the centre of sympathetic attention. Spectator raked ham actor with ruthless gaze. There was no more than had regarded me in the mirror that morning; black bobbed hair, green eyes, a face a little paler than was normal. Nothing to suggest incipient panic.

I stood up and my ears roared, the lawn, trees, and greenhouse tilting and spinning crazily. Somehow I carried on walking towards the stables where I knew Mark was getting his horse ready for a ride.

"Faith, the woman's drunk," said a voice close behind me, and then laughed when I broke into a run.

"Who laughed?" asked Mark, leading Marcus, his horse, out into the sunshine.

"Freddie," I replied, leaning on a wall.

"I can't imagine why Dad employed such a lunatic."

"Old Bill recommended him," I said and stroked the chestnut, remembering how I myself had used the same expression not so long ago.

"Really? I wonder how much money changed hands."

Marcus danced at the shadows, snorting, and then wheeled around with a squeal when a pigeon flew up in his face. Mark, hopping around with one foot in the stirrup, swore and then led the animal down the drive for a short distance to calm it down.

I watched him. The similarity in name was no accident, the horse had been an eighteenth birthday present. But not the kind of animal, I reasoned, that could be expected to behave itself when ridden perhaps only one weekend in four.

"You keep away!" Mark shouted when he saw that the gardener was making as if to help him mount the plunging creature. "Clear off!" he yelled. "You'll only make him worse."

I did not stop to witness the outcome of this but quickly ran up the wooden staircase on the outside wall of the building. The door into the loft room must have been ajar for I do not remember opening it, only becoming aware of sitting on a bale of hay and feeling not scared but sick and faint. Already the plans had gone wrong. Mark had gone out earlier than expected. He was to have witnessed our play acting.

I gazed around me. Most of the space in the roof was taken up with bales of hay and straw, sacks of animal feeding stuffs, both cubes for the horses—Marcus and Emma's mare, Queen—and dog meal and biscuits for the Newfoundland, or Newfie as it was nearly always referred to. A thin partition across one end separated the store from where Freddie slept.

I simply couldn't believe that Old Bill had inhabited this sleazy corner. There was a camp bed with rickety legs, the blankets on it smelling of wet dogs and mothballs, a chest of drawers, one corner propped up by a couple of books, a tap dripping into a filthy sink with nothing to clean it. This was how a wealthy British family housed their supposedly mentally retarded employee. I seethed, not just because the man involved was my husband but for all people thus treated. It seemed that the padlock on the cupboard containing skeletons was already well and truly off.

And, of course, the magazines, a great pile of them by the bed. They dated back several years. In spite of myself I flipped through a couple and probably received the same kind of shock that comes to any woman who has previously regarded herself as broad-minded when she first encounters hard porn. Had he really lain in bed looking at these?

In a kind of daze I flipped the top blanket aside to reveal grey sheets and a pillow lumpy with age. There was a thin mattress of sorts. I slid my hands beneath it and, kneeling at the side of the bed, felt along its length. In the middle but at the foot end was a sock rolled up around something hard. It was the gold Rolex watch I had given Patrick shortly after we remarried.

I wept, wondering, "Fool, fool, what's the matter with you?"

Standing up, I took a knife from the draining board, wiped off the stickiness on a dirty tee-shirt and, back on my knees, examined the floor. There were several loose boards and after prising up three I found what I was looking for.

At this point the man called Freddie nudged me quite gently on the bottom with a toe.

"That's a damn stupid and obvious place to hide a gun," I said, dangling the Smith and Wesson under his nose.

"Mark will be back," announced the man in my life. "He's just been thrown and hurt his wrist."

"No mikes up here?"

"None. You'll have to scream quite loudly."

"You bastard," I whispered, surprised by my own venom.

Grinning at my good acting he lunged at me and bore me down onto the campbed. I think I went a little bit mad myself then without knowing why, and this was what really frightened me. I fought him off, at one point remembering my training well enough to send him hurtling to the floor. And all the time I screamed until he silenced me with his mouth, an altogether too brutish, bruising kiss.

At the moment that he realised I wasn't acting and drew away, perplexed, Mark ran into the room and beat him off with his riding crop. Such was the state I was in that, for a few moments, I let young Hartland's temper run riot. After that few moments Mark himself would have been in danger. Something cold and calculating within me allowed the whip to fall once more across Patrick's shoulders and then I got up and grabbed Mark's arm.

"You filthy bastard," he mouthed at the sordid figure lying on the floor, backing away, white with anger.

Somehow I bundled him out of that squalid room and down the stairs. Then I must have fainted.

CHAPTER 6

Perhaps that cold calculating quality within me was the prompting of my writer's brain, the same mechanism that functioned as a watchdog over my own behaviour and at the same time collected data and memorised faces, mannerisms and information for future use. Whatever the true nature of this phenomenon it carried on quite ruthlessly presenting me with a picture of the world while I was, to all intents and purposes, unconscious.

I was lying on the sofa in Emma's room, covered by a blanket and in the company of several hot water bottles. This much I knew to be fact and not dream even though at the same time I felt many miles and many years away.

"Stalky," whispered someone, and then closer, "Stalky—Stalky's coming!"

Then, perhaps in dream, perhaps in reality, I wept for the second time that day, seeing a skinny boy going through a school gate and out into the street. That was the first school rule he broke on that fateful occasion. The second was to approach a member of the public and shout, deride, jeer and insult him until the infuriated man chased him away. Patrick had run slowly. Stalky, being what he was, travelled behind at a shambling canter, arms waving. At that speed he had seemed even more terrifying to me than when he had crept up on us behind hedges and peered at us through holes in the playground wall, and made signs to us girls that most of us couldn't understand but which frightened us witless all the same.

"Oh, God forgive me," whispered what sounded like my own voice.

"He'll have to go," said Emma, and I heard a door close.

Mark sat on one end of the sofa, still breathing rather quickly, a frown on his normally good-natured face. "You weren't apologising to us," he said when he saw me looking at him.

"To Freddie," I told him. "He didn't mean it."

"He tried to rape you and didn't mean it?"

"He resurrected a childhood nightmare without meaning to," I corrected him softly.

"Mother's gone to phone the doctor."

"There's no need. How's your wrist?"

"It aches a bit. If it hadn't been for that I'd have really given the bastard what for. I'd swear in court he threw a handful of gravel at the animal's hind legs."

When the doctor arrived, in her early twenties, black and with the kind of fizzing energy that always makes me feel old and utterly exhausted, it soon became apparent that Emma had not told her the reason for my present fragility. I couldn't really blame her, no one likes to admit that a member of their staff has violently attacked a guest in their house. Thus I was examined and told there was nothing to worry about. Afterwards the doctor departed. I did not imagine for a moment that we would have to call her out again that same night.

Freddie had very wisely made himself scarce by the time Hartland arrived home. But it seemed to me, watching and listening while pretending to read in the living room, that the search for him was perfunctory and that Hartland had other more pressing matters on his mind. So he contented himself with bawling out Emma for allowing it to happen and demanding to know of me why I had visited Freddie's quarters in the first place.

"I never dreamt that he'd be housed over the stables," I

retorted. "I went up to watch some swallows nesting in the roof." This glibness came regrettably easily but at least the birds had taken up residence over Freddie's head, they had been skimming in and out through a broken window. But I was not happy. If Patrick had obeyed orders and worked from within the house then there would have been no necessity for our charade. But he had insisted that he had his reasons and breaking his cover by a fake rape also had a purpose. Would the Hartlands sack him quietly, call the police or hire a couple of thugs to run him out of town?

"Robin Hughes," said Hartland, gazing at the man using that name as he entered the room having just arrived with all the others. "That isn't your real name, is it?"

"You know it isn't," replied Terry. "At your own request you—"

"Is that so-called gardener one of your subordinates?"

"Most certainly not."

"Do I have your word on that?"

"Of course," Terry said, getting just the right tone of injured surprise into his voice.

"I was told there would be two of you," Hartland persisted.

"He is not working for me," said Terry in a manner that made Hartland change the subject.

Mark, however, was made of sterner stuff. "So where is he then?"

"Behind the third spruce tree along from the left. How the hell should I know?"

"That's no answer."

Terry held Mark's gaze until the youngster flushed. Further silent scrutiny caused him to jump up from his seat and slam out of the room. Emma and her husband exchanged glances.

"I'm sorry," Terry said to them. "But you know I can't discuss that kind of thing."

I turned my back on the room and looked out of the window. It seemed to me that the most innocent parties were the only ones being hurt and that the entire mission was swinging crazily between tragedy, ineptitude and pure farce. And why did I imagine that working deeply in cover was turning Patrick's brain?

"Any clues as to whether the writer of the threatening note was a nutter?" Hartland asked Terry after dinner, quite mellow after several glasses of claret.

"No clues of any sort," Terry replied, relaxed and carefully polite after one glass. "London postmark—posted in Ealing the previous night."

"Where does Fraser live?"

"Yelverton—Devon. About twenty minutes' drive from Plymouth," McAlister answered after Terry admitted that he didn't know.

"Has something happened?" I asked.

"His cars had acid thrown over them."

"When?" Drew shouted to make himself heard over the cries of dismay.

"Yesterday."

"Not his lovely Lotus and Range Rover," Margaret Howard said in a low moan, and suddenly I wanted to know exactly how upset she had been by Andy's death.

"Outside the office?" enquired Paul.

"No, his garage was broken into."

"But there are dogs!" This again from Margaret.

"Apparently they didn't make a sound."

"Then surely that suggests that they recognised whoever did it."

Hartland clearly did not want to be drawn into a discussion about Chris Fraser's dogs. "I've no idea. The police are investigating."

"But you don't understand," she went on. "They're Dobermanns. Even the post and papers have to be left in a box at the gate."

"Postman and paperboys can't afford steak," commented Terry wryly.

"The Germans use them as police dogs," Margaret said dismissively. "Quite the most savage dogs."

"That's correct," Terry replied. "When they're trained never to take food from strangers. The average Dobermann kept as a pet will run for its life if you slap it over the muzzle or be your friend if you produce a lump of beef."

"Experience talking," Paul smiled. "My guess is that it depends heavily on who is doing the clandestine visiting."

"Have the police—?" McAlister started to say but was drowned out by the Newfoundland, an animal which until that moment had resembled nothing more than a friendly hearthrug. It lumbered to its feet and let out the loudest bark I had ever heard. Then it careered to the window, paws skidding on the polished floor, and from there to the door. Finding it shut the animal commenced to howl like a banshee.

In the general confusion of everyone running into the hall, falling over each other and the dog, finding coats and becoming even more agitated when we heard Marcus frantically neighing and the unmistakable sound of him kicking at the walls of his box, I was aware of Terry quietly strapping on his gun harness and slipping out through the kitchen. I followed him.

Our subtlety proved to be of no avail for we all met outside and it took every ounce of Terry's authority to quieten the babble of voices and slow everyone down. He went on ahead and I contrived to be just behind him.

"There's a pick-up parked behind the stable," I heard Emma say.

"Probably ours," Hartland grunted.

"Don't be stupid, David. It's piled high with lobster pots."

My inner watchdog noted a sky bright with stars, a faint nimbus around the moon promising frost and the smooth lawns silvery in its light. I ignored all of this and focussed my attention on the squares of light that were the door of the stable and the two windows, one on each side of it.

Marcus neighed again, angry and frightened, and there were more bangs as he kicked out at the wooden partition. As we reached the doorway Mark ran out, almost straight into Terry's arms nearly knocking him over, recoiled hesitating and then dashed off into the dark.

"What the devil . . . !" Hartland shouted. "Mark? Mark!"

The first thing I saw when I ran into the stable behind Terry was Marcus, eyes rolling with fear but still thankfully secure in his box. Queen was in one of the two stalls, alarmed and staring over the top of the partition at what was taking place in the empty one next to her. More correctly, she was boggling at the man in the hay rack in the stall next to hers, Patrick, trying to evade the lunges being made at him with pitchforks wielded by three men built like wrestlers. Then, two of them threw these aside and with greedy grasp hauled their victim from on high and threw him onto the floor.

Emma screamed.

Patrick's answer to this was effective and, in the circumstances, quite stylish. Lithe as a ballet dancer he uncoiled upwards from the floor, a fist ramming into the side of one man's jaw sending him sideways and down. His other hand, quite independently, swung up to shoulder height to smash bloodily into the nose of another who had been coming from behind to grab him by the throat. The third, who had had a foot raised to kick his ribs in, fell to Terry.

I loathe violence but this astounding affray, a kind of antithesis of a nightmare, the frog turning into a prince, the happy ending after impossible odds, caught at my throat. I glanced around at white, shocked faces, saw Terry grinning like the Cheshire Cat, and then had to get out of the way quickly as the three thugs were on the run.

"I enjoyed that," murmured Terry, twitching his sweater straight, but no one was looking at him.

"You lied to me," said Hartland, not taking his eyes off his erstwhile gardener who was dusting himself off, reminding me irresistibly of a bird of prey rearranging its plumage after a kill.

"No one has lied to you," Terry said.

"I very much regret that my son has been responsible for forcing him into the open like this," Hartland bellowed at Terry, "but I insist that you confirm that this man is one of yours."

"He's one of mine," said Patrick, still fastidiously picking strands of hay from an otherwise unspeakably dirty tee-shirt. The voice was now the one I knew so well, no longer Freddie's nasal whine. But deceptively quiet, with just a hint of a cutting edge.

"And you are?" Hartland enquired.

Patrick told him.

Emma struck a theatrical pose and, with resignation, I waited for her little scene-stealer. "Your husband!" she cried, staring triumphantly at me.

To my fury, I blushed as seven pairs of eyes fixed unwaveringly on me.

"Oh dear," said Emma with a giggle. "Poor Mark."

"Who are those characters?" Patrick asked Hartland.

"They take him fishing," Emma chimed before he could reply. "I'm cold—can we talk indoors?"

"There's blood on your leg," Margaret told Patrick. She had been one of those tossed aside when the attackers had fled and was also removing hay from her clothes. She was remarkably cool under the circumstances.

Patrick glanced down. "A few prods with a hay fork."

"Tetanus," I said. "Jabs up to date?"

The grey eyes regarded me in a fashion that made Margaret's coolness look like hysterics. Talk about laid back. "Are you all right, Ingrid?"

"I'll make out my report in triplicate," I said, getting the message right across.

CHAPTER 7

Emma insisted on calling the doctor to attend to Patrick's ugly-looking puncture wound. Also, having watched her carefully since my arrival and aware that Hartland might have told her more about Patrick than she had mentioned, I suspected that she wished to get as much mileage from the situation as possible.

The heating having mysteriously gone off when the doctor arrived, Patrick had to have his leg dressed in the living room. It was too cold anywhere else, Emma insisted. So we had to have the whole rigmarole: Patrick having to remove his jeans behind the scant privacy of the settee with its back turned to the room, a tetanus jab, everything, while I sweated with embarrassment for him.

Not that he is particularly coy concerning the result of his injuries in the South Atlantic, long hospitalisation has seen to that. Also, had his disability been made known previously to those present I'm sure they would have taken themselves off to bed. Now it was too late.

I felt like an extra in an extremely third-rate movie sitting alongside him on the settee waiting for the young black doctor's interest to penetrate the buzz of polite conversation behind us. She asked him about percentage mobility and a lot of other technical questions that he seemed to be able to answer, and by the time the wound was dressed everyone in the room must have been aware of the man-made construction of the lower part of his right leg.

The doctor departed and the patient was once more attired, this time in clean clothes provided by Terry, when Emma produced the apparent cause of all the trouble, piloting him in Patrick's direction with a shove.

"You've been sick," said Patrick observantly, one eyebrow quirked.

It occurred to me then that the best kinds of pleasure and the worst of cruelty involve anticipation, and that this young man had been thoroughly prepared by Emma for his comeuppance at the hands of an expert.

Mark, it seemed, was beyond making a reply to this.

"You were sick before you even came into the stable," continued Patrick in a quiet voice. "Those men—the biggest one was Bryce, the dark-haired one Lanny . . . Who was the third?"

"Rab," whispered Mark, and then his legs buckled.

Patrick caught him, dispelling any lingering doubts as to his mobility, and lowered him on to the settee with his head between his knees. "Give him a brandy with some ginger ale," he said to the room at large. "I wouldn't mind some as well."

The elegant reproduction clock in the dining room struck eleven in the silence that followed. Emma turned away with a small frown.

"The Gaspereau brothers," Patrick went on. "It was written on the side of the pick-up."

Irritably Hartland said, "He told them you tried to rape a guest at the house, and then the whole damn fool lot got drunk and decided to do something about it. You have my apologies." He didn't sound sorry.

Patrick took the drinks from McAlister, placed one on a table and succeeded in getting Mark to swallow most of the other. He choked and leaned back with a groan, his head on

Patrick's shoulder. Quite naturally Patrick's arm went round his back, keeping him in a secure upright position.

Hartland said, "If you know who they are, then why ask?"

"Checking on the level of co-operation," he was told.

Mark sat up with another groan and put his head in his hands.

"If you throw up again in here you can pack your bags forever," Emma said, tight-lipped.

"Beer and a Chinese take-away is a dreadful combination," Patrick observed, placing a metal waste paper bin at Mark's feet and tapping him on the arm to draw his attention to it.

I smiled behind my hand. Even after all this time, familiar as I am with his methods, I find myself in awe of Patrick's gift of handling people. I had no doubt that had Mark displayed any lesser degree of co-operation, either by making a rude remark or refusing to reply because of his nausea, he would have received a box around the ears that would have guaranteed his vomiting on to the carpet. Now, Patrick would draw his gun rather than permit anyone to lay hands on his charge. Recognise and acknowledge his authority and you come under the aegis of Patrick Gillard. It is like joining a select club.

Margaret's voice broke into my thoughts. "I can't understand why he knocks around with such a rough bunch."

"They take him fishing," said Emma, not for the first time.

I looked at Mark, the educated son of a wealthy influential family, and then across to Hartland who had a boat but would concern himself more with stocking the bar than providing fishing tackle. I had seen pictures of the *Dancing Sprite* and could not imagine that bait and fish scales would ever be permitted to sully its gleaming decks whereas it was easy to picture a young Mark in the Gaspereau brothers' fishing boat, a lobster pot at his back, a tin of beer within reach, enjoying long, lazy, sun-soaked afternoons a million miles from his

studies or his parents' social graces. In exchange for a few
dollars to buy the beer, and the chance to chip away at Mark's
middle-class good manners, the three Maritimers would tolerate his company.

But would they risk beating up his father's gardener? The
answer to this surely, was that drunk they would do anything.

"I'm sorry," Mark said to the floor.

"That's not good enough," Emma snapped.

I was thinking that their son's lapse had definitely brought
out the worst in his parents when Emma spoke directly to
me, unrecognisable as the pleasant woman who had met me
at the airport.

"You're not saying much. I suppose what happened over
the stable started off as a furtive amatory frolic."

I felt like being immensely rude to her but, since coarse
quotes always find their way into the media, refrained. "No,"
I said with a smile. "He and I have never felt the need to
play at being furtive." Make of that what you will, I thought.
Perhaps it was sufficiently obtuse to make you forget to be
beastly to your son for a while.

Mark gazed somewhat fearfully at Patrick but before he
could speak was pulled to his feet.

"There's nothing for which you have to apologise. My
reaction would have been precisely the same if I'd found you
lying on top of Ingrid. Go to bed."

Whereupon someone shrieked with laughter. I'm afraid
that person was me.

Mark wanly wished everyone goodnight and went from
the room. I was inwardly promising him explanations and
apologies when it occurred to me that they might be unnecessary. Mark's sports car had been parked by the fishermen's
pick-up in a position that suggested he had arrived first. Had
he come to warn Patrick, terrified of the trouble he had stirred
up? His full tilt exit from the stable certainly suggested that
he had been on his way to get help.

The DARE people collectively took the hint and went to

bed. Paul lingered and then bashfully came over to Patrick and held out his hand.

"You'll think I'm daft," he said, "but that was absolutely bloody marvellous. Thank you."

Patrick can be seen to be lost for words perhaps once in every ten years. This was one of those occasions but he smiled and gripped Paul's hand warmly. No more was necessary.

That was where the pleasantries ended. Emma sat tight until an unrelenting stare from Patrick unnerved her. Even Terry was caught in the fall-out from this and rose to go.

"Sit down," said Patrick.

Terry sat.

David Hartland meanwhile had been going through the motions of reading a newspaper, turning the pages with angry jerking movements. When the door closed behind his wife he threw the paper down and commenced to swear at Patrick with all the ingenuity and verve of a man who has been made a thorough fool of.

Patrick sat, left leg crossed over right, toe swinging gently, and waited for him to finish. Finally, Hartland ran out of steam and was reduced prosaically to demanding an explanation.

Patrick said, "When you request help from home base, it doesn't mean you can call the tune. You know that."

Hartland took a deep breath. "Tell me one useful piece of intelligence that you discovered whilst engaged in this ridiculous and, I take it, self-motivated exercise."

Helping himself to a big handful of peanuts from a dish on a side table, Patrick said, "Well, for a start your Newfoundland's likely to be in pup, courtesy of the Great Dane down the road."

For a moment I thought Hartland was actually contemplating physical assault. This possibility came alarmingly closer when Patrick delivered his next remark.

"Also that your wife seems to possess roughly the same

inclinations as a bitch in heat. A security risk, wouldn't you
say?''

I began to see why he had ordered Terry to stay.

''She's had every man in this house barring McAlister and
myself. And you, of course.''

I couldn't help it. I glanced across at Terry who steadfastly
refrained from looking at me.

''You're lying,'' Hartland said.

''Why should I? Anyway, you knew about it. You suspected her and had microphones installed in every room.''

''No—no. They were already here. I took this place over
from the Canadian Secret Service.''

''But still operational. Several thousand dollars' worth of
equipment humming away behind a false wall in the laundry-
room. Even a child would want to know why a cupboard
door has such expensive locks on it.''

''It facilitates certain—'' Hartland began, but Patrick cut
him short.

''I'm sure it bloody does. Perhaps Emma's in the know
too and gets them talking if she can. In return for which you
allow her certain freedoms.''

''That's filthy slander, Major!'' Hartland burst out.

''Andy Quade was on his way to meet her at a motel the
evening he was killed.''

''Kitchen gossip?''

Patrick nodded gravely. ''You find out an awful lot when
you live backstairs. But I did check. She was careless enough
to book the room in her own name.''

Hartland gazed wildly around the room and seemed to find
inspiration. ''This has absolutely nothing to do with your
brief to ensure that the DARE team stay alive.''

''Carte blanche,'' Patrick drawled. ''I'm still trying to
work out why you invited them here. Were you hoping there
was a rotten branch to be discovered by you—with Emma's
help, of course? Does the prospect of an eventual knighthood
make personal torment worth while?''

Was this revenge for a cold, damp room, I wondered, or was he trying to goad Hartland into some kind of confession? Or was he hoping for an excuse to get really tough? I didn't have long to wait for the answer.

Hartland got to his feet, deadly calm after his initial outburst. "I suggest to you, Major, that your behaviour is as outrageous now as it was when you were posing ineffectively as my gardener. I further suggest that you are taking this matter to a quite unwarranted personal level. For a moment I shall do likewise. I would be interested to know if your present attack on me is fuelled by something you yourself just said. I take it that McAlister is faithful to his wife—was your forbearance something to do with the injuries you received during the Falklands War? The grapevine did hint at serious genital damage . . . '' Hartland's voice trailed away and he smiled sadly at me. "Forgive me but I did a little checking on Ingrid's private life and husband when I knew she was coming.''

The fool. With the kind of mandate Patrick has he could have put a bullet between the man's eyes, there and then, and probably got away with it. Terry, still painfully learning to keep his dearest and most blood-thirsty ideas to himself, would have lovingly laid Hartland out on his own carpet and not begrudged the two cent pieces to keep his eyes closed.

But despite Patrick's knowing that being left with only part of one testicle has not affected his masculinity and that those who matter, in this case Terry and I, are fully aware of it, I saw the taunt strike home. The expression that I had witnessed that morning flickered across his face and suddenly he wasn't Patrick any more but the epitome of choking hatred and disgust. He's only human and to him Hartland represented his deepest fears.

Then Terry cleared his throat and Patrick followed his gaze to where the bullet had splintered the woodwork of the door frame. There was no magnificently moral sequel to this for Patrick then progressed with deliberation to the laundry-room, opened the cupboard by deftly bypassing the locks with a credit card, and then proceeded to inflict terminal damage on the equipment concealed inside it. But, whatever Hartland thought, here was not a man mindlessly smashing but a thoroughgoing professional who knew what he was doing.

At last, he twitched out a final electrical lead and looked around in the manner of a small boy hunting for another bubble to pop. Then, having tossed a few cassettes of tape over his shoulder into a corner by way of an encore, he sat on the washing machine and regarded Hartland solemnly.

What could anyone say?

CHAPTER 8

I have learned since my remarriage to Patrick not to bombard him with questions or demand explanations when he is tired, no matter how strongly I feel. Not that I particularly wanted to do either at the moment, there was just an overwhelming need to communicate. Nevertheless, when he came into the room and threw on to the bed an armful of clothing that Terry had hidden away for him, I kept quiet.

He began to undress. Lack of sleep and nourishment for the past week or so had produced dark shadows under his eyes, and an unhealthy pallor. His stamina is not so good as it used to be.

"How's the leg?" I enquired when I could bear the silence no longer.

"Which one?" he said from the inside of his sweat shirt.

Patience really is a virtue. "The one with the hole in it."

"Fine."

"Please have a bath."

"The bandage'll fall off."

He smelt so robustly of compost heaps, horses and heaven alone knew what else that right then, so long as he had a wash I didn't care what fell off.

Then I looked at him properly and got out of bed. "Is that where Mark hit you?"

He winced as my finger traced one of the welts on his back. "He's a strong lad."

"I'm sorry," I said huskily.

"What for?"

"For not stopping him sooner."

As usual he sat on the floor to remove his jeans. "I must admit you did have me worried a couple of times today."

"I fainted."

"Fainted!"

"You know who Freddie is, surely?"

He gave me a very straight look then. "Who?"

"Stalky."

Patrick tensed, still looking at me. I did not have to remind him or explain further. Then he said, "I'm starving."

I raided the kitchen, feeling both guilty and vindicated, and returned bearing a plateful of cold roast beef, ham and chicken, bread rolls, butter and one of several bottles of white wine I found in the fridge, the removal of none of which was likely to inflict mayhem on Dot's menu planning for the following day.

"I'm glad you're working in the open from now on," I said, running hot water into the bath while he finished up the last morsels. "Especially now an attack's been made on Fraser."

Patrick grunted.

"How are you going to keep that injured leg dry when you haven't a spare to stand on?" I asked a few minutes later.

"Pass," he said and got into the bath.

I had run a bath for him because I wanted the hole in his leg to be immersed in hot water to draw out the dirt I thought might remain. Neurotic of me perhaps but I wasn't taking any chances. Both of us knew it would hurt like hell. So I hugged him until the worst was over, poured him another glass of wine and then let him get on with washing himself. I was glad to see when I removed the soaked bandage afterwards that there was a dark stain on the dressing and the wound had started to bleed a little.

"Was it really worth it?" I wondered aloud, applying one of the clean dressings left by the doctor.

"Oh yes."

"But too tired to make further comment?"

He stroked my cheek with a long index finger, an extraordinarily gentle and delicate gesture after the night's violence. "I got most of my information from Bill. The Gaspereau brothers have been here before—or, at least, Bryce has. Inside the house, too. The old chap whispered darkly of "goings on"—other men, people he'd never seen before. But he knew Bryce, everyone knows him."

"I take it you weren't pretending to be Freddie then?"

But Patrick was smiling to himself, staring into space, remembering. "He was in the war, of course—stationed in Yorkshire for a while. I suppose you could describe him as a modern loyalist—he was more than happy to give me his job, retire to Vancouver and keep mum for five hundred dollars."

"Patrick, you told him who you were!"

"Sort of. But he wasn't surprised. The place has been crawling with security people ever since Quade was killed."

"Then surely they were the men he saw."

"No. The 'goings on' he referred to happened before, and were spread over quite a long period of time."

"Emma's boyfriends."

"Some of them might have been. I've got to be sure, that's all."

"I can't believe Andy was having an affair with her."

Patrick was silent for a moment. Then he said, "If I say that ordinary normal women like you can't understand the effect that women like Emma have on normal ordinary men like Andy, Paul and Terry then I know you won't be offended. If I then say that she had a go at me the first morning I started work on the garden, then you'll get an idea of her attitude to the male sex."

I battened down prurient curiosity and said, "So where did Andy meet her if he wasn't living here?"

"That's easy. Hartland had invited the team to dinner on a couple of occasions."

I was nearly asleep a while later when he said, "In case you're worried, Terry did ask me if he ought to sleep with Emma."

"An unusual decision for you to make," I commented.

"We both agreed that it was in the line of duty."

"Please don't make it sound as though he was about to go before a firing squad."

Later again, I realised that he was still wide awake. "Does your leg hurt?"

"I want you."

But he wanted reassurance and comfort, not pleasure, and proof that Hartland's words were only empty malice. Sadly, the lovemaking was a disaster.

The next morning most of my worries returned. There was no doubt that Ravenscliff was a safer haven than ever for the British engineers now that there were two armed guards instead of one. But I still seemed to be looking at Patrick through a glass darkly, and so I suspect was everyone else. He stayed in bed that day, a Saturday, not expressly resting his leg or saying that he was tired, not making any statements at all, just deeply asleep as though drugged. Saturdays being treated as a normal working day this did not matter, Terry acted the chaperon as he usually did.

At about four Patrick rose and such was his demeanour that I risked all and rang Terry to warn him of possible boiling oil and flaming arrows treatment on his return. This proved to be perfectly justified. The minder walked straight into a fairly ruthless test of his reflexes and security arrangements.

The exercise left everyone, me included, in a state that could only be described as elated mild nervous collapse. British stoicism rose to the occasion marvellously, the hungry and tired contingent only protesting slightly upon being shoved down in a heap under the stairs when the lights suddenly went out as they entered the house. What they didn't see was their protector being hauled outside again, cuffed silly, and then required to shoot at various targets that had been fixed in the trees. Terry, murderous and still upright in the dusk, slaughtered an awful lot of pieces of cardboard.

The senior member of British Intelligence got up early the following day and went to church. He returned, thoughtful and delicately exuding the scent of Communion wine, and ate a huge breakfast. This meticulously trained and highly paid connoisseur of security then mooned around for a while before wandering into the garden where he pruned a couple of shrubs. Properly though. I am very pleased with my pupil and how our combined efforts are really making something of the cottage garden at home. After this, and smiling like a shark, he commenced to stalk Mark around the property armed with that young man's riding crop.

There is no more exquisite embarrassment than knowing that everyone is embarrassed for you.

The day continued to evolve like a West End farce. Lunch was consumed at the appropriate hour, the Hartlands ignoring the most recent addition to their table, the rest of us animatedly talking amongst ourselves. All the while Patrick ate like a horse, occasionally pausing to grin at Mark who was ostentatiously sitting on a cushion and who, astoundingly, grinned back. After the meal Emma retired to her room, complaining of a headache, and Hartland to his study, making it known that he was going to ring London.

"What," I demanded of Terry when we were alone, "the hell is going on?"

"I still seem to be learning," he replied.

"I'm certain that Hartland's complaining right now about the standard of personnel. Suppose Patrick's recalled?"

"He won't be."

"You seem very sure."

"I'm sure of the Major too."

"You always were slightly besotted," I said, perhaps cruelly, but he only smiled.

"Every job involves different methods!"

"You call this shambles methods."

Terry flexed his broad shoulders against the confines of the gun harness. "I can assure you he was ice cold normal when he was giving me my orders last night. If you ask me, he's acting a bit loopy with the Hartlands to get them really twitchy. He's not convinced that they're on the level."

"So I understand," I replied. "But say what you like, I don't think he's . . ."

"What?"

But I'd said too much already. I simply had no business discussing Patrick's behaviour with a subordinate. "It doesn't matter," I finished lamely.

When I had almost reached the door, Terry said, "I do know that he's trying to make it up to Mark for all the trouble he got into."

"With a riding crop!"

"That was hellish funny! Marcus bit his backside when he was mucking him out this morning. For pity's sake, Ingrid—haven't you ever seen the Major clowning around before?"

No, I hadn't. Not like this. Not when a man had been killed in strange circumstances. And now a seemingly promoted Terry was calling me by my Christian name.

Patrick and Mark were just about to drive off in the pickup.

Patrick called to me, "We were just on our way to have another look at the accident spot. Coming?"

"I'd like a word with you first," I answered. When he reached my side I said, "I've had enough. I'm going to try to get on a flight home tomorrow."

He took my elbow and walked me further away from the vehicle. "You can't."

"I can," I informed him. I was genuinely surprised. There

had been previous occasions when my presence had proved superfluous and I had simply returned home.

"I want you here," he said.

"I'm not stating a preference," I said, through gritted teeth, "but a fact. I'm going home."

"Aren't you well?"

"I'm superfluous," I said. "I'm an imposition on these people."

"To hell with that!" Patrick exploded. "Hartland gets a massive entertainment allowance from London. Those in his position have to put up with all sorts of strangers staying with them."

Looking at him, I prepared myself for what was about to happen next, when he would switch on the freezing authority and remind me that I had no choice in the matter, Queen and country over-ruled our relationship. It had happened before. Once. Unaccountably my sight blurred and I discovered with a shock that tears were running down my face.

He spoke very gently. "You didn't answer my question. Aren't you well?"

"I can't cope with this," I blurted out.

He put his arm around me and again spoke softly, but not as though trying to humour me, I have never been that kind of woman. "Look, I do need you. Can we talk about it later?"

I nodded, aware that Mark was watching us.

"Will you come with us to Quispamsis? You won't have to cope with anything—just sit in the truck."

It was a bit of a squash with three of us but I was oddly comforted by their close proximity.

After a couple of miles Mark said, "This Freddie was a real person, wasn't he?"

"Oh canny, canny child," Patrick breathed, but Mark didn't seem to mind.

"You were fourteen," I said, memories flooding back.

"Tell him about Stalky."

"You tell him."

"Not a lot to relate really," Patrick began. "He lived next door to the school we both attended and was the son of a couple who were by this time rather elderly. All the children called him Stalky because he was so thin and walked like a wading bird. His mental age was pretty low. When he started to make suggestive signs to the girls over the school wall I decided to mount my own crusade and get him away from them. I should have told a member of staff instead."

"You were famous," I sighed. "The Headmaster looked out of his window just as you were doing your bit, yelling and doing a wonderful imitation of Stalky's funny walk, and he was running towards you to chase you away."

"Lolloping, not running," Patrick corrected. "At the end of it all I got the cane, and then my Dad belted me because my dear little brother had heard rumours about drugs at school, didn't know what had really happened and put two and two together to make several million. Meanwhile all the mothers were phoning the school demanding that something be done about the sex maniac. It even got into the national press."

"Vicar flogs son for tackling man pestering girls," I intoned.

"It's an ill wind," Patrick laughed. "The church was full to the gargoyles for months afterwards because of the publicity. The collections raised enough money to repair the roof, and the Bishop bought me a racing bike."

"It was when I first noticed him," I explained to Mark. "All the girls thought him a real hero and bought him sweets from the tuck-shop."

Mark was laughing so much that, strictly speaking, he was a hazard to other road users.

"The bike was mainly to appease my mother—she and Dad nearly split up over the belting he gave me."

"So this guy really made an impression on your young days," Mark observed. "What happened to him?"

"He was put away—in a home."

"I suppose I can laugh about it now," I said. "But I used to have terrible nightmares that he was after me. He used to hide behind hedges and jump out on us when we were going home from school."

"Probably quite harmless really," Patrick said in my ear.

I thought about it. Yes, probably quite harmless, a lonely, flawed man with a child's mind. But nevertheless, resurrected by someone else in possession of a vivid imagination, had turned him into what Stalky had been to *us*. An object of fear.

"I wish I felt less bad about the other night," Mark mumbled.

"What can you remember?" Patrick asked him.

"Very little. Eating too much. Drinking too much. I haven't the first idea how I got home."

"You drove."

"Jeez," Mark groaned.

"You arrived about ten minutes in front of your friends and spent most of that time throwing up behind the stable."

"Right under your window, I suppose," commented Mark bitterly.

"No—round by the manure heap. That's where I took you after you'd tried to climb the stairs and failed."

The pick-up swerved slightly.

"You had something on your mind but couldn't even begin to tell me," Patrick continued. "You were kind of upset about it so I pushed my fingers down your throat and then held you while you suffered the consequences. After I'd ducked your head a couple of times in the horse trough you managed to get out that people were on their way to give me a going over."

"I can't remember any of that," Mark said.

"Just as well," Patrick said with a sideways smile at me. "I wasn't exactly tender with you."

"You must have come to warn him," I said. "Was it to make up for asking them to do it?"

"I don't know. I can't remember anything."

He became very quiet after this exchange and did not speak until we arrived at our destination. I had an idea that talking about that night had brought some of it into his mind, and how afterwards he had almost fainted from sheer fright upon beholding Patrick in the living room. The finely drawn taunt: "You've been sick" had brought from his subconscious what it was like to be handled by those wiry, wringing fingers and thus ensured his complete co-operation.

When we were parked at the side of the road, Mark removed the keys from the ignition and sat still, staring at nothing. Finally he said, "What's the word? Wimp? Spoiled brat? You tell me."

"Where did you find them?" Patrick said, speaking rather sharply.

"I didn't. They found me. In Bob's Deli."

"But that's not where you ate."

"No. I'd gone in there to buy some sandwiches to take to the trotting races. I knew I'd miss dinner. Bryce came in and asked me to go to Jasper's Creek with them for a few beers. I didn't really want to—I don't usually drink with them other than when they take me fishing. But I did, and it all got out of hand."

Frowning, Patrick got out of the truck and strolled away from it, hands in pockets. Then, in mid-stride he turned and walked quickly back to rest both arms on the wound down window, staring at Mark penetratingly for a moment. "Tell you what—I don't believe you bleated to them about me at all." With that, he commenced an examination of the roadside by the burnt out trees.

"What you must bear in mind," I said in an undertone to Mark, "is that you encountered the very, very best. Not even trained soldiers can withstand him when he's after information. The MoD let him loose on people accused of spying."

"But now he's being kind."

"Oh no, never think that. Patrick is never kind. He gets right to the truth in the most ruthless fashion and doesn't care if he strips people psychologically naked."

"Then why did he say that?"

"Because as far as he's concerned, it *is* the truth."

"Fair enough," said Mark, preparing to get out of the cab.

"Of course I'm only speaking about those things that he regards as part of his job," I said, detaining him with a hand on his arm.

"So where do I really stand, having given him another hiding for imitating Stalky?"

"You're still confusing the issue," I told him. "That was duty, and when he's working he always plays with fire. Getting singed is part of the job." I couldn't help smiling at the worried expression on Mark's face. "Right now, if you want the moon go and ask him for it and he'll give it to you."

Young active people always want self defence lessons from Patrick and Mark proved to be no exception. When Patrick had come within earshot he said, "Bryce'll come back. He's never run away from anyone. When he does—"

"You'll keep out of the way," Patrick interposed.

"You could teach me a few tricks of the trade in case you aren't around."

"I'd be court martialled if you so much as bent an eyelash."

Mark coloured but persevered. "No one need know."

Patrick took a deep breath. One day, perhaps, he will set up a survival school. In the meantime he is kept very busy teaching nephews, nieces and cousins how to beat off would-be rapists, bank robbers and other law breakers.

"If my leg allows it," Patrick said. "And if I have the time I might, for a small fee to make it legal as strictly speaking I am free-lance . . ."

Mark was grinning.

". . . teach you the rudiments of looking after yourself."

They went away to examine closely the ground at the place where Andy had died. I had seen enough. So I listened to the birds, catching a glimpse of a blue jay dipping and bowing as it scolded the two men slowly quartering the ground. Self-defence lessons notwithstanding, I was pretty sure that the first person whom Patrick or Terry would remove from the battle arena should the Gaspereau brothers arrive waving axes would be Mark.

From their actions I could see that they were trying to reconstruct the accident, if indeed it was such. Following Patrick's instructions Mark paced the distance from the skid marks that were still visible on the road to the tree that had taken the full impact. They returned in a few minutes dusty and slapping at insects, after hunting around in the undergrowth near where the car had burnt out.

"I'd like to have had a look at the wreck," Patrick muttered.

Mark said, "They're kept in a locked compound until the police say they can be disposed of."

We exceeded the speed limits all the way back into Port Charles.

My sensation of horror returned at the sight of the remains of the car. Inside there were just the bare frames of the seats, the crumpled driver's wheel. The headlights had gone, leaving holes like empty eye sockets in a skull.

"Surely the police . . ." I started to say, but Patrick was already right inside the wreck, his shoes crunching on broken glass and rusting metal.

Mark, examining the tyreless rear wheels, said, "I wouldn't say, looking at these, that he'd had a tyre blow out and driven along on the rims."

"What about the front ones?" Patrick asked, intent on the dashboard area.

"I've already looked. The left one flew off on impact and wasn't burnt—it's over there. Seems all right. The other's

really chewed up. It must have sort of folded up underneath.''

''There were only skid marks,'' Patrick mused. ''It can't
have folded up there or the suspension would have gouged a
hell of a groove in the road, and the car would have probably
turned right round in a circle. But it didn't—it carried on as
though the bend wasn't there. That suggests driver failure to
me.'' He exclaimed softly and beckoned us over.

''What is it?'' I asked, already almost certain that the mark
on the left hand side of the windscreen mounting was the
result of a bullet having ricochetted off it.

''Murder,'' said Patrick. ''I would guess that the shot came
slightly from behind, through the rear right-hand window.
Whether it caused a flesh wound in his face, creased his scalp
or only frightened the living daylights out of him the result
was the same—the car crashed.''

''Wouldn't it have been noticeable that he'd been shot?
Even after . . .''

''Not necessarily. If his skull was damaged they might
have assumed he hadn't fastened his seat belt and been thrown
forward.'' Patrick shot a quick glance in my direction. ''I
won't bore you with any details of what happens to the human
body in extremely high temperatures.''

But I knew, writers are a fund of that kind of knowledge.
Indian funeral pyres, cremation, people trapped inside burning cars . . . in a situation of intense heat the skull usually
explodes.

I went back to the pick-up leaving them to inspect the rear
right-hand door. When they climbed back into the cab Patrick told me that there were no bullet holes or other ricochet
marks that he could see on any other part of the chassis so it
was fairly safe to assume, as he had already put forward, that
there had been one shot through the rear right-hand window.

''We're talking about someone who is an extremely good
shot,'' he went on. ''I'm sure that the decision as to how the
job was going to be done was taken right at the last moment.

You have to make all sorts of last-minute decisions when you're going to kill someone. What was the weather like?'' he snapped at Mark, obviously regretting the indiscretion.

''Warm,'' he replied. ''The whole week had been warm. Unseasonably so. It took everyone by surprise.''

''Not so difficult then,'' Patrick said. ''I suggest we go back and work the area again.''

I helped them search for a while but in the end was driven back to the pick-up by insects; minute black flies that sucked my blood without me feeling them but which left holes from which I continued to bleed afterwards, and mosquitoes that whined and stung.

From where I was sitting I could see Patrick and Mark. Both had raided the forest for sticks with which to probe in the undergrowth. Patrick, I knew, was suffering. On the flat he is nearly as mobile as anyone. Make him walk through thick matted vegetation and, shockingly, he is suddenly a man with an artificial leg. Mark was probably learning some new adjectives.

They found what they were looking for. By the roadside, much further away from the point where the car had left the road than anyone expected, was a patch of grass still flattened, a few ground out cigarette stubs and three empty beer cans.

''I could drink the harbour dry,'' Mark said, grimacing as he wiped away the evidence of black fly bites on his face and arms.

''We'll report this first and then you can dive in,'' Patrick told him.

At a little after five-thirty we left police headquarters where no one had offered us so much as a coffee, the entire building apparently bereft of coin-in-the-slot drinks machines.

One hand on the door handle of the pick-up, Patrick slowly removed it to eye Mark narrowly. ''If you like we'll have lesson one in staying alive.''

"Here?" queried Mark with commendable politeness. "In the car park?"

"Why not?"

"OK," Mark agreed.

Patrick indicated that I should climb aboard and then got in after me. He spoke to Mark through the open door. "Get in."

Mark sat behind the wheel. "I'm ready."

"Drive us home."

When we had travelled about a mile during which nobody spoke, Patrick reached behind me and clapped Mark on the shoulder. "Well done."

"I don't understand," Mark said.

"Lesson one in staying alive is to do as I tell you, however unreasonable the orders seem . . . and without asking questions."

There was to be no opportunity for Patrick and I to discuss anything in private for that evening Paul Rogers was poisoned.

CHAPTER 9

At first no one realised how serious it was. But after a while, when he was still ceaselessly vomiting, my blood ran cold. It had started with horrible suddenness. One moment he had been joking with Terry; the next doubled over with agonising stomach cramps, his dinner splattered widely across the floor. McAlister and Terry had half carried him to a downstairs cloakroom where he had continued to be devastatingly ill.

I found Patrick with Mark in the basement, interrupting concentration during a deadly *pas de deux* to the extent of being responsible for Patrick being upended ignominiously into a settee.

"Sorry," I said in response to his glower, "but Paul's been taken terribly ill."

"Have you called the doctor?" he asked when I had given him a few details.

"Margaret's doing it now. I told her that I thought an ambulance would be more appropriate but she said that he's prone to violent bilious attacks."

Hands on hips, slightly out of breath, Patrick said, "What is your diagnosis?" He was not being sarcastic. All D12 operatives are trained to recognise the symptoms of many illnesses.

"I think he's been poisoned," I said.

These five words were sufficient to put into operation one of our rehearsed routines. I didn't have to be told, it was enough to see him unhook his gun harness from the antlers of a stuffed moose head and strap it on. We mounted the stairs to the ground floor, I to close all outside windows, lock all exterior doors and locate a powerful flash lamp that I knew was kept in the kitchen. This was in case the power supply was cut off deliberately from outside. It is not unknown for a diversion such as a poisoning to be created within a household before armed men break in.

Emma, with a bucket of hot soapy water and a cloth, was down on her knees on her precious polished floor, frantically mopping and half crying with misery and disgust. "Where's David?" she called when she saw me.

"At the boat."

"I know he's at the boat," she wailed. "Surely someone's rung the marina by now and left a message that he's to come home?"

Not surprisingly no one had, so to keep her quiet I did, at the same time making a mental note to tell Patrick that Hartland would shortly be banging on his own front door.

Paul had by now collapsed, barely conscious, complaining that his face and hands were going numb. Between them McAlister and Terry had removed his soiled outer clothing and wrapped him in a blanket. I called the doctor's number again and spoke to her partner who agreed that the case sounded sufficiently grave to warrant an ambulance.

It made a strange tableau, the blanket-wrapped man lying on the rug in the entrance hall, Patrick crouched by him, gun drawn, the DARE staff back in their hideaway under the stairs sitting on the floor, Terry behind the front door, also with gun ready. Emma stood looking over the bannisters from the living area above, her floor washing completed. She did not seem to have noticed the splashes of vomit on the tiles in the cloakroom.

Patrick's gun trained quickly when Mark ran in from the dining room, causing him to come to a dead stop.

"Walk—don't run," said Patrick softly.

"What did he throw up?" enquired Mark.

"Everything, I should imagine," Patrick said coldly.

Paul groaned and writhed, twisting himself partially out of the blanket. I went to him and covered him again. He didn't seem aware of my presence.

"Oh, come on! Come on!" cried Emma, beating her clenched fists on the bannister rail, but whether she was referring to her husband or the ambulance I was not sure.

Mark had gone into the cloakroom and now came out, rather pale. "Clams," he said. "It was clams. You can see it was."

"Mark! Must you?" Emma shrieked at him.

But Mark ignored her, staring at Patrick. "If it was bad clams then he's a gonner."

"Surely he wouldn't have eaten them if they were bad," Patrick reasoned.

"No!" said Mark angrily. "Shellfish poisoning. Haven't you been reading the papers?"

"It would seem not."

"I have," Terry said. "There's a minute poisonous plant that the shellfish ingest which makes them toxic. You can't taste it and cooking doesn't eliminate the poison. Three people died last week."

Paul was still alive at six the following morning. That was the hour when Terry relieved Patrick at his bedside. Terry took with him the information that an Inspector Le Blek had called with two of his men, one of them a forensic scientist, soon after Paul had been taken to the hospital. Le Blek had questioned everyone briefly while the man from the forensic department had collected specimens.

"Le Blek has to investigate, even if it's only a straightforward case of Paul eating the wrong clams," Patrick said, very tired and obviously haunted by what he had seen. "If you're interested in the scientific stuff it's a plant called Gonyaulax-Tamarensis. The boffins refer to it as a dinoflag-

ellate, and it produces a poison fifty times stronger than cu-
rare.''

He smiled wearily. ''I wrote it down. I can always remember things when I write them down. Clams and mussels eat
this plant and it makes them pretty deadly, but periwinkles
aren't affected as they graze on larger seaweed. Scallops consume it too but we throw away the poisonous part and only
eat the muscle.''

''Does Paul have a chance?'' I asked, getting to the point.

''Depends. As Terry said, cooking doesn't affect the toxin. There's no antidote.''

''No antidote!''

''That's what the doctor was careful to impress on me.
Another point not in Paul's favour is that local people can
build up a resistance to it. They might be unaffected by a
meal that would make a visitor very ill.''

''I don't understand why Le Blek has to investigate if it's
an accident.''

''Because these plants stain the sea red and clam collecting
is automatically made illegal in any area where this is observed. A special watch is mounted in the summer months
when the danger's at its height. And three people died last
week, don't forget—it might just be accidental.''

I broke the silence that followed by saying, ''Paul is the
real brains of this outfit.''

''He's also the only one in the team who likes clams so if
anyone's going to be poisoned accidentally it would be Paul.
We mustn't become carried away by thoughts of murder.''

I felt quite useless. With no meals to plan and cook, no
garden to tend, and quite unable to write a word, I read until
my eyes ached—mostly light fiction of Emma's of the kind
that had driven me to writing in the first place, and the better
English Sunday papers, available at certain outlets at three
times the price at home. The latter probably saved my sanity.

After four hours sleep Patrick went to find Mark, who was

spending the week at home as the college was closed for a half-term break. They both disappeared to the basement and neither emerged for nearly twenty-four hours. David and Emma's disapproval of what they knew to be going on down there settled over the household like a chilly miasma. It was typical of Patrick, however, to give everyone something to think about.

Before he departed he asked me if I was feeling better and I think I answered him truthfully because, when a man is dying, one accords one's own minor health worries the same sympathy due to a spoilt whining child. But in quiet moments I had to admit to myself that in a vague, unhappy way I felt decidedly ill.

I was glad that Emma kept away from the basement. Not many mothers, even when the fire of maternalism does not burn unquenchable in their bosoms, will willingly witness their son being taken apart and put back together again, no matter how artistic or necessary the ensuing redevelopment. At the end of this time Mark emerged more exhausted than he thought possible and told me all about it. He was surprised that the tuition had not really been about the martial arts but self-control, admitting to losing his temper four times without being touched. The penalty for this was thirty press-ups on each occasion, his mentor all the while lethally demure.

"Chris Fraser's flying out," said McAlister to Hartland that evening. "Our managing director," he elaborated after Hartland had looked at him quite blankly.

"What does that achieve?"

"It's a gesture of support—that's all," Drew replied, surprised.

"To be with us in our time of need." Hartland spoke slowly, his voice tremulous with false emotion.

Terry walked out, hands clenched.

"Have you been drinking?" McAlister said sharply.

"I might have been," Hartland observed, and also left the room.

"Nerves . . . I hope," I commented, closing the book I had been unable to concentrate on. The phone rang and was answered on an upstairs extension.

"How's Paul?" asked Margaret.

"Very weak," I told her. "They don't hold out much hope for him."

"But he's a fighter," said Patrick who had entered without any of us noticing.

"Who, Paul?" said Margaret. "I wouldn't have said so."

Patrick sprawled on the sofa. "When I was with him—that first night—he was in terrible pain a lot of the time. But I could see just by looking at him that he wasn't going to give in easily."

McAlister repeated the news that Fraser was joining us and Patrick pulled a wry face.

"More worry for you?" Drew hazarded.

"He was the one to whom the letters were addressed. Who knows? This might be exactly what somebody wants him to do."

"Shall I wire him not to come?"

"I'm not sure that I ought to make that kind of decision," Patrick said. "Is it of practical help to you if he does?"

"Certainly. Paul's the computer genius, but the project's all Chris's brainchild. People tend to forget that."

Margaret said, "Chris can produce the technical drawings. If you carry on writing the design documentation, perhaps we can borrow a programmer from Nasonworth."

"That's fine until we hit snags," McAlister told her. "But we can work on like that for a while. Chris might decide to send someone else out from UK."

"That's it then," Patrick announced. "He comes." He frowned as Mark came into the room. "What's wrong? Have you heard from the hospital?"

"No," said Mark. "It was Le Blek. He wanted to know if I'd seen Lanny Gaspereau lately."

"What did you say?"

"I told him the truth."

Patrick gave no reaction. "Go on."

"He asked me if I was aware that he'd served eight years for manslaughter in 1972. I told him no—of course I wasn't."

Patrick said, "I'd already mentioned our small fracas the other night. What else did he say?"

"Lanny's prints were on the cans."

"Lanny's prints were on the cans," Patrick echoed in a whisper. "How interesting. He was the dark-haired one, wasn't he? The only one of the three who was more muscle than fat. Blue eyes, small scar on the left cheek that was probably a legacy from a knife fight. More intelligent than the others so therefore the most dangerous."

"That's Lanny," said Mark.

Patrick subjected him to an unwavering stare. "Did you tell him everything you know?"

"Of course."

"Nothing you deliberately left unsaid?"

"What do you mean?"

"I *am* speaking English."

The basement lessons certainly hadn't cowed Mark. He met Patrick's stare defiantly. "I don't know where Lanny is."

"I'm not really suggesting that you do." The human lie detector was well into his stride by now, his expression intent, never taking his gaze off Mark for a moment. It is a side of Patrick that I do not like at all. "Perhaps there's somewhere he *might* be."

Mark looked at me for support and I said, "Even if you omitted to tell Inspector Le Blek for the best possible reasons."

"Leave him alone!" Margaret said. "He's telling the truth."

"He's lying," Patrick replied. Then, to Mark, "Be warned."

"I was going to talk to you in private about it," Mark mumbled.

Ye gods, even I could see it now. My heart went out to him for I knew Patrick would be utterly merciless.

"Could it be," murmured Patrick, each word a diamond on glass, "that you were hoping that you and I, Hawkeye and the last of the soddin' Mohicans, would track him down and bring him back alive?"

I thought for a moment or two that Mark would burst into tears.

"Go and ring Le Blek back," Patrick said. "Apologise for forgetting to mention the mooring, hut, cabin, hunting lodge, his Aunt Agatha's or wherever else Lanny might be."

"That was really cruel!" Margaret cried when Mark had gone. "It was a perfectly natural thing for him to do after all the attention you've given him."

"And I have enough on my plate," he told her, equally cruelly, "without the complication of hero worship from a teenager neglected by his parents. No, you listen to me," he continued when she opened her mouth to argue. "Do you really expect me to connive with him in concealing information from the police and then scamper all over the boondocks looking for some guy who might or might not have thrown three empty beer cans away in Quispamsis?"

CHAPTER 10

Emma's Morgan mare Queen quivered all over as Patrick lowered himself into the saddle, then snorted and sidled, mouthing the bit. Mark put a hand on the rein.

"It's all right," Patrick told him.

"She doesn't usually take to strangers."

"I'm OK."

A two and a half hour drive was behind us, a slow, hot journey because Queen had kicked the sides of the trailer if Mark drove faster than fifty kilometres an hour. She was to be Patrick's right leg, his own description. The walk was not a long one, perhaps a couple of miles, but along a steep and rough logging track.

Patrick went off down the road for a short trial spin, Queen picking up her small delicate hooves with precision.

"Relax," I told Mark. "Patrick's ridden before."

He watched anxiously. "The mare's used to Mother riding her Western-style. I wish he'd let me put the Western saddle on her then he could have used the pommel to hang on by when the going gets steep."

How do you explain without sounding like a know-all that body strength, a good sense of balance and wrists like steel hawsers can control any horse?

Queen tossed her head a couple of times and tried a little humped-back buck. After all, her rider was far heavier than the indulgent Emma who nursed her through various small alarms by crooning to her in French. Then I saw that Patrick held the reins as though they were a single strand of gossamer but his thighs were unmistakably keeping the animal under control. Shortly afterwards he halted her, turned her round and then laughed delightedly as she responded to his touch by breaking into a sedate armchair canter.

I had been prepared for arguments when I asked to be permitted to accompany them—that is from Mark, not Patrick. I am part of Patrick's back-up team to the last degree, in theory the last one to fire the last bullet if that is how a mission ends. In theory. There had been a couple of exercises along these lines with the SAS as enemy, situations that at the time had seemed twice life-size and twice as bloody. Deliberately made so.

"Ingrid can stay with Queen," Patrick told Mark before he could protest. "Then she can ride and phone if anything goes wrong."

At this moment Ingrid was hating the flies, the sudden heat and a nasty little jingle that was going round inside her head in time to Queen's dancing hoof beats. *Don't ride Emma, ride Emma's mare. Don't ride Emma, ride Emma's mare.*

In fact I hadn't wanted to be present, merely to keep Patrick in my sight. Even to myself I could not explain why. Something to do with the jingle perhaps, and a pile of magazines and disobeying orders and . . . No, I didn't exactly feel differently about him, perhaps it was that time of the month even though the internal processes had gone haywire as they often do when we are on a job.

Paul was still stubbornly clinging to life, slipping in and out of coma. It had not as yet been confirmed whether he was suffering from shellfish poisoning or had had some other form of toxin administered to him. Until such time that this was known Le Blek had mounted a guard over him.

Mark had visited us in our room the previous evening, as we were getting ready for bed. I think Patrick had been expecting him and apologised for not wandering lonely as a cloud in the garden after dinner.

"It was that or crawl up the wastepipe into your shower in the morning," had said Mark, poker-faced, and with apparently no ill effects from the encounter earlier on. It occurred to me then that his education was still in progress and that he was doing magnificently.

"I'm tired," Patrick had said quietly and sounding utterly exhausted. "I'm also aware that you did as I asked and gave Le Blek certain information. But grassing on friends isn't a very pleasant thing to have to do and you're not the kind of person who would make a habit of it. It's better, isn't it, to go after him yourself, even if you take reinforcements, than to bring down the law on him? He'd understand that—your anger that he might be mixed up in the murder of someone who was known to your family."

Mark had nodded, speechless.

"Is Le Blek likely to be able to find this place easily?"

"It's an old bus the brothers use as a hunting lodge. I gave the best directions I could but it's right out in the sticks."

"How long will it take to get there?"

"Three hours—drive and then walk."

"We'll leave at six."

Which was why a trainee architect and the Prime Minister's part-time body-guard were engaged in a manhunt. I was sure the latter had been planning it ever since Le Blek's call.

When we had gone a short distance Mark suggested that he precede us by about fifty yards in order to put Lanny at his ease if he was there. Reluctantly, Patrick agreed.

"Would you like a horse?" I asked, walking at Queen's shoulder.

"If I could have this one." Patrick was not giving me his full attention but ceaselessly scanning the trees and undergrowth.

"Morgans must be available in UK."

"At a price."

The track became steeper, no more than ruts caused by the wheels of vehicles. Water running off the hill had washed soil from between the stones which had then been split and crumbled by frost. The going got very rough indeed. I hung on to Queen's mane but she tended to hurry over the worst parts and I had almost to run to retain her support. Soon we were all sweating profusely.

"Why were you so mad with me that day over the stable?" Patrick enquired, without taking his eyes off his surroundings.

"I thought you were hamming everything up dreadfully."

"And?"

"And nothing. Except perhaps that you seemed to be positively relishing the squalor."

"You called me a bastard."

"Like the old days," I muttered, under my breath, but he heard me.

"At the time I thought you were merely being realistic. Then I realised otherwise. Yes, just like the old days."

"Let's just call it diminished responsibility and leave it at that," I said savagely.

He looked at me. "I simply don't see how I can be accused of—"

"Me!" I interrupted. "It's me I'm talking about. Suddenly I can't face the sight of you looking like Stalky, disobeying Daws' orders, reading filthy magazines and discussing with Terry whether he should bed Emma. Your mind never used to slant that way."

There was a long silence. A heron that we surprised staring into a ditch at the side of the track took off and flapped away like an affronted umbrella.

"I do believe you're right," said Patrick. "No excuses. Not even about the girlie mags. I found them hidden behind the feed sacks—they must have belonged to Bill."

"I can understand that," I said, but heard my grudging tone.

"No, you can't," he replied. "Let's have all the dirty washing on the line. I thought they'd take my mind off Emma."

I made myself view this statement dispassionately, even went so far as to pretend for a moment that I was Terry and we were talking on a man to man basis. Not so long ago, and still fighting an agonising battle against his injuries, Patrick had been so terrified of sexual failure he had shunned the company of all women. Then we had met again and, together, solved the problem. And what a woman like Emma could do to ordinary men like Terry and Paul she could also, it seemed, achieve with the more strong-minded.

"Squalid," said Patrick, looking between his mount's ears. "That's a good word for it. She said she'd show me where I was to sleep and as soon as we got there behaved in a fashion that I won't go into details about. Not even in the army—and I found myself in some pretty awful places after I joined up, you do, it's part of growing up—had I come across anything like it. She wanted me right there and then, standing up, you name it. I managed to get away. I kept thinking of you but that didn't stop me wanting to give her everything she was after. I was on a sort of obscene high for days—couldn't stop thinking about it. I'm sorry."

I hadn't really been after an apology and there had been doubt at the back of my mind that I was right to press him. I just wanted an explanation, reasons perhaps. Now, it appeared that I had them but I felt very cheap. I had made him apologise for being human.

"Still love me?" he whispered.

"Yes," I said, no louder.

Neither of us spoke again until Mark halted and waited for us to catch up with him. The trees had closed in over our heads, excluding even a whisper of a breeze. It was stifling.

"Are you armed?" enquired Mark when still some yards away.

"Howitzer and two mortars," Patrick replied.

"Engage brain before opening mouth?" Mark queried.

Queen stopped before she trod on Mark's toes and gave him a friendly shove. Her rider dismounted and handed the reins to me.

"I saw the bus through a gap in the trees back yonder," Patrick said. "Kindly shed the *Shane* demeanour. I don't intend to take out the windows of the damn thing, and neither do I want to see so much as a hair of your head when I approach it. Is that understood?"

To my relief it was. We left the track and entered a small glade where the trees had been cut down. From there we could just see the back of the vehicle, an old ex-school bus parked not in the clearing but further up the hill, right in the forest. It had been there for many years judging by the way the trees had it in their embrace. From a distance it looked like a fat yellow beetle caught in an insect eating plant.

"Be ready to mount," Patrick said to me. "No, on second thoughts, get on now. If you hear me shout your name, or if there's any shooting the outcome of which you're not sure about, then ride like hell for the pick-up. Tie the horse to a tree and get to a phone. I've put a cross on the map where we parked so you can give Le Blek the reference, and I've written his number on the cover."

I climbed into the saddle. It was a long time since I had done any riding. By the time I had adjusted the stirrups to my shorter legs Patrick and Mark had disappeared. I held my breath and listened for a moment but all I could hear was Queen munching grass and swishing away flies.

From where I was I couldn't see the bus, which, I reasoned, was just as well for it meant that if anyone was inside it they couldn't see me. I fervently hoped that Mark would remember his undertaking to keep out of the way.

The flies became a torture, causing Queen to kick at her belly and swish her tail incessantly. She swatted the ones on her chest and front legs with her nose. I prayed that she wouldn't decide to remove us both back to her trailer.

Resurrecting the Stalky episode was bringing back other old memories.

When the fuss had died down Patrick had once again merged into the untidy howling mob of boys which made life at school so difficult for every eleven-year-old girl. This was not to say that he joined in with the plait yanking, beret snatching and general ribaldry. He was merely male so as far as I and my friends were concerned, inhabited the same black pit as all his contemporaries, beneath our notice.

Then, when we all began to grow up and take an interest in each other, the three year's difference in our ages yawned like a chasm. All of a sudden he was eighteen, Head Boy, captain of the cricket eleven, a member of the water polo team and in possession of a maturity that prompted the staff to send miscreants to him rather than worry the overworked Headmaster. Rumour had it that he listened, advised the timid, awarded lines on a sliding scale to occasional offenders and took bullies and real criminals, male, into the gym for a couple of rounds with him in the boxing ring, thoughtfully providing gloves. Troublemaking swiftly went out of fashion.

Fate had decreed that my father be co-opted on to the Parochial Church Council and he had soon found himself Treasurer as no one else admitted to knowing the first thing about accountancy. Dad was a stockbroker, the typical something in the City with bowler and briefcase. In appearance, he was an orchid amongst a field of cabbages: rare, colourful and slightly outrageous. After one of the PCC meetings, and following a conversation between the two men, the Rector had suggested that his son could help me with my physics homework. The Reverend John Gillard had been almost beside himself with gratitude at the time for my father had just announced that he had discovered the existence of a savings account of church funds, long forgotten about, that had accrued several hundred pounds in interest.

The following Thursday Patrick had arrived, eyed my

muddle of exercise and text books scattered over the kitchen table, seated himself and simmered. Then, appearing to notice my existence for the first time, asked me heavily what my problem was.

Total confusion, a new sensation for I was a very organised person in those days, had come over me. It was only afterwards that I made the decision that here was the man I wanted, for ever and ever. There was also the realisation that he was unattainable, not a male to be won by thrusting my adolescent bosom under his nose. This knowledge, a kind of instant acquisition of womanhood, materialised in less time than it took to draw a neat line beneath the words "Specific Gravity."

"Would you like a glass of white wine?" I had enquired, outwardly concentrating on my text book but in reality not seeing one printed word. I had glanced up, schooling my expression to one of polite disinterest. One black eyebrow had quirked and those unholy grey eyes of his had bored into mine. Somehow I had held the look. If I giggled, I was finished.

"OK," he had drawled. "Thanks."

I had penned a few lines concerning Specific Gravity and then addressed him again. "You'll have to open it." The Hock was to have accompanied the Sunday dinner and I had been involved in some frantic mental arithmetic as to the state of my Post Office savings account with which I would have to replace it.

"Perhaps we'd better have coffee," Patrick had decided and himself put the kettle on. I had stood around feeling useless while he had asked my parents, watching television in the living room, whether they would like some and had then returned to make it, beans, grinder and all—we never drank instant—unerringly putting his hands on china, spoons and all the ingredients. It was not until several weeks later that he had confessed to being given coffee by my mother every week when he delivered her butcher's order, and had watched her make it.

We had tried to score points off one another for the rest of the evening but then it had become unnecessary for what we had become involved with was not physics but chemistry.

We rode our bikes, took the dogs for walks and went for long rambles over Dartmoor. I discovered that his main attraction, other than looks, was his ability to make me laugh. He was then, as now, a superb mimic. One day we both laughed until we cried, hugging each other under a hot summer sky.

We were both quite innocent until that moment when I felt the warm skin of his back through his shirt and the way the sinews of his body flowed beneath my fingers. I had drawn back, shocked speechless by the delicious pang that had shafted through me.

Both innocents, we had not so much as kissed before. One moment we had never touched one another and the next were as close as it is possible for two human beings to become. It seemed a logical conclusion for suddenly he was my man and I his woman. There was nothing planned or furtive, it was the only way we could express this discovery of possession.

I can remember nothing of removing clothes, no awkwardness, fumbling or embarrassment. Gazing up at the sky I had fleetingly wondered what it would be like and then he had touched me and I had known. A little later, gentle but strong, he had entered me and there had been bright, blazing pain. He had paused, kissing away the few tears, but then I had urged him on. Subsequent pleasure had taken us both by surprise and we had lain paired for a long time, greedily drinking the last few drops of nectar.

For a week it had been our drug. In scorchingly hot summer weather we escaped whenever we could to the empty open moor and extracted every possible moment of pleasure from our young bodies. By this time of course we knew that we were doing wrong, our upbringing had seen to that.

Patrick had then suffered a severe bout of conscience and offered to marry me. My reply that I was under age had caused him to attain a shade of paleness that I had not believed humanly possible. Then he had repeated the proposal, come hell, high water, horsewhips and jail. I had accepted.

After this there had been an unspoken understanding that we would behave ourselves and wait. Then, when his three "A" levels and considerable ingenuity had made him acceptable material for the police, I did not see him so often. After a few months he left to join the army and I hardly saw him at all for two years.

We married when I was twenty-one. By that time the Gillards had moved to Hinton Littlemoor in Somerset and the ceremony was performed there by the Bishop of Bath and Wells. It was a wedding that the village has talked about ever since; military uniforms, a horse drawn carriage, the ancient church aglow with flowers. If only my father had lived to give me away then my day would have been really perfect. He had died shortly before of a crippling disease that had turned him into an old man in his forties.

Perhaps we had never stopped to think before we were married. Patrick simply wasn't the marrying sort by then; too many places to visit, too much to do, a real professional soldier. We began to have rows—about his long absences from home, his holier than thou attitude when he *was* around—all culminating in total war when he discovered I had been taking the pill without telling him. Then we had split up.

Now we were together again, had come full circle, and things still weren't right.

I glanced at my watch and saw that six minutes had gone by. Queen was taking me too close for comfort to some overhanging branches as she grazed so I picked up the reins, nudged her with my heels and turned her away from them. She made for a lush patch of grass and tugged at it greedily.

I had forgotten that animals have their own early warning systems. All at once her head shot up and her ears pricked forward. She stopped chewing to listen, long strands of grass hanging from her mouth. Just as I was about to dig her with my heels again she recommenced grazing but warily, looking into the trees. I grabbed some of her mane, preparing for flight but just then she sighed noisily and a small brown porcupine trundled out of the undergrowth and went across the track like a clockwork toy.

I felt weak, sweat trickling down my back.

"Please don't let it be much longer," I whispered. Every day, every moment, it seemed that a mirror was being held up before me, forcing me to view my own inadequacies. What on earth had a colonel in MI5 seen in me to convince him of my usefulness?

Queen threw up her head and to my horror let out a ringing, brassy neigh. Then I saw that she had seen Patrick and it only needed me to pick up the reins again for her to set off at a jaunty walk in his direction.

"He's dead," Patrick said. "Someone cut his throat."

CHAPTER 11

I stared at him stupidly.

"Looks as though he drank himself into a stupor and was then murdered. There's no sign of a struggle."

The greens of the trees pressed into my eyes, the buzz of insects grew louder.

"It happened a couple of days ago I should think . . . there are plenty of flies."

It became imperative that I dismount but when I had done so there was no strength in my legs. I suppose Patrick caught me for the next thing I was aware of was him mopping my face with his handkerchief soaked in water from a ditch.

"I'm not at all the fainting sort," I mumbled and then pure shame made me cry. Survival training in the Cairngorms had come to this.

Patrick was concerned but also impatient to report to Le Blek. He scrubbed at my face with the moistened handkerchief, tilted up my chin and kissed me. "Don't fret. I know you're not. Is it that time of the month?"

How could I sit there blethering that I was no bloody good at my job when a man was lying dead with his throat cut not a hundred yards away? I got to my feet, regretted it, took several deep breaths and went over to Queen who frisked me busily for sugar.

"You ride her."

"No, your leg'll chafe raw in this heat." Even after all this time there was not the courage to talk of stumps.

Every step of the way back I wished I had taken up his offer. "You're too old," whispered an inner taunting voice, "stick to writing." When we reached the pick-up it was like an oven after standing in the sun. Was I going to faint again, be sick or die? I didn't particularly care.

We stopped at a store we had passed on the way out and Patrick phoned Le Blek. I knew that the instructions how to find Lanny's remains would be precise to an obsessive degree; the exact number of telegraph poles from a certain landmark to where the narrow track joined the highway, a compass bearing, perhaps a report on the condition of the track as to its suitability for police vehicles, any information that could be of the slightest use.

I sat in the truck, resting my head on the side of the cab. Mark was not over-communicative either, fiddling with the radio, trying to find some music. This proved to be saturation bombing heavy rock and after I had given him a long suffering look he switched it off.

"Never seen a dead body before?" I enquired.

He rubbed his palms across his face wearily. "Only a guy that got knocked down by a car in Port Charles and I didn't get that close. When I saw Lanny I thought at first that he was smiling, then I realised that the smile was across his neck. He was all sort of stiff and bloated and there were flies coming out of his mouth."

"Nasty," I agreed, failing to convince myself that I was not after all going to be sick or faint.

Mark said, "When I phoned Le Blek back another bloke answered, one of his men. He said his boss had been called out to a robbery. That's probably why we haven't seen him."

"Mmm."

It was strange how I could converse like this and at the same time be engaged in hectic calculations.

* * *

One might be forgiven for picturing a man called Le Blek as short, dapper and prone to making expressive Gallic gestures whilst speaking. Nothing could be further from reality. The RCMP man, for this was what he was, not from the local police, was nearly as tall as Leander Hurley, wore his clothes like a scarecrow in a gale and when sitting, like now, his hands rested in his lap. But the fingers clasped and unclasped as though they might be more usefully employed holding a gun or twisting a suspect's arms up his back. In the jargon of the Wild West, he looked mean.

"You're sure you touched nothing?" he said to Patrick.

We were in the dining room at Ravenscliff; Le Blek, Patrick and myself sitting around the table, Hartland leaning on the wall by the door as if to prevent anyone escaping and Mark standing just to one side of and behind Patrick's chair. I found it interesting choreography.

"The door of the bus was open," Patrick told him. "I went in, saw what had happened and came out again. Mark took a peep and decided to give it a miss. Then I went in again and looked around for a little longer. Neither of us laid hands on anything." He took his time before he continued but Le Blek, surprisingly, did not interrupt or try to hurry him. "I can understand your irritation with us. I'm not trying to do your job for you."

Le Blek looked at Mark for a moment, who squirmed, and then said, "Well at least you had the decency to give me a bell and tell me what you found. Can't say that I understand your methods though, taking a woman along. Does the British Army have female scouts these days?"

"Only on night sorties," said Patrick.

Le Blek did not smile. "You guys on some kind of assignment over here?"

Patrick said, "I believe I mentioned that my brief is to—"

"I know all that," the other interrupted. "You've just told me about it and I reckon I've got it off by heart. Give."

"OK," Patrick said after a pause. "I exceeded my brief."

"Is that all you have to say?"

"Yup."

Le Blek leaned forward. "Mister, I could have you run in as a suspect, and young damp-round-the-ears hiding behind you."

Mark's hands gripped the back of Patrick's chair but his face remained expressionless.

"Why did you tell Mark that Lanny's prints were on the cans we found near Andy's accident?" Patrick asked.

"Ill-judged," Le Blek agreed.

At this moment Emma came in to tell Hartland that London wanted him on the phone.

Le Blek said, "I made Gaspereau's record known to him for the same reason—to frighten him off any detective work."

To Mark, Patrick said, "Please take a short walk in the garden for five minutes."

When he had gone out Le Blek said, "Mister, if I want to interview that—"

"It's Major, or didn't you learn that bit off by heart?" Patrick cut in. "You're wasting my time as well as your own. I'm answering none of your questions in front of Hartland and members of his family. In a nutshell this is the state of the game: the marine consultancy earning its living helping to haul your navy out of the birchbark canoe era is heavily involved at home with work on the Trident programme. So when the managing director is threatened, MI5 become very interested. Furthermore, when one of the company's top engineers is killed on a road here in a manner I have proved fairly conclusively not to be an accident, everyone at home gets slightly jittery.

"Then," he went on, "the real whizz kid with the brains is poisoned. This *might* be accidental, but you said yourself that even if it is shellfish poisoning you want to know where he ate the clams. Right?"

"Agreed," said Le Blek stolidly.

"Going back to the Gaspereau brothers . . ."

"They're real filth," Le Blek interposed and Patrick paused, frowning. "Been terrorising the whole neighbourhood since they were knee-high. Any amount of folk would queue up to cut their throats."

Patrick nodded. "Can I rely on your discretion?"

"In what connection?"

"In connection with the fact that David Hartland is involved with the British security services."

"I already knew that."

"How?" Patrick rapped out.

"I got it from Hurley—he should know."

Then, I was convinced, Le Blek could have bitten off his tongue. He had never before come across the Gillard method of retreat, charm and pounce. Patrick glanced at me and his eyes were smiling. But he gave Le Blek his reward.

"Bryce Gaspereau has been to this house before."

Le Blek swallowed his pride. "When, and who saw him?"

"The old gardener, though he was a bit vague about it. There were other men as well."

"Hurley did mention . . ."

"I'm sure he did," Patrick said dryly. "Women like that tend to stick in the memory."

"You think something's going on here?"

"Quade was on his way to meet Emma the night he was killed."

"Can you prove that?"

"Definitely. She booked the motel room in her own name. I'm convinced that Mark didn't set those thugs on me either."

"It's not what you've said," said Le Blek slowly after a short silence, "but what you've left out." He brooded. "I appreciate that people in your line of business don't have to get a bloke drunk before you rub them out but—"

"Yes, I noticed that in the bus too," Patrick interrupted. "One pile of empty cans neatly stacked in one corner with the pull-rings dropped inside, the others—those near Lanny—just dropped on the floor."

"You said you didn't touch anything."

"I carry a small flash lamp," he was told. "All the best burglars do."

"Any idea why he wasn't killed with a bullet?"

"You know why—bullets can be traced to weapons."

"D'you carry a small knife too?"

"Ask a sensible question . . . like why worry about bullets being identified when only an hour's drive away is the border with a country where it's every citizen's right to carry arms?"

The corners of Le Blek's mouth turned down but nevertheless conveyed the impression of a smile. "Let's stick to what we know. Lanny Gaspereau is dead. Some time before that happened he might have stood by the side of the road to Quispampsis, smoked a few cigarettes and drunk three cans of Labatts. There is a possibility that he was waiting for someone and that he took a shot at that person and the guy was killed. Are you saying that the Hartland woman fixed it all up?"

"It was no secret where Quade was going."

"That's an evasive answer. Did she then arrange to have Lanny killed to prevent him talking?"

"Whoever did would be aware of his drinking habits and that he might shoot his mouth off if he had a skinful."

Le Blek gave an impatient shrug, as if he was trying to shake off the entire line of reasoning. "This doesn't feel right to me. It just doesn't tie in with a guy in Britain getting a threatening letter."

"It was probably made to look like that."

But Le Blek was off on another tack. "What you said just now . . . about identifying bullets. What did you mean?"

"The KGB prefer to use the home made product."

"Here? Don't make me laugh. I think I might learn a lot more by asking the Hartland boy about the Gaspereau brothers' friends and acquaintances."

Patrick stood up just as Hartland re-entered the room. "He's clean. I've talked to him. They only took him fishing."

Le Blek also rose and for a moment there was a bizarre

vision in my mind of two characters in a Wild West film reaching for their guns. In reality neither of them moved a muscle for several seconds. Then Mark came in.

"Sonny," said Le Blek to him. "You nearly got yourself into a load of trouble. Next time, ignore what some foreigner tells you and leave police work to those whose job it is."

"My son is a British subject," Hartland said. "Have you finished with your enquiries?"

"For the moment," Le Blek said and left.

Hartland rounded on Mark. "I hope you realise what he meant. His notion of trouble is to take you to a quiet place and paste hell out of you."

I bit back the retort that sprang to my lips, that over Patrick's dead body would Mark have been removed from the house for more questioning.

"Well?" rapped out Hartland. "Will he be back?"

"He might," Patrick said. "When he discovers, or someone tells him, that Lanny's hunting rifle wasn't in the bus."

"Did you take it?"

"Of course I didn't bloody take it! You seem to forget that I'm trying to solve this business."

"I do sometimes wonder, Major."

But at least we had discovered that Leander Hurley was with the Canadian Security Service.

Chris Fraser's presence could not fail to be supportive. Although several inches below six feet in height he was a big man, barrel chested and with a small pot belly. His appearance was deceptive however for he moved like a cat and had graceful precise hands. Fascinated, I sat in Emma's favourite chair in the living room and watched him light his pipe, the actions slow and methodical, his gaze straying now and again to admire the view through the window. He had grey eyes, greying fair wavy hair and a slow charming smile as he turned to speak to me.

"I read *One for Sorrow*," he said. His voice, like the tobacco in his pipe, was a rich and deep nut brown.

I said, "I hope you took no notice if anyone told you that I'm reputed to be read mainly by women."

He chuckled. "I read pretty well anything about Devon, including fiction. My sister is a great fan of yours—she gave it to me to read. I hope you're working on *Two for Joy*."

This was not telepathy on his part of course. The titles come from an old country saying concerning the sighting of certain numbers of magpies;

> *One for sorrow,*
> *Two for joy,*
> *Three for a girl,*
> *And four for a boy.*

I told him that I was, adding that I couldn't work on it in Canada, the life style was too different.

"Oh yes," he agreed. "You'd have no problem, though, if you were telling a tale of Scottish border skirmishes."

Talking of skirmishes, I thought, seeing Patrick approach us in a manner that suggested he had lost his wallet and found a run over skunk. I introduced them to each other.

"Pleased to meet you, Major," said Fraser. "Seeing as your good lady has just informed me that she can't concentrate on the writing, I assume she's helping you keep your powder dry."

"Wavy navy?" Patrick enquired, neatly side-stepping the remark with a broad smile. From the way his expression had changed I knew he had assumed me to be alone.

Fraser clapped Patrick on the shoulder with the hand not holding his pipe, quite hard I reckoned. "Territorials actually. My guess is that you're Royal Engineers and were down in the South Atlantic. In command of your own reconnaissance section, were you?"

It was either a real fluke or Patrick had met his match in placing people.

He said, "I was down in the South Atlantic but not with that outfit."

"So you didn't tread on a mine," Fraser responded. "I've a confession to make. When the taxi delivered me out front you were on the far side of the garden. You've a swing to your step like an oppo of mine who did just that and got his foot blown off. My apologies."

"Tin right leg below the knee," Patrick said. "Grenade."

After dinner and fuelled with rye they yarned solidly for three hours. Everyone listened, me included, for the simple reason that Patrick does not very often talk about his service experiences as he is afraid of boring people. But when he does, like all good stories, one tends to learn more from them about the man recounting them than why Britain had won the wars but lost an Empire.

I went up to bed at a little after midnight leaving Patrick, Chris and Terry still talking. The others had retired earlier and Mark, it appeared, was staying with a friend's family for the night. After a while I heard Terry come upstairs and yes, it was his own room he went into. The hinges of Emma's door squeaked, his didn't.

The frogs, crickets and other rural night life were in fine voice. I tossed and turned, a suspicion growing in my mind that downstairs an age old contest was in progress. Take an intelligent man of moderate habits—well, fairly moderate—place him among his contemporaries, provide alcohol, and lo and behold their collective mental ages plummet to a figure indicated by holding up the fingers of one hand.

I went down.

The empty whisky bottle stood on the table between them, together with several Moosehead beer cans, also empty, and an overflowing ashtray with Fraser's pipe resting on the top. Fraser himself seemed to be asleep, fists propping up his chin. Patrick lounged back pensively smoking one of Mc-Alister's half coronas, eyes slitted against the smoke.

"Are you never coming to bed?" I hissed from the doorway.

He considered. "Truly," he agreed solemnly. "One day I shall come to bed."

"You can't even stand," I informed him heavily. It was yet another clip from one of those bloody cowboy films, the hero drinking all the baddies under the table. The scenario seemed to be falling into the general pattern for suddenly Fraser's head fell off his fists and thundered into the ashtray. Patrick gazed at him serenely for a moment and then smiled at me, innocent as a newborn boa constrictor.

"The first thing that goes overboard," I told him, "is the hard won co-ordination of your right leg."

Patrick laid down the cigar, gripped the edge of the table and stood up. Then he transferred his right hand to the back of the chair, let go of the table with his left and manoeuvred himself behind the chair.

"Use it as a walking frame," I suggested. "I'll go in front with a red flag."

"Ingrid," he said plaintively. "I'm not drunk."

I took the chair away and smiled broadly at the inevitable result. "Then why lie on the floor?"

He giggled. Why do I always love him so much when he giggles?

However, under no circumstances does a husband of mine spend the night in the middle of the living room floor. A swift raid and a strategically aimed squirt from a soda siphon got him to his feet with a yell and I piloted him upstairs praying that no one would investigate the noise.

Once upstairs Patrick subsided onto the bed and then in response to my look sheepishly onto the floor where he distastefully set about removing his damp nether garments.

"Fraser's a soldier," he murmured, more to himself than to me.

I gave him his bath robe. "So he said."

"He spent a lot of his childhood in India, is an excellent shot and has been trained in jungle warfare methods. According to Daws he's very highly thought of in the Territorials."

Even though his eyes weren't properly focussed it wasn't the drink talking. "So?"

"What if Andy was going to pinch Fraser's ideas and make a lot of money out of them?"

"Never. He wasn't like that. Besides, Paul has the brains."

"But Quade was the businessman. And he could have persuaded Paul to join him without much trouble. Paul's a genius but like so many egg-heads a bit naïve. He wouldn't have taken much convincing that his work would bear more fruit under Andy's guidance."

"It's all supposition."

"But suppose again that someone told Fraser that he was going to do it?"

"Who, for God's sake?"

"Margaret Howard, for example."

"You've been on the phone to Daws," I whispered.

"Yes—when I went down to the airport to find out if our friend really did get off the Halifax plane. Margaret Howard was engaged to Andy some years ago and he broke it off because she was seeing another bloke."

"Fraser!"

"Precisely."

"So she *is* a bitch," I said, and Patrick grinned at my vehemence.

"It has to be fully checked out but according to Daws she now has an East German boyfriend."

CHAPTER 12

Paul did not die. At about the same time that he began to respond to the heroic and unrelenting efforts of the nursing staff a weighty and detailed report was presented to Le Blek. It concluded that Paul's illness had been caused by shellfish poisoning, its severity, taking into account the small amount of poison ingested, the result of a weak constitution and other contributing factors. The author had thoroughly covered the latter, writing at length on such subjects as unseasonal sea temperatures, fluctuations in tide patterns and the patient's blood pressure.

"But I haven't a weak constitution," Paul protested when Patrick read some of it out to him a couple of days later. "Just prone to biliousness—I always have been. Bloody hell, I run marathons."

"Never mind, old son," Patrick said. "Just get better and keep well away from everything in shells except eggs."

As are all who have had a very close brush with death, Paul was vibrant with life when we visited him. He seemed quite oblivious to the drip tube in his arm and if anyone had shown him his reflection in a mirror, a black stubble of beard growing on a gaunt face the colour of tallow, he gave no hint of concern.

"You stayed, didn't you?" he said to Patrick. "All that first night. I'm sure I didn't dream it. Did I dream the bit where they tried to make you leave and you drew a gun on

112

them and said that it was your job not to let me out of your sight?"

"Definitely," Patrick answered with a smile.

Paul smiled back knowingly. "A real dream was that it was weeks that I'd been lying here and I opened my eyes and you were still sitting by my side. There was a nurse as well. I felt sort of numb all over—like just after it first hit me— and then it seemed that I was floating away. Suddenly you grabbed my hand and rested your forehead on it so I couldn't see your face. The pain came back and even though I thought I was going to die I knew you were praying for me. Then all I could feel was your hand gripping mine. It hurt like hell. Then I woke up and there was a copper by the side of the bed."

"Hallucinations," Patrick said. "It's a symptom of the poisoning. Do you feel up to answering a few questions?"

"Fire away. But it won't be much help—Le Blek's already asked them all."

Patrick quirked an eyebrow at me. "Like where you got the clams, for instance?"

"He already knew that. Commander Hurley had rung him and told him I had had lunch at his place that day. I don't know what the fuss is all about really, Hurley ate some too. He nigh-on lives on the things at this time of the year. I suppose his body is used to the substance that laid me low."

I said, "I thought he was staying at the Delta."

"Was," Paul replied. "He cleared out a week ago when he realised he was going to be in Port Charles for quite a while. He has a first floor flat in Manawagonish Road. It's really nice—looks out over the river."

"Must get a goodly dose of pong from the pulp mill when the wind's in the east." Patrick mused. "Did he cook these things himself or did they come from a take-out?"

"Surely you still don't suspect anyone of—"

"I'm suspecting anyone who singles out DARE engineers

for special treatment, whether it's for bullets or clam lunches.''

''I was planning on going to Market Square with the others for a lobster roll but Hurley said he had these clams a friend had given him. We'd been talking about sea-food.''

''It does look fairly innocent,'' I said. ''Especially as he phoned Le Blek when he heard what had caused Paul's illness and told him.''

''It's undoubtedly perfectly innocent,'' Patrick said with some asperity. ''But do remember that all well-planned murders are intended to look that way. Tell me,'' he said to Paul, acknowledging a signal from a nurse that it was time to go, ''did Andy Quade make any business propositions to you?''

''Business propositions?''

''Offers.''

''You mean set up with him on our own?''

''Anything like that.''

''Not really.''

''You don't sound all that sure.''

Paul frowned. ''Some while back he nearly left the company. Had a terrific row with Chris and raged around for a week or so making a lot of noise, saying he was going to leave and take as many of us with him as he could. He was a bit like that.''

''Was it over Margaret Howard?''

''You know about it then.''

''Only from an outsider. So it all blew over?''

''Things usually did with Andy. He'd met his present wife by then.''

I remembered how Peter used to laugh about Andy blowing hot and cold, one day talking non-stop about some scheme or other, the next totally abandoning it.

''You should have asked him if there was still anything between Fraser and Margaret Howard,'' I said to Patrick when we were outside.

''There isn't. Fraser brought up the subject himself the

first night he arrived when the whisky began to lubricate his
tongue a bit. He can't stand her now and only keeps her on
because she's good at her job and McAlister has no com-
plaints.''

"Hurley's been keeping well clear," I commented.

"Wouldn't you if you'd been indirectly responsible for
someone almost dying?"

"Yes, but is he on the line?"

"Until we find out otherwise we must assume that he is."

"It's his country too."

"Too right. It would be stupid to forget that. Canada might
be an old ally but he won't welcome Brits conducting their
own private war on his territory any more than Le Blek
does.''

"Hurley's a very attractive man," I murmured, again picturing him and Emma together and to my shame experienc-
ing a purely lascivious gut thrill. I instantly wished I hadn't
spoken.

"And not over modest," came the retort. "Three times a
night—so he informed Terry—no problem at all. D'you fancy
being . . ." and here he used a very basic expression he does
not normally utter in my presence, ". . . by a man with no
problems?"

"Quite a lot of woman fantasize about men like Leander
Hurley," I told him.

"Do they?" asked Patrick stonily. "While their husbands
are making love to them?"

"Some do. I don't have to."

From the way he was looking at me I knew he thought I
was lying.

"I heard them going hammer and tongs," I said. "And
frankly it turned me on. But I didn't want him, I wanted you.
No one could be a substitute for you."

Mark suggested a small celebration in honour of Paul's recovery. This found general favour, possibly because every-

one felt a need to return to some kind of normality. There is nothing like an emergency for bringing out the real characters of people but few desire to remain thus revealed. And we had all been living on our nerves for far too long.

It was a relief to Emma to discover that she was not expected to provide the food. The DARE group and their two minders dug deep in their pockets and I volunteered to do the preparation. Emma, in fact, did turn to on the morning of the party, the following Friday, and made two gigantic Pavlovas: meringue, mountains of thickly whipped cream flavoured with Cointreau and, piled on top, two pounds of fresh Californian strawberries.

Inexplicably, the party mood grew from there. David provided champagne when it became clear that Paul was being discharged from the hospital that same afternoon, Patrick, McAlister and I shopped at the covered market in Port Charles and bought the rest of the food and drink on the way back at a shopping mall while Terry, now called that by everyone, assisted Viv, the daily woman, in cleaning and moving furniture.

"Thirty-three," said Margaret Howard, squinting at a list without the benefit of her reading glasses. "I counted the dog in too because I understand she always filches things when no one's looking."

"Thirty-three!" Emma exclaimed.

"Blame your husband and son," Margaret said, pulling a face at Mark. "One appreciates that the two secretaries have been recruited from Port Charles and can't be left out, but their husbands . . ." She broke off with a sigh.

"Just a couple of friends of mine," Mark said. "And their girlfriends, of course."

"And their girlfriends," Emma echoed in a doom-laden voice. "I hope they're not like the last bunch who smoked pot."

"One did," Mark said, colouring. "I kicked her out. You know I did."

Emma gave a dramatic shudder and went away to look for paper napkins.

"Dad's invited the neighbours too," Mark revealed defiantly to her back. "It saves him from asking them at Christmas in return for the housewarming we went to."

The day progressed at a steady trot until about lunch time when the kitchen had to sacrifice a tray of sandwiches and a quiche as I had forgotten all about interim refreshments. I was regretting that Dot had gone to Prince Edward Island on a rare long weekend visit to her sister. The Newfoundland, presumably eating for at least eight, then gobbled a whole plateful of vol-au-vents which had been laid aside to cool before subsequent re-heating and the cook came to the conclusion that there simply was not enough to eat. I sent Terry out to buy more frozen vol-au-vent cases and my life continued at a brisk canter. Come eight o'clock that night and with the guests arriving thick and fast, the bit was well and truly between the teeth and we were all at a pell-mell gallop. I grabbed Patrick, several French loaves, garlic, parsley butter and a knife and press-ganged him into making garlic bread so I could dash upstairs and get ready.

The food was laid out as a buffet on the extended dining-room table but as with so many gatherings when people stand talking in the way of others trying to find something to eat, three of us had to hand it around or it wouldn't have been eaten. This job fell to Terry, Jon, a friend of Mark, and myself with the inevitability that all such tasks arrive at the doors of the meek at heart who shall then inherit the washing up.

Paul, inhabiting the sofa from whence he emitted a kind of regal glow, was piled with sensible nourishment by the three of us. At a little before eleven he was put to bed in Mark's room by Terry when it became clear that the noise, heat and cigarette smoke had exhausted him. He was left with a glass of champagne as a nightcap.

The half-hour I had spent getting ready had been intensely

precious. In the mall that morning I had bought a pregnancy testing kit. In one tiny phial of coloured liquid I had stared at a host of imaginings, nightmares and failings. A wash, change of clothes and make-up had been achieved in moments, the rest of the time I had sat on the bed both at peace and numb with shock.

Every atom of my being urged me to go to Patrick and tell him the news. It was what he had always wanted, a dream come true. Since the Falklands War I knew that this yearning had taken on another, deeper dimension for him, and like every other woman on this planet I wanted to be able to tell my husband that he was all man, virile, potent, a child in his wife's womb to prove it.

I hung back and not because I was not convinced of the accuracy of the testing kit. Do you tell a Grand Master in the middle of a chess tournament that he was won a million in a lottery? In his job, even on this assignment, he uses the same kind of concentration. A moment's distraction might result in more than the loss of a pawn. I found to my surprise that as far as Patrick was concerned I was on foreign ground. I had never been in a position to give him momentous news. How would he react? My inner voice told me that my velvet hand in the iron glove man would cry.

I decided to choose my moment very carefully, if necessary postponing it for a quite a long time. It was the most difficult decision I had ever made.

I am not really a party person. It gives me satisfaction to plan, cook and then watch the results of my efforts being appreciated but then I expect people to sing for their supper and work at making it successful. But if I am expected to stand for hours on end with a glass in one hand and a plate of jumbled food in the other whilst engaging in polite conversation, I tend to become waspish and bored. When I entertain at home I always make sure it is a dinner party.

Because of this I had every sympathy for a young woman,

at a guess one of the secretaries, standing quite on her own in a corner, an empty glass in one hand.

"Follow me," I said and she did, gratefully.

I refilled her glass, piled her with some eatables and led the way to the conservatory. I had the key in my pocket. Emma had asked me to take charge of it because she didn't want any horseplay amongst her fragile and very expensive orchid plants. The familiar warm earthy scent welcomed us both.

"Peace, perfect peace," sighed my new acquaintance. "Sorry—I'm Carol, Mr. Hartland's secretary when he's in Port Charles."

I introduced myself and asked her what she did when he was in Montreal.

Carol laughed. "Oh, dogsbody. Now David's here most of the time Nasonworth have hired a temp to do what I do normally and most of the time I can give her a hand. The work's really beginning to hot up now DARE are getting into their stride. There's the phone, post, stuff coming through on the Fax and telex machines. It's a mad house most of the time."

"Is your husband the red-haired man talking to Drew McAlister?"

"How did you guess?" she answered with another laugh.

"There's a red hair on your shoulder. It shows up rather well against black satin."

"Are you a detective in a real life?" she asked in a mock serious whisper.

"No—I write. But sometimes it can amount to the same thing. My curiosity, for instance, makes me ask you why you said 'real life'."

She wrinkled her nose in a way that must have proved too captivating for red head to resist. "Parties are so artificial. I'm sorry—I shouldn't have said that."

"It's not my bash," I told her. "As a matter of fact, I agree with you."

Carol carefully examined an orchid, a breathtaking crea-tion of purple, cream and brown with leopard spots in its throat. "I was hoping to have a word with Robin on his own this evening—no, it's Terry isn't it?—I've had no opportunity until now. D'you think . . ." She tried again, "If you said you'd like to see him for a moment he'd come, wouldn't he? Oh dear—this all sounds so dreadful."

I had already decided that she wasn't the kind of girl to betray red head's trust in her. "I'll fetch him for you if you want me to," I said.

Her round brown eyes stared into mine, assessing me. "It's about something that happened at work. I know he's been hired to protect DARE. I thought of talking to the other one—he called in the other day and I think he's Terry's boss—but I couldn't quite pluck up the courage and I haven't seen him here tonight."

I said, "The last I heard he was taking on all-comers at arm wrestling in the rumpus room. Don't be put off by ap-pearances. Underneath he's like Paddington Bear—complete with a craving for marmalade. We'll go and find him if you like, if there's anything to be said it ought to be said to him."

"It's probably nothing at all," she said with a shrug. "I'm sure people will say it's because I don't like Margaret How-ard. But that's not true. Now I'm not all that sure I saw what I thought I did."

"Look, Patrick won't eat you," I said, standing up. "And no one will know what you've said to him. If you want me to I'll stay within range and hit him if he even breathes hard on you." The levity, I knew, must have sounded forced. I was too tired and had too much on my mind to be convinc-ing.

Still uncertain, Carol followed me to the door. "I'd like you to be the judge of it first, though. I know that you'll keep it to yourself."

I turned and faced her. "You can confide in me or him—

it doesn't matter. We're married. Does what you have on your mind involve the possibility of murder?''

The question broke through her reserve. ''It might. The day that Paul was taken ill Margaret brought in blueberry muffins for the mid-morning break and offered to make the coffee. It wasn't like her really—she hadn't done it before. I went to help her take the mugs around and just as I arrived I saw her drop something in Paul's mug. At the time I thought she'd made a mistake and given him a sweetener—both David and Earl Lawrence take sweeteners in their drinks but Paul takes sugar, two spoonfuls, he has an awfully sweet tooth.''

''Did she see that you'd noticed?'' I asked, my pulse beating like a drum in my head.

''No. At least, I don't think so. I was wearing flat shoes— they don't make any noise.''

''Did she then put sugar in Paul's?''

''Not while I was there. I didn't like to stand over her watching.''

We left the conservatory and I put the key back in my pocket. Then, not hurrying, I found Terry and issued the instruction that he should check on Paul and stay with him until ordered otherwise.

Thus, unwittingly, I ensured the death of two men that night.

CHAPTER 13

I have never been to a cockfight but the scene in the basement of Ravenscliff as I descended the stairs with Carol brought to mind one I had seen in a film. But for the absence of the birds all was the same: an air of tense expectancy, sweating humanity crammed together, hoarse shouts and a lot of money changing hands.

The spotlights which illuminated the room had been adjusted to direct the beams into the centre of the room, creating a pool of light like a small stage in which had been placed a small table and two chairs. These were at present occupied by Leander Hurley and a man I knew to be a neighbour of the Hartlands. To a chorus of cheers and groans Hurley smacked the other's fist back on to the table.

Carol nudged me and indicated with a discreet index finger. She had already caught the mood, her face tight with suppressed excitement. This was understandable. She had unburdened herself of something that had up until then spoiled her evening, and the information she had divulged had not been laughed at.

Our quarry lounged with his back against the wall in one corner, the darkest one I couldn't help but notice, a tankard of beer in one hand. He had removed his sweater and rolled the sleeves of his shirt up to the elbows. Despite the gloom I could see that the thin cotton material was soaked with sweat and that his hair curled on his neck and forehead in damp ringlets. There was not the slightest chance of reaching him without drawing the attention of the entire gathering.

Critical of the lax state of security I then observed that his shoulder holster was hanging within reach and when he moved into the circle of light to take the seat vacated by the loser he removed the gun from it and tucked it into his jeans pocket. Tangibly, the excitement of those watching mounted.

"Hiya Major Freddie!" roared Hurley despite his opponent's nearness. He seemed unlikely to die of thirst within the next few moments. "Shall we do some gardening right now? I might even prune your balls for you sonny boy."

During the roar of laughter that this produced Patrick leaned across and said something in Hurley's ear. Hurley didn't believe what he had been told and became helpless with laughter which was just as well, Patrick had taken a decided risk that he would impart the knowledge to the room at large.

"Hurley only arrived a short while ago," McAlister said quietly to me. "We insisted that he work his way up through the rest of us like your husband had to and now there's just the two of them."

"Was he as drunk as that when he arrived?" I enquired.

"Don't imagine that he's as drunk as he looks. From what I've seen of him he acts pretty crazy when he's only had one or two. I should like to be able to warn the Major about that."

There was no need, I thought, Hurley was sitting opposite one of the British army's most exalted interpreters of the human condition.

"Twenty dollars Gillard loses," offered Earl Lawrence, rudely leaning across Carol.

"Are you speaking to me or Drew?" I demanded, wondering if he had postponed flying home to Montréal for the weekend because of the party.

"Fifty," said Nelson Redding's voice from somewhere nearby before McAlister could reply. "You give me fifty if he wins."

"Done," said Lawrence, ignoring me.

"Yes," McAlister said thoughtfully into the hush that settled over the room. "I'll make it fifty too."

"That's a lot of money," I heard Mark whisper to Jon.

"Don't look at me, friend," said Jon sadly.

I nudged Carol. "Tell Mark I'll back him."

The two men seated at the table clasped hands, sheer beefcake versus lean wiriness. For a few moments nothing happened and then Hurley went in for surprise tactics, a sudden ferocious burst of strength that knotted the magnificent muscles of his back. Patrick's arm went about six inches from the vertical and then righted as Hurley relaxed. They smiled at each other with teeth only across their raised hands.

I tried to evaluate how much Patrick had had to drink. Watching him move and remembering how he had walked to the table I found myself smiling. He was merely drunk on his own body chemistry. Hurley didn't stand a chance.

So it proved to be. Inch by inch, Hurley lost. He sweated and swore, panted, raved and sweated again. Inch by inch his arm was forced backwards on to the table, three times, the final bout an indignity, a walkover for the winner.

"I must admit that I don't understand," said McAlister, nevertheless delighted with his handful of money. "Hurley is so incredibly muscular."

"It seemed more like hypnotism to me," Carol said breathlessly.

But I didn't want to enter into a discussion of how looking at Patrick makes some women feel weak. Nor for that matter that there was a lot in what she had said. Weasels do it too.

I said, "I've a notion that Hurley pumps iron for an hour or so a day. There's nothing to indicate that he comes from a long line of men who could crack walnuts with their fingers. And Patrick had to rely on the strength of his arms and hands to haul himself around when he was recovering from his injuries."

I caught Carol's eye but no one was moving to disperse. Chris Fraser struggled through the throng holding aloft a can

of beer and gave it to Patrick. He drank it straight from the
can this time, with hardly a pause. Then he removed his shirt
entirely, used it to dry off some of the sweat then rolled it
into a tight ball and threw it overarm at Mark.

"I withdraw," said Mark, tossing it back.

"Out here," Patrick ordered, smiling.

"Now what?" I said, desperate to go to bed and sleep for
a week.

"Ah," said Drew's soft brogue. "Well, it seems that young
Mark was denied tuition on certain aspects of unarmed combat on the grounds that he was not strong enough. He begs
to differ so your other half has told him that if he can hang
from that beam by his hands for five minutes he will concede.
As you might imagine, people are betting on the outcome."

The basement at one time had been fitted out as a gym-
nasium and the beam, a smooth piece of maplewood set
several inches below the ceiling, had been incorporated into
the building and so could not be removed. Everyone settled
themselves as comfortably as possible, a few of the women
laughing loudly at Patrick when he dusted the top of the beam
with his long suffering shirt and then dropped it on the floor.

Mark slowly went forward, round-shouldered, hands in
pockets.

"He won't do it if he doesn't want to," I heard Emma
say, and I turned to locate her. She was sitting at the top of
the stairs behind me and was obviously quite unable to tear
her gaze from Patrick's naked torso. Perhaps, after all, she
was only a lonely, rather silly woman, with good and bad
points like everyone else, who found solace for her loneliness
and boredom in the arms of any willing man.

Patrick approached Mark who miraculously ceased to kick
his heels and then removed his shirt as requested in case the
seams cut into him. It was agreed that Fraser be made responsible for time keeping.

"I suppose this will do wonders for his drawing ability,"

said David Hartland when his son had been in position for a minute without the slightest sign of strain.

Patrick fielded the remark. "Of course. Any exercise that strengthens the fingers and wrists must improve manual accuracy."

"This seems to me to be more of a feat of endurance."

"I shall take him down before any damage is done." Patrick said patiently. "And that's also why I've forbidden him to take any cash inducements."

"So what does he get out of it?"

"I promised I'd show him how to knock a man over with his feet."

But Hartland wasn't finished. "Can you do this?"

"Three minutes," called Fraser.

Patrick began to show irritation. "I never ask people to do things that I can't. As a one time naval officer you ought to know that it's one of the golden rules of command."

"Oh God," sighed Emma, displaying for the first time how much gin she had consumed that evening. "Aren't people who take themselves seriously bloody tedious?"

Don't throw him that kind of opportunity, I inwardly warned her. You'll get more back than you bargained for.

Mark's fingers began to slip and on Patrick's advice he changed his grip, one hand at a time. But he was in trouble, breathing in grunts.

"Come down," Patrick told him softly. "Before you fall down. You've already done better than I thought you would."

"Four minutes," Fraser said.

Mark silently appealed for a few more agonised moments and then let go of the beam. Grimacing with pain from his cramped fingers, he acknowledged the loud applause.

"Cash inducements!" announced Leander Hurley, and those who had been moving towards the stairs ceased to do so.

"He's not really an extrovert," I whispered to myself. "Leave him alone—he only played along to make the party go well." Seemingly of their own volition my feet were taking me down into the pool of light.

"Ten dollars you can't do it," drawled Hurley.

Patrick appeared to give it serious thought. "I already earn more than that in five minutes," he said finally.

"Surely not," I murmured, still carrying on a one-sided conversation and by now standing at the front. Then, louder, I said to Hurley, "Don't turn him into a sideshow."

Hurley glanced at me. "Ma'am, I wouldn't dream of it. This is a business transaction."

"Damn you," I retorted but the remark was lost in the response he knew his words would have. From all sides offers were thrown at Patrick, a clamour, not particularly pleasant to listen to, the real frenzy of a cock fight.

I understood that no man with red blood in his veins could walk out of the room without facing up to the challenge. After the Freddie fiasco, and the fact had to be faced that from the point of view of an undercover operation this was what it had been, Patrick had won back a lot of respect just by being himself. Anyone heading a security mission needs all the respect and co-operation he can get from those around him. Therefore he had no choice but to offer himself as a sideshow.

He rubbed his palms down the sides of his jeans and relied on his left leg to provide impetus to jump up to grip the beam. Chris Fraser hurriedly looked at his watch.

During the first three minutes, which passed amazingly quickly, Patrick accepted a total of sixty-four dollars for five minutes, someone's mother-in-law for two seconds over that time and a pick-up with all four wheels missing for a minute on top of that.

Well into the next five minutes he swopped the mother-in-law for a jar of peanut butter and gave the pick-up to one of Mark's friend's girlfriends, whose father was a scrap merchant, in exchange for a kiss. Not from Daddy though, he emphasised, just smiling at the girl who had called out that she had an old lorry to dispose of and what would he give her for that?

At eleven minutes Hartland said, "Two hundred you can't stay there for twenty."

"I'm not taking bets," Patrick told him. "You give me two hundred to stay here."

"That's my offer."

"Makes it more interesting," Hurley said.

"This is getting too crazy," Mark said to me in an undertone, "I wish I hadn't opened my big mouth."

"Twelve minutes," Fraser intoned into what had been a long silence.

"On my terms then," Patrick said. "Two thousand for twenty-five."

"Done," Hartland replied, and this really set it alight.

At fifteen minutes all business seemed to be over with Patrick due to gain or lose four thousand three hundred and forty dollars. This settled he removed one hand at a time from the beam to wipe the sweat from his eyes. I was trying to remember the final figure on our most recent bank statement.

Fraser had just called nineteen minutes when Patrick's right hand began to slip. He immediately changed his hold as he had advised Mark, so that his palms faced him instead of the backs of his hands. I didn't try to catch his eye, no more than I did when someone gave him hell with an electric cattle prod during interrogation resistance training sessions.

The more sensitive members of his audience regretted their lighthearted offers during the following four minutes. By this time I was sweating with him, almost feeling the racking pain in wrists, forearms and shoulders. No, he wasn't doing it for the money.

There was one minute to go when Bryce and Rab Gaspereau shoved their way down the stairs.

CHAPTER 14

The hunting rifle was pointing at my head before anyone could move, and the situation by then was utterly hopeless as the only person in the room with the ability to do anything about it had been surprised with his eyes closed.

The weapon swung away from me and came to rest about a foot from Patrick's stomach.

"Bryce! No!" This from Mark in an appalled whisper.

He received a tremendous back-handed blow from Rab that sent him cannoning into me. I grabbed at him to save him from falling but he was already down, sobbing with agony, crouched on the floor.

Bryce spoke inches from Patrick's face. "Stay right there or I might do to that woman what you did to Lanny." The rifle swung back to me again. "I'll shoot her in the legs first to give a little music to your damned party." He was as drunk as Rab appeared sober.

"I'm getting the police," Hartland snapped.

"Cool it, halfwit!" Hurley bellowed at him.

"Lanny was already dead," I said, doing Patrick's talking for him. He was beyond speech.

Bryce hit him, quite gently in experimental fashion, just below the ribs and then stood back to assess reaction. The result disappointed him so he hit Patrick again, harder.

"He had been dead for days," I said, and for some reason my voice sounded perfectly steady.

"It was in the paper," McAlister said. "Don't you read the local papers?"

"I read the papers," said Bryce very quietly, swaying. "I also know how the law runs this town, the papers, radio station . . . everything. Those who don't behave get rubbed out and the guy who does it gets given a medal. Did they give *him* a medal?" Here he jabbed Patrick again with the barrel of the rifle.

"His throat was cut," Mark said thickly from the floor. "Two tries. The Major doesn't need two goes at cutting someone's throat."

Perhaps we were all mesmerized by these two men, by their almost obscene obesity and pig stupid bloodshot eyes. For during the next couple of seconds during which Rab kicked Mark twice and Patrick reversed his grip once again on the beam no one moved or spoke.

"Bloody pongo," said Bryce to Patrick. "Someone said you were a bloody pongo. Tell me what that is." He gave the rifle to his brother.

"It's British slang for soldier," I said.

Bryce took a knife from his pocket and moved in my direction. "What kind of soldier?"

I stared at him, trying not to see the knife, my mind an utter blank.

Patrick said, "A soldier from a special unit trained to fight without weapons."

Bryce forgot about me and went back to Patrick. "Fuckin' lyin' bloody pongo." The knife point drew a red line down Patrick's breast bone and then jabbed, twisting slightly. Blood welled and trickled and there was a thud behind me as someone fainted.

A small sound escaped through Patrick's clenched teeth and he had to grab for a hold. Bryce chuckled at the desperate endeavour, hands reversed again, thumbs gripping the bottom of the beam, fingers curled right over the top.

"I'll show you," Patrick whispered and spat accurately right in the big man's face.

Bryce involuntarily took a couple of steps backwards and thus positioned himself to receive both of Patrick's feet in the mouth. He went over backwards like a poleaxed bullock.

I went for Rab, intent on getting the rifle away from him. He kicked out at me, hacking me on the shin, but I kneed him in the groin and he dropped the weapon. But he wasn't finished. He grabbed me in a bear hug, obviously with the idea of turning me into a shield. I can deal with bearhugs but hadn't reckoned on another knife. It was held to my throat, I could feel the blade against my skin.

Aligning an armed attacker for a heart shot involves committing to memory a series of complicated movements, split second timing and surgical accuracy on the part of one's working companion. This degree of accuracy had, for obvious reasons been assessed with a pistol armed just with a laser light beam. I had only my memory to rely on at this moment but I performed the movements wondering if Hurley would have the presence of mind to hit Rab over the head with a chair.

It was a shock then to hear the Smith and Wesson fire, and to know that the soft nosed bullet had taken Rab under the right arm, through ribs, intercostal muscles, pulmonary vein and then into the right atrium.

Rab died.

For a moment there was silence but for Bryce gargling on blood and smashed teeth. Then, uproar.

Patrick bent over Mark who was still choking from the kicking he had been given and had badly cut lips. Then he came to me.

"I don't know how you did that," I said, and he knew that I meant holding the gun. It had fallen from his hands and directly into Hurley's as soon as it had fired, Hurley told me afterwards.

"I think Bryce is dead," Fraser said during the next confusing moments when I had my arms around Patrick and seemed to be holding him up rather than vice versa.

He was. The grossly overweight man had suffered a heart seizure.

It was another bad blunder. The very last thing we needed, as Patrick so succinctly put it just after midnight, was for the whole of Port Charles to be made aware that the British Army, special operations variety, was in residence at Ravenscliff. He didn't mention what we were all thinking, that he himself was about to suffer the adulation of the entire neighbourhood for finally ridding it of long standing bully-boys.

To Le Blek, however, Patrick was not a hero and he took him away for questioning.

"Took him away?" queried Leander Hurley when I tracked him down in his office in the Naval dockyard in Port Charles the following morning when Patrick still had not returned.

"Careless sentence construction," I said. "He went with them when requested to do so. Can you do anything?"

"To get him out?"

"Don't you know any words with more than two syllables this morning?" I raged. "What else could I damned well mean?"

Hurley doodled on an otherwise virgin blotter. "I don't think he'll come to any harm, and that's the opinion of an honest man."

"We're talking about something a little further into the grown-up world than your department zapping MI5."

He laid down the pen. "Even if Le Blek does get a little impatient, and perhaps doesn't let him have much sleep or anything to eat—"

"Or wash or relieve himself or sit down," I interrupted. "No, you're right, he's had plenty of dress rehearsals along those lines. But didn't it strike you that those drunken lunatics rolled up rather neatly on cue last night?"

He nodded slowly.

"D'you know where the expression pongo really comes from?"

Hurley showed slightly more than polite interest.

"It's Royal Navy slang for a soldier," I informed him. "I'm surprised you haven't heard it before. Someone described Patrick to Bryce Gaspereau in those terms and I reckon whoever it was arranged for them to arrive when they did. They would have killed him."

"I think Le Blek realizes that."

"So why has he taken Patrick in?"

"He might be suspicious that your husband knows a lot more about what's behind this whole business than he says he does. The RCMP don't like foreign agents on their patch."

"How about you?"

"Me neither," he agreed. "If your government is conducting in-fighting on Canadian soil we want to know about it—every last detail. Put yourself in our position."

"I believe you've been given sufficient information to satisfy protocol."

He sat back in his chair and looked me straight in the eye. "Where do you fit into all this, Mrs. Gillard?"

"Nowhere," I said. "But it was you who kept the party going by making Patrick perform for money last night. You also fed Paul the clams and just happen to be in a position to call someone a bloody pongo."

"Ouch," said Hurley, looking out of the window.

The dockyard siren wailed an invitation to a lunchbreak that had begun unofficially some five minutes earlier when cars had begun to stream past the window and out through the gates. Moments later the hooter of Port Charles Shipbuilders, next door, seconded it eerily into the thick Fundy fog, a tin whistle to a bassoon.

"Then there's Emma," I continued.

"What about her?" Hurley asked carefully, giving me his full attention.

"She's spiteful enough when the mood takes her to fill your mind with all kinds of rubbish."

"Ma'am, I take no notice what a woman says when I'm bedding her."

"No? Then why bother with her? You can have any woman you like."

Hurley's eyes bulged slightly. Then he smiled, more of a leer really. "Why—are you game?"

"No," I snapped. "Was Margaret Howard?"

"Even if she was, let me ask you something. Is it your job to do the same as Emma, find out what you can and report back?"

I had to look away from him, recollecting how Patrick had clung to me and thanked God that the bullet hadn't hit me too.

"Perhaps not," said Hurley. He picked up the pen again and recommenced doodling. "The KGB was mentioned to Le Blek . . ."

So the conversation at Ravenscliff *had* been reported to Hurley. I kept quiet.

"Don't say that you're not involved. If you weren't the Major would have sent you packing when he was telling Le Blek to get off his backside. I think that everyone agrees that you're both here to keep an eye on these guys, but whether the threat was really made or whether you're doing something else on the side . . ."

"Ask Fraser," I said. "He received the letter."

"I have."

"Well?"

"He showed me a photocopy of it. Anyone could have cobbled it together in five minutes."

I grimly hung on to my temper. "Hasn't there been *any* communication between MI6 and your department over this?"

"Not that anyone's managed to trace."

I gazed at him in utter disbelief.

"But you don't know anything about it," Hurley mocked in a sing-song voice.

"I go with him on some of his assignments," I told him. "It gives me a break and I find plenty of material for my novels. He likes having me around if all he's doing is socialising and keeping an eye on things. It makes his presence less obvious."

"It won't do," Hurley said shaking his head. "I was there when you kneed Rab Gaspereau in the goolies, remember?"

"For heaven's sake!" I exclaimed. "Don't Canadian women attend self-defence classes?"

"To learn commando holds and place a man in position for a difficult heart shot? You learnt your lessons well, Ma'am, you didn't pick up that rifle afterwards the way any housewife would. It was all ready to blast the head off any friend of the Gaspereau family who might have burst in."

I wanted to convince myself that Hurley was merely totally unsubtle, a stickler to his job and could therefore be trusted. But there was a streak of irresponsibility about him. As Earl Lawrence had said, he was like a big kid. And a big kid with power was highly dangerous.

In the aftermath of the killings I had forgotten to draw Patrick's attention to what Carol had told me. At the time, I suppose, it had hardly seemed important. Now, I had no intention of giving this information to Hurley, nor for that matter buying Patrick's release by co-operating in any way.

It did not seem too rash to assume, in fact, that Hurley was responsible for Patrick being taken in for questioning. Also, if Six hadn't smoothed the way for a small unit in Five to do a job then we had deliberately been thrown in the deep end. There could be several reasons for this but one might be that someone was now working for the wrong side and given enough rope would hang himself. In no circumstances should Hurley be made a party to this.

But I saw no reason why Patrick should be hanged first.

Hurley said, "The poisoning was an accident. I ate some

of the clams too. Quade's car hit a tree because he wasn't used to our vehicles and roads, and that mark on the chassis was where a stone hit it in the crash. Lanny was standing around on that spot because he was going in for a spot of illegal hunting, it's a well known place where white-tailed deer cross the road. Then one of his many enemies caught up with him on a dark night. This story can be re-written in many ways.''

"Teach your grandmother to suck eggs," I said. "Where was Lanny's rifle when his body was found? Has anyone mentioned to you that Fraser's cars were sprayed with acid before he flew out here? Did you actually bother to look at Fraser when you were asking him questions? Beneath the bland exterior he's half out of his mind with worry.''

Hurley stood up. "I'll take you to your husband. We'll both check that he's still smiling.''

I had no choice but to go with him.

"Of course this is just what an enemy would wish," I said when we were seated in his car. "Suspicion, confusion and time-wasting among allies.''

"I have to be quite sure that we are allies.''

The impatient retort sprang to my lips but I didn't utter it. If Six hadn't ensured a security clearance for us because of an internal investigation all Hurley had to do was make a few phone calls. David Hartland was the most accessible representative of Six but might not have the seniority to vouch for this. It was possible that he himself was the one under scrutiny.

We took the Fredericton road and then branched left towards Tracy, crossing by a quirk of topography from King's County, across part of Queen's, nipping a corner of Charlotte and then into Sunbury. I didn't need a map to know this. I had memorised the countryside around Port Charles in a radius of a hundred miles.

Two miles after Blissville, Hurley swung the wheel and we entered a long driveway that wound for about two miles through the trees. Always the trees. In every direction, everywhere one looked, were trees. And on the coast, where they grew with precarious hold on eroded cliff edges, it seemed that they only gave way reluctantly to the ocean.

We drew up at a house clad in the familiar white weather boarding. I opened the door of the car myself and stepped out. If I was to be delivered like a parcel then I would walk in front and Hurley could follow. He did nothing to prevent me.

I went straight in without knocking and felt a glimmer of satisfaction when my sudden ingress caused a man standing in the hallway to start violently. He began to smile at me but changed his mind when he saw Hurley, thought about shaking hands and then chickened out on that as well.

The ground floor seemed to be an office of sorts; phones rang, people wandered around with files tucked under their arms, through an open doorway near where I stood I could see a woman typing. The general aura of the place was pleasant enough, a lot of white paint, prints on the walls, a few expensive house plants well looked after. It was a bit like the reception area of a secure mental hospital I had once visited.

Inspector Le Blek came down the staircase directly in front of me, not at all surprised to see me, obviously having watched my arrival courtesy of security cameras.

I said, "I take it you're a visitor too."

He smiled politely at me and gave an envelope he was holding to Hurley. He didn't confirm what I already knew, that we weren't at the local headquarters of the RCMP. He didn't say anything, just regarded Hurley in hostile fashion.

Hurley slit the envelope open and walked away a few paces to read what it contained. "Nothing else?"

"That's all," Le Blek replied grittily.

Hurley screwed the sheet of paper into a ball. "You'd better take her up."

"I think I'd rather you brought Patrick down," I said.

"He's sleeping," said Le Blek.

"What would you do if I walked right out of here again?"

"Nothing. You're free to do as you like."

I turned to Hurley. "Would you drive me back to Port Charles if I asked you?"

"I'll take you both back when he wakes up." Hurley wasn't really listening to me, frowning to himself, still kneading the ball of paper in one hand.

The three of us went up the stairs, Le Blek leading, then me and Hurley bringing up the rear. They had been honest with me. In a front bedroom Patrick was asleep on a double bed, fully dressed. I heard the door close and lock behind me but paid no attention.

He had been laid down in the first aid recovery position, on his stomach, left knee drawn up slightly, his head on one side. A towel had been placed beneath his head. I removed it and folded it so that the patch of vomit was inside, cleaning his face with tissues from my bag before I put it back.

I was sitting on the bed when the door opened. I didn't look up. It didn't take much intelligence to realize that they were about to do the same to me.

CHAPTER 15

"Have you any idea," I said to Leander Hurley, "of the effect of this stuff on an unborn child?" He was, for the first time, looking slightly out of his depth.

"Not very original," commented the female paramedic, the needle almost touching my arm. "They all try that one."

"Are you pregnant?" Le Blek asked.

"Yes," I replied and wrenched my arm from the woman's grip. Her nails raked my wrist. "Not beyond the wit of the Canadian Army Medical Corps to check, surely?"

She straightened up and glared at me. "It'll take ten minutes, that's all—you'll have gained nothing."

"There could be one hell of a row," mused Hurley, gazing down at Patrick.

The woman hooted in derision. "She's his trollop? Not a chance. Didn't you read Doctor Reid's report? He only has half a testicle."

And with that she repossessed my arm and banged in the hypodermic.

My free hand connected with her head, a real sideswipe with my arm straight and rigid. She lost her balance and toppled sideways. The pain was so bad when the needle was dragged out that I screamed. I really saw red then, thought about how my wedding ring was there as large as life for the bitch to see and kicked her on the side of the jaw when she tried to stand up. This time she stayed down.

"Is that it?" I yelled at Hurley. "I'm a criminal? An undesirable alien to be filled up with your filthy drugs? And I suppose that afterwards you'll deny having brought us here, so that Canada and Great Britain can carry on being buddies for ever and ever. Until the next time MI5 sends someone who just happens to be able to arm wrestle you to the floor and doesn't have to rely on screwing and drugging women as his sole source of information."

While all this had been going on Le Blek had been lounging against the wall by the window.

"Perhaps you'd better check," he said.

"What exactly did Gillard say?" Hurley barked.

"I gave you the report."

"All three lines of it. People talk when they've been given the truth drug. What did the guy actually *say*?"

Le Blek levered himself off the wall. "We asked him all the usual questions. He said who he was and who he was working for, just what he told me when we first met. He said why he was here and who his wife was and when it was her birthday and what he was going to buy her. Then we lost him for a bit—he's a very bad subject—didn't listen, kept singing to himself and trying to go to sleep. I told you, if you remember, that I thought he was too tired.

"Then he came on stream again and sang a bit more. Rather good. I should imagine he used to be in a choir. Said that his Dad was a priest and how he was thinking of doing the same one day. We asked him about Fraser and he said that the man was a part-time soldier. Gillard didn't sound as though he trusted him all that much. I wrote that down. It is the only really interesting thing as far as you're concerned. Listen to the tapes if you want to, there's a hell of a lot more—about the army, how he's meaning to collect all the Beethoven symphonies, all sorts of stuff. They're in the next room with the recorder."

"God damn," said Hurley softly through his teeth.

"You can forget any other methods too."

"I'm not stupid!" Hurley snarled. "For Chrissake get her out of here!"

"Which one?" Le Blek enquired, straight-faced.

The moaning paramedic was carried out by two men, with no more ado than if they had entered to empty the wastepaper basket. I made a pad of my handkerchief to stem the bleeding from my arm.

"Did you ask him about her?" Hurley persisted, jerking a thumb in my direction.

"Listen to the damn tapes!" Le Blek said, voice rising. "The answer's right under your nose. She writes. She goes with him sometimes as company when the job isn't expected to get too close to the coalface. I imagine she's been given a little basic tuition in self-defence in case there's trouble. Why should she be lying about being pregnant?"

"According to—" Hurley started to say but I cut in, addressing Le Blek.

"We've been trying for ages," I said, and such was the pain in my arm that my voice sounded strange in my own ears. After my burst of anger I felt weak and tired. I hadn't had any sleep the previous night either.

"There's no security clearance for them," Hurley shouted. "For all we know they might be a plant by the bloody Communists to disrupt the frigate programme."

Le Blek's lip curled. "Oh sure. As soon as the first boat drops into the Saint John river Moscow waves the white flag. Do you really think," he went on and it seemed to me that as his temper rose the less Canadian and the more Irish his accent became, "that the KGB employs a couple who are trying to start a family? Thought about seriously, would they be permitted to go all out for babies if they were working as a team?" He noticed the blood-stained handkerchief. "This is all the support you can get from me. Call a car and I'll take them home."

"The Mounties always get their man," said Hurley in a dead quiet voice. "I can just picture you standing on a bloody

mountain top dressed in your red jacket and fancy pants hol-
lerin' for Rose Marie.''

What happened next startled me greatly and woke Patrick.
Quite cold-bloodedly Le Blek drew his gun from a shoulder
holster and put three shots in the floor at Hurley's feet. The
result of this was Hurley going through the door at some
speed, somehow preventing an armed inrush, and five minutes later Patrick, Le Blek and I were in a car and speeding
down the drive, Le Blek driving as though all the fiends of
hell were after him.

"I don't give a damn if you're the fairy on the KGB's
Christmas tree," he said, choking with anger. "When you
said you were pregnant back there, the fear of death was in
your eyes."

"Please slow down just a little," I urged.

"Janice and I have been trying for fifteen years for kids,"
he continued, but heeding the plea, "And that stupid bastard
behaves as though everyone but Canadians are reds. It's the
brainwashing they give them. Trouble is, they forgot to give
him his back after it went in the tub."

"Will you get into trouble?"

After he had straightened the car when it had slewed round
a sharp corner Le Blek glanced sideways at me. "I guess
not. My boss calls the security boys hickory heads. Besides,
the Major is my responsibility."

"Then either slow down some more or give me a brown
paper bag," Patrick said weakly from the back seat.

Le Blek lifted his foot off the accelerator and switched off
the ignition so that the vehicle rolled to a standstill. Then he
got out, opened both rear doors and laid the pliant passenger
on his side, ordering him to take deep breaths of fresh air.
When Patrick felt better he closed the doors and opened the
windows.

"Gets to you, doesn't it?" Le Blek muttered. "They tried
it out on me once during training." He got back behind the

wheel and twisted round with his arms on the back of the seat. "Is Daws someone important?"

Patrick swore fluently.

"It's important that he stays unmentioned," I said, wondering with a sinking feeling how much damage had been done by blowing Colonel Richard's cover in Canada. Enough, probably.

Le Blek faced front again and re-started the engine. "That's what I thought. I'm not convinced that a lot of stuff doesn't get to the ears of the Yanks via the likes of Hurley just to show the CIA that they aren't all horns and balls. That's why I scrubbed the tapes."

"But there were others present," I said, refraining from hugging him.

"Only the medic and right then she was listening to someone give her orders over the radio."

A few miles further on towards Port Charles we pulled into a lane that led to a group of houses, a new development set in a copse of white birch and beech trees. At the house nearest the road we stopped and two women came out into the garden. The youngest was Le Blek's wife, Janice, surprised to see him home so early from work; the second his mother who looked as though nothing concerning her son would surprise her.

Patrick was beyond caring if the distaff side of Le Blek's family assumed him to be inebriated. Once out of the car he leaned on a handy tree, still taking deep breaths. I went to him but was beaten by a short head by the elder Mrs. Le Blek. With bright blue eyes she gave Patrick a long, penetrating appraisal.

"Steve is a very bad driver," she announced at last. "But to be sure you aren't the type of person to make a fuss so it must be something else."

"It is herself of the Irish," murmured Patrick, kissing her hand. "So help me I've been felled not by his driving but the poteen he brews up in the garage. If you have another drop of the same . . ." He gave her a wan smile.

"I'll get it," Janice said, eyes on my makeshift bandage. "You all look as though you could do with some."

In the end I had real English tea and drank it sitting on a seat in the garden. Patrick had by this time slid to the grass and was leaning on his tree, sipping from the Waterford crystal tumbler that had contained at least a triple of Irish whisky.

They left us alone in the sunlit garden.

"Come and sit over here," I suggested after a while.

"You'll have to provide a crane."

Between the two of us, the tree and I got him to his feet and I steered him to where I had been sitting. There was a reason for moving him. I didn't want him to fall asleep again outside. There are notes in Patrick's file in red letters an inch high emphasising that under no circumstances is he to be given drugs during training or for any other reason. Since the Falklands and the resulting two years in and out of hospital, his constitution overreacts to alien substances.

Patrick broke the silence first. "Don't blame Hurley too much."

"Ladies don't spit," I said.

He took my hand.

"Ever get the notion we've been set up?" I asked.

"Yes."

"Is that all you can say?"

"What else can I say? If it is like that then I'm sure Daws doesn't know."

"Despite the fact that there's supposed to be co-operation, Six didn't clear the way for us. Hurley said so and the way he worded that to me suggested that people have been checking. You're always so sure of Daws but we didn't ask. Aren't we supposed to be grown up now and think for ourselves?"

"No, no and yes," Patrick replied absently, lifting the stained handkerchief from my arm. "How did this happen?"

I told him, not giving the real reason for my resistance.

"Ingrid one, paramedic nil," he said. "They waited until I nodded off before giving me the works. I must be losing my grip."

Some time later Janice took us both indoors where we showered and rested and then were invited to sit down to dinner. Through the window the sun was setting in a magnificent sky of orange, pale pink, translucent aquamarine and blue, tiny clouds looking as though they were floating on a lake of colour. In the garden crickets zithered frenziedly.

"Wishing you'd never come to Canada?" enquired Le Blek, but his wife silenced him with a look and asked Patrick to say grace. Clearly, there had been some feed-back.

"Red herrings everywhere," Patrick said suddenly, getting into bed that night.

Le Blek had driven us back to Ravenscliff where we had met several local newspaper reporters, and found a large pile of cash in coins and notes that Terry had tipped into an antique chamber pot. Patrick's winnings.

"I think I'm going out of my mind," I said. "Everything's either black tragedy or pure farce. One minute the third degree the next a pot full of money."

"Blood money at that."

"You mustn't—" I said, and then stopped for he was smiling at me, untroubled. No, the killing of two armed thugs holding your wife hostage was not murder.

"Your father could find a use for it," I said lightly. "Organ fund, dry rot, rising damp."

"I'll have to see what else I can get up to," Patrick interrupted. And he lay down on the bed and laughed, slightly hysterically, winding down like a clock. "Oh God," he muttered. "Am I going mad too?"

I sat on the bed with him. "Patrick, do Five check up on Six?"

We had said nothing of what had transpired, not even to

Terry. As far as he was concerned it was unnecessary. Anyone with service insight looking at Patrick could see that he had been drugged. I was fairly certain that he had been given a shot of LSD as well to hurry the process.

"What did you say? Hell, Ingrid, am I really as high as a kite?"

"I was just thinking the same," I told him. "Yes, and I asked you if Five check up on Six, to try to bring you down to earth."

He frowned ferociously, thinking. "No, not really. You know our Richard. If he got even a sniff of a rumour he'd be on to it. But you can say what you like—if he had had suspicions he would have warned us. My bet is that it's nothing more than incompetence—someone in Six overlooked getting us cleared."

"Here's another red herring for you then," I said, and told him what Carol had related to me the previous evening.

"Sherlock Holmes where are you?" Patrick said with feeling when I'd finished. "According to the boffin it was shellfish poisoning but the report was very vague in places. I'm not keen on questioning Margaret Howard until we get more from Daws on her East German boyfriend. Now I've a red herring for you—when I went down to the airport to check on Fraser's plane, I discovered that he'd had a three-hour wait in Halifax to get the Port Charles connection. But he could just as easily have got off a plane from Montreal that arrived an hour after the one he was supposed to have come on from Heathrow."

"Was his name on the passenger list?"

"Not on either—but he could have been travelling under another name for security reasons. I intend to ask him."

"You keep coming back to Fraser. Does your funny feeling tell you he's in the pay of the Russians and that he's going to ruin his own firm and kill people to achieve it? If so he's hating every minute of the job."

"Not so fast," Patrick admonished. "Here we have a man

who wouldn't bat an eyelid at seeking out the likes of Bryce Gaspereau, who would be more than familiar with the expression bloody pongo, and could have slit Lanny's throat with no more qualms than swatting a bluebottle. The really important bit of evidence is that Fraser drinks Oland's Schooner beer and drops the ringpulls into the empties—like the ones in the bus. I'd put money on him killing Lanny.''

"But that means that the threatening letter was a fake.''

"Not at all. But he could have received another one as well with instructions to hand over only the first to the police. It's possible that he's under appalling personal pressure. Do we know if he has a family? Have they been kidnapped? Anything might have happened.''

"It's mayhem,'' I said. "MI5 are being made a laughing stock because people are being done away with under our noses. DARE's being put out of business and that means the Trident programme will suffer.''

"Not to mention the Canadian frigate programme and a new patrol boat for the Dutch Navy that DARE have just won a design contract for.''

It seemed far too complicated for three people to sort out. I said, "We ought to include Terry in this discussion.''

"But almost more important in my view,'' Patrick went on as though I hadn't spoken, "is that it might destroy D12 as well. We've built up too good a reputation over the past months for Moscow to be happy.''

"So what do we do?'' I asked, repeating the question because he had closed his eyes and there was no response.

"I'm not asleep—I'm thinking.''

"Perhaps Fraser hadn't cut a man's throat before,'' I said, half to myself. And shuddered.

A full minute went by before Patrick said anything. "Despite what Mark thinks I never have either. It's messy, melodramatic and only indulged in by those ignorant of tidier methods.''

He didn't know it but he wasn't telling me anything new.

"How's your arm?"

"It throbs a bit."

"Did you really floor that clone of Stalin's mother?"

"Two of them carried her out," I told him.

"I had a dream that you said you were pregnant."

I experienced a kind of weird glow all over. "You're using your methods on me, Major Patrick. First the soft approach and then slam in with the big question. You weren't asleep in the car."

"I haven't been able to think of anything else," he whispered.

"According to a testing kit," I said, trying to control the wobble in my voice.

"And fainting all over the place and behaving as though you were moon-struck," he added, and enveloped me with his long arms and kissed me until my bones turned to water. Nineteen forty-seven was a very good vintage for kisses.

"I'll get Fraser in a corner and ask him," said Patrick after a while when we were in bed, not making love, just smoochily hugging. "Take him out crow shooting in the boondocks—get him on his own."

"Make sure he doesn't kill another raven," I said.

"What?"

"It doesn't matter," I murmured, nibbling his ear.

CHAPTER 16

Despite all the tension and unpleasantness, DARE continued to work doggedly at their Machinery Control Functional Design Document, or McFUDD, putting in long hours of overtime, every Saturday and most of Sunday, with Terry roped in to file, sort, fetch and carry. The McFUDD was the second paper to be produced by the team. The first, the Machinery System Operational Design Document, quaintly referred to as M.SODD, had been presented to Nasonworth very soon after their arrival in Canada, some of the work having been done in England.

These facts were provided by McAlister at a meeting called the following morning, Sunday 18th May, with a view to tightening security even further. He then disquieteningly spoke of deadlines.

"Oh, yes—the first of June," Drew said in response to Patrick's query. "I'm sorry, should I have mentioned it before?"

"Someone should," Patrick said, glancing up as Fraser entered. "Will you meet it?"

McAlister politely gave us his chair at the head of the table for Fraser to sit down but found himself still spokesman. "Er—we should do. There's nothing to make me think otherwise. Paul's doing the really difficult stuff and Chris is helping him where necessary." He looked at Fraser as if

149

hoping that he would verify what he had said but Fraser was filling his pipe, in a brown study.

"Are you going in today?" Patrick asked him.

The pipe was lit and drawing satisfactorily before Fraser replied. "After lunch. There's no need for anyone else to come. Paul's staying in bed—he's tired out."

"Only your minder," said Terry.

"If you insist," Fraser replied without emotion.

Patrick then outlined his new proposals: that in future he would travel with them to work and spend the day in the near vicinity, invisibly, adding to the security cover, then make his own way home, probably in a taxi, to the rear of their vehicle. On occasions where the team were split up, as they would be that afternoon, those remaining at home were to stay indoors.

"It's like prison," said Margaret Howard, making her first contribution to the discussion.

"Let me know where you did time," Patrick said shortly, turning to speak to Terry. "On second thoughts, I'll go in with Chris—you have the afternoon off."

"If you say so, sir," replied Terry bleakly, going down with guns still blazing.

There had been a short, fierce encounter between him and his commander over the latter's plans to take Fraser into the forest, hunting. In the end Patrick had been forced to pull rank on him, something he loathes doing.

"I don't intend to turn my back on him," Patrick had said into an unhelpful silence. "Ingrid will be two minutes behind us with the homing device sounding loud and clear."

Terry had glowered.

"You haven't fully recovered from that slug you took in the shoulder last year," Patrick had continued winningly. "Just because you managed to take a chunk out of Hartland's door frame it doesn't mean that you're fast enough against a bloke armed with a hunting rifle."

Now it seemed that the plan had changed. Fraser was about to be abducted instead.

It was with a sense of mild foreboding that I changed after lunch into jeans and sweater, packed several small indispensable items about my person, found my light waterproof anorak and went downstairs. Foreboding was accompanied by a feeling of unreality. The sun shone, birds sang, leaves were bursting from buds on the trees—and I was about to be a party to taking away a man against his will and interrogating him about murder.

In my view Terry was quite correct in his censure and I said so, not so much getting Patrick in a corner as giving him a wifely embrace in the garden as he waited for Fraser.

"I realise that," he agreed, having pecked my cheek and then kissed me properly.

"It was monstrously unfair to tell him he wasn't fit after what you've been through lately."

"That too," said he blithely.

"Fraser's had plenty of time to get on the phone," I told him, lowering my voice.

"This *is* my fault."

"Patrick, I'm not nagging."

"I know that too. It's my fault for not asking about deadlines. If Fraser's been given a date for the job being finished then the same deadline applies to the threats. For all I knew he might have been planning to set fire to the portable cabins that they work in and destroy the second paper. The first's no good without the second."

But for the first time since I had known Patrick I doubted his judgement. And why had he spoken in the past tense?

"Are you OK today?" he enquired.

"Better now I know why I'm feeling bad," I said nonsensically, still feeling a dreadful inclination to cry at hourly intervals.

"We must talk," he said, giving me another but rather absent-minded hug. "There's a hell of a lot to talk about . . .

the future . . . whether I give up this lark. God . . ." He swallowed. "I can't really believe . . ." With that he let me go abruptly and dived into the car. This, of all moments was the one when Fraser arrived.

"I'll go away again," he said, turning on his heel.

"No—please," I said. "It's—"

His eyes brilliant, Patrick said, "Don't mind us. Ingrid's expecting and I can't get used to the idea."

But Fraser didn't smile or congratulate us. He just got in the car.

Sweating gently but persistently I drove the pick-up out of Moss Vale, only a reassuring bleep from the homing beacon for company. Beneath my anorak on the seat beside me was Mark's hunting rifle but I found its presence less reassuring. If Fraser got away from Patrick and tried to make a run for it in the car, my orders were to take out his front tyres. Similar endeavours on my part during training and under ideal conditions had resulted in an extremely frightened Royal Corps of Transport.

Mark had taken the morning plane back to Toronto as his college re-opened the following day. The techniques that Patrick had taught him had ensured that he was only mildly bruised from the kicking and the use of cold compresses had reduced the swelling of his mouth. Obviously mentally buoyant he had caused his tutor no concern at all. Better than that, he had promised to visit us in Devon after he had qualified.

There was no real plan of action for Patrick's approach to Fraser. I had no idea how he intended to deviate from the road to Port Charles nor how he would make the initial suggestion to Fraser. Overpowering him, I knew, would be a last resort and also quite out of the question at the moment as Patrick was driving.

Despite my usual state of nerves those last three words stayed in my mind. At home Patrick has an automatic BMW 635i with the pedals adjusted so that he can drive using his left leg. In Canada where vehicles are left-hand drive and nearly all of them automatic there was plenty of room for him to stretch his right leg out of the way. And despite rumours to the contrary he has always been a level-headed, even cautious, driver.

The bleeper's sound became piercing and I pulled into the side of the road, cursing my inattention, and hurriedly held up a map in front of my face. The Buick had drawn up at a gas station some two hundred yards ahead of me. Peeping over the top of the map I saw Patrick get out, pay the attendant and then go round to Fraser's window and speak to him. Then Fraser got out, went round to the other side and sat behind the wheel. Now I would have to be really careful. Fraser was in a position to see me in his driving mirror.

I allowed the car almost to vanish from sight before I followed, stationing the pick-up behind a truck loaded with tree trunks. Unfortunately this large comforting screen turned off after about a mile, forcing me to drop back as the road was quite straight. One consolation was that pick-ups were ten-a-penny. There were two others besides the one I was driving at the rear of the Buick.

Suburbs gave way to the grounds of the Forest Lawns Motel, then more filling stations, a Super Burger take-out, St. Hubert's chicken restaurant, a school, and still the Buick kept to the road straight towards the city centre. The traffic was quite heavy for a Sunday afternoon and I wasn't particularly worried that Fraser would spot me. He would be far too busy looking where he was going.

Slowing down to make way for a truck that had forced its way out of a side road, I almost missed seeing the small red blob ahead of me that was the Buick suddenly turn off at a left fork. I tucked in behind the truck, a wondrous artifact of glittering stainless steel and chrome plating, the whole thing clean enough to eat off, hoping that it would take the same road. But it didn't and neither did any of the other vehicles in front of me.

It immediately became apparent why. The road was a rural route to Sussex and beyond. Beyond lay Fundy National Park. *Parc National de Fundy* announced the bi-lingual signpost.

It was a narrow twisty road and I had to be content not even to catch a glimpse of the Buick. The bleeper intimated that the men were no further than a third of a mile in front of me but I closed the gap a little, hating not knowing what was going on. I could imagine them arguing. How long before Fraser stopped the car, refusing to go any further?

The sun was sinking towards the horizon, casting shadows over small valleys dotted with farms. But I was not in the mood to enjoy the scenery nor to notice other than in a vague way blond Belgian horses and fields glossy with new grass grazed by herds of South Devon cattle, the lovely animals that during the summer months can be seen from my cottage windows at home. Another time.

The car did not stop. It carried on until the road joined Route 114 and then turned right on to it towards the park. Again, I had to be careful. This was a main road, wide and straight, the traffic now sparse. I risked a short burst of speed and then another when I still could not see my quarry. Then amazingly I caught sight of it just coming to a standstill in a car park of an attraction that had been advertised on hoardings for several miles. The Mystery Crater.

I drove past, reversed into a logging track and parked where I could see the car. Both men alighted and strolled, stretching, to a soft drinks stall where they bought cans of Coke. I could see the colour of the cans from where I was. They then sat on a picnic bench under the trees.

"Ye gods," I moaned under my breath, resting my burning forehead on the wheel for a moment. I flicked a switch, silencing the bleeper's ceaseless clamour. From what I could see of Fraser he remained in total ignorance of Patrick's reason for bringing him out here. Indeed he seemed relaxed, happy even, a man out for an afternoon drive.

I began to feel rather angry.

After ten minutes or so they sauntered back to the car and drove off in the same direction, Fraser still driving. As soon as I saw them make a move to leave I reversed for a short distance up the track until a curve hid the pick-up from the road. Then I set off after them.

I switched on the bleeper again, just to make sure, but there didn't seem to be any danger of losing them. Patrick had the homing beacon around his neck on a piece of cord, well hidden by the thick lumberman's jacket he was wearing. I still wasn't quite sure why he had opted to wear such a warm garment on a sunny afternoon.

Ahead of me, just visible in the distance, the Buick entered the park. I slowed right down and followed, the change in speed necessary to obey a forty kilometre an hour limit and also to adjust my eyes to the gloom, the road passing through a glade of sugar maples, hemlock and pine which almost met overhead.

To the left and right, signboards indicated paths and trails to places of interest. Tracey Lake, Caribou Plain, Bennett Brook, Third Vault Falls. All at once I didn't want to be driving, hot and bothered, but wandering where my nose led me through silent, cool trees, watching the birds, with not a thought in my head.

I was to remember this longing with some bitterness.

Here, near a sheltered coast, spring was merging imperceptibly into summer. The ditches at the sides of the roads were spiky with lupins just beginning to tint pink and blue. Snowberry trees were in full flower, a light breeze waving the delicate white blossom to and fro. Moon daisies and wild iris would soon appear to turn the margins of the roads into ribbons of colour.

Again, I had to force myself to concentrate and direct my gaze back on the job. The Buick was just disappearing into a dip in the road about a mile away. It didn't emerge and I floored the accelerator.

They had turned left towards a picnic area at Kinnie Brook.

At the first opportunity I parked and concentrated on the
bleeper. It became fainter and then steadied at the same volume. So they too had stopped. Now came the dilemma. Firearms are totally forbidden within the park and anyone seeing
me carrying a rifle would immediately report me to the game
rangers or RCMP. I decided to leave it in the pick-up, working on the theory that if Patrick was expecting that kind of
trouble from Fraser or anyone else he wouldn't have chosen
to make a National Park his destination.

I rolled the rifle in the anorak, thrust it under the seat and
locked up. Then, walking on the grass at the side of the path,
I went in the direction of where I guessed the Buick was
parked. It was much closer than I thought, about a hundred
yards away, and they were still sitting in it. Just as I caught
sight of it through the trees they drove off again. I'm afraid I
swore.

We traversed the picnic site and set off along a so-called
wilderness trail signposted "To Bear Mountain." Now I
simply dare not allow the vehicle in front to appear within
my sight. The trees thinned to a few scraggy spruce and fir
and then as we climbed higher came to an end. I soon realised that this had nothing to do with altitude when I noticed
a few blackened and rotting stumps here and then. The trees
of the upland had been destroyed by fire.

I braked to a standstill and slowly counted up to fifty before I set off again. There seemed nothing to worry about.
The bleeper was still loud and clear. I crept at stalling speed
over a rise and surveyed a landscape devoid of life, the trail
winding gently down to a valley floor, once again thickly
wooded. In between the trees I could see the glint of water,
almost certainly the Upper Salmon River.

A covered bridge spanned it. Just like a barn and constructed of hefty timbers it set up alarming booming echoes
as the pick-up rumbled over the slatted floor. I passed a camp
site with a couple of parked trailers and a tent though not a
person in sight, and then the trail entered a gully, its steep

sides host to magnificent spruce of such evenness of size that they looked like a green army petrified in mid-stride.

The gully opened out into a natural amphitheatre some two hundred yards across. At least it struck me at first that the phenomenon was natural but when I looked around more carefully it occurred to me that it was an old mine, the heaps of spoil, now overgrown, forming the sides. The Buick was stationary over on the far side, with no sign of Patrick and Fraser. I reverse into a glade and parked on the far side of a thicket.

I sat at the base of a tree overlooking the open space and for ten minutes it seemed that not even an insect moved. Then, somewhere behind me, a blue jay uttered its harsh whistling alarm call. I kept quite still, recalling what I had read about the birds in a book at Ravenscliff. Blue jays are afraid of very little, the shrill intensity of their calls tending to drive away small predators and even man.

Small predators wouldn't be snapping twigs the way this intruder was.

Keeping to the cover of the scrub covering the spoil heaps, I moved off, going as quickly as possible without making much noise. But the ground was dry and covered with fir cones and twigs that crunched and crackled as I trod on them. So I headed right to the top of one of the mounds of spoil, more intent now on warning Patrick of possible danger than anything else.

Once at the top I threw aside all caution and ran down the other side. A gentle wooded slope lay in front of me, the trees more mature, a path of sorts, more like a game trail, winding through them. But almost blocking my way was a gigantic rock. I had noticed several similar and from the way they were rounded and smooth knew them to be glacial debris. This one uncannily resembled an enormous doughnut. There were even flecks of marble on the surface that looked like sugar.

I carefully picked my way over the spiny plants that were

growing around the stone and once on the other side, at the point where the path began, paused. There was no point in blundering around wildly and I had no means of knowing if Patrick and Fraser had come this way. Not for the first time in several weeks I found myself unsure of what was going on in Patrick's mind. Why had he come here? Was he waiting for something to happen? Or the someone I had heard in the trees?

I don't like playing cat and mouse especially when I'm not sure who is in which rôle. Just then, and with a suddenness that made my skin crawl, Leander Hurley stepped from out of the trees right in front of me and on to the trail.

"One sound," he said to me, "and I promise I'll shoot."

He walked towards me slowly, not lowering the rifle by so much as an inch.

"I'm not armed," I told him, but nevertheless he turned me round to face the rock, made me put my arms over my head and searched me diligently for weapons. Finally I was allowed to face him again.

"Congratulations on being so quiet," I said.

"It helps to know the terrain," he answered. "Where are they?"

"You mean you didn't overtake me?"

"No, I came up from the other side," he replied irritably. "Answer the question."

"Someone was right behind me just now."

"If you—"

"Violence doesn't work with me," I broke in. "I go all weepy and bloody stubborn if people get rough."

No, he had never met a woman like me before.

I continued, "I've no idea where they are or what's going on. I wish I did, and also that you'd point that rifle somewhere else. We are on the same side, after all."

"Then what is Gillard doing out here with Fraser?" he ground out.

I stared him down and after a few moments the rifle jerked away from me.

"Talking to him," I said. "Patrick's sure that someone has a hold over Fraser. Threatening his family—something like that."

"Something like that," Hurley repeated with a grim smile. "Oh, brother."

"Are you allowed to drink on duty?" I asked, keeping my tone light.

The look he gave me was one of pure hatred. "I am not on duty."

"Tell me one thing," I said. "Are you alone? I wasn't imagining things when I heard someone following me."

"Well now," he drawled, "I'm really glad Fraser phoned and let me in on this. It did seem a little unfair—him, a middle aged company director, against that husband of yours. Damned unfair, if you ask me. Almost vicious. I'm beginning to see a little light in this murky business. I reckon this whole damn mess has been cooked up by your government. Did Fraser's company bid for the contract against orders? I should imagine that working for Canada takes quite a bit of time away from the Trident stuff. DARE are already involved with design work for Type 23 frigates for the Royal Navy and platforms for North Sea oil. But then again—I wasn't supposed to know things like that." Hurley simpered, an extraordinarily fatuous expression in a man of his appearance. "No comment for once?" he chided.

It was then that a movement caught my eye and I glanced quickly at Hurley. But he had seen the two men already. They were in a clearing in the trees above where we were standing.

"Down!" he said.

I got down but even from a crouching position could see Patrick and Fraser. They were standing still facing one another, perhaps conversing, perhaps not.

I said, "I suggest you get right out of sight. You stand out a mile in that blue jacket, and although he's only armed with a pistol he's quite capable of killing you from there if he thinks you're holding a gun on me.''

For answer Hurley gripped his rifle and checked that it was loaded. One drink or many, alcohol seemed to have blown his brains.

And then Fraser ran for it. I heard Patrick shout his name just before both of them disappeared from sight.

"Are you alone?" I asked Hurley, only aware that I had shouted when he started violently.

"Yes," he answered, amazingly meekly.

"You must help us!" I yelled, trying to penetrate his fuddled wits. "Patrick won't hurt him but others might—people who don't care about your navy or anything else Canadian. Find that person I heard—make sure he isn't armed and out to kill Fraser. Please!"

Fraser was coming straight down the hill towards us. I knew because I could hear him crunching dry spruce needles underfoot. Then he burst into view and what we were looking at was not a middle-aged company director but a fit part-time soldier. He saw Hurley and then me and slid to a stop. He had a hand gun which he aimed at us and opened fire.

He got Hurley at the second shot, before the Canadian had time to move. He fell back into the undergrowth, and when I crawled up to him looked at me, sober and terror-stricken. The bullet had taken him in the right shoulder.

"He didn't phone you, you bloody idiot," I found myself shouting at him. "Someone else did. Fraser didn't expect you to be here."

But Hurley had fainted.

I grabbed the rifle with no clear idea of what I was going to do with it and turned just in time to see Fraser framed against the skyline as he ran towards the car. I tore after him.

From the top of one of the mounds I had a perfect view, the Buick a close target. Trying to remember what I had been told, holding my breath and trying not to shake, I took aim at the front tyre closest to me and squeezed the trigger. The recoil nearly broke my shoulder but from that range even I couldn't miss. The Buick sagged over on one side.

Fraser, strangely, had been standing motionless by the car, not attempting to drive away. He swung round yelling something I couldn't hear and took a shot at me. It went wide but I had already flung myself down. I could still see him though. He seemed to go crazy. He started in my direction, stopped, hurled down the gun, took something from his pocket and lobbed it beneath the car. Instinctively I put my hands over my ears. Seconds later came an explosion and a battering wave of hot air.

Before I knew what was happening Fraser was running towards me through the thick black smoke. He was waving the gun, looking desperate, mad, terrified.

"Throw that down or I'll kill him," he yelled.

I twisted round and there was Patrick not ten yards behind me. He didn't seem to be armed. I laid the rifle down on the grass and stood up. As soon as I had done so Fraser shot him.

I must have turned my back on Fraser because I was running to where Patrick lay on the ground. But all I could see was the events of those past few seconds playing over and over again in my head. One moment Patrick had been standing there, his arms relaxed at his sides; the next flung backwards into the pine needles like a rag doll.

No amount of training could have prepared me for what happened next. I supposed I stopped running as I approached Patrick, fearful of what I might see. Yes, I *had* stopped when something hit me sickeningly on the head from behind. Everything became as in a dream, larger than life and preposterous. I fell and there was soil and dead leaves in my mouth but I still saw Fraser walk up to Patrick and shoot him again from point blank range.

"Have fun, soldier," said Fraser, and then smoke or darkness swallowed him up.

CHAPTER 17

The dream continued. We were in Hell and burning, I could smell my own hair singeing and was a prisoner in my own immobilised, cramped body, staring stupidly at Patrick's right shoe smouldering gently. Anger, the only emotion I could feel now, goaded me to my feet and I staggered over to where he lay and looked down upon him. His eyes were closed which was not right at all.

"You shouldn't be here," I said. Or at least thought I did, my voice sounded far away and slurred. Around me flames crackled, creeping forward.

I felt a lot happier when his eyes opened although I knew this to be very selfish. We were still together. But conscience nagged. "You shouldn't be here," I repeated.

"Sorry I passed out," he mumbled. "Is there any blood?"

"God knows with that red jacket on," I replied, suddenly feeling very light-headed and flippant.

He noticed the fire and struggled to sit up, caught his breath and then floundered, writhing, in a private agony that was horrible to watch. It brought me partly to my senses. People like Patrick who wear a cross and chain, I reasoned sluggishly, aren't allowed into Hell.

By the time I had reasoned myself back to reality I was crying and beating out the flames which were by now busily devouring the sock covering his artificial right foot. It was

162

odd how I hadn't noticed before that I was coughing on the smoke and could hardly see for eyes full of smuts.

In the end I simply got him in a fireman's lift and took him away from the flames. How this was achieved, where the strength came from or even how far I carried him, I don't know.

There were animals all around us, like something from a Walt Disney film. I can remember a deer with her fawn, and the way she looked at me, unafraid, as if we shared a common bond. There were herons picking off small rodents and insects as they fled the flames, and who also ate those who twisted in the blackened grass when the fire had passed. I saw all this but was not aware of carrying a twelve stone man. After a while I must have collapsed for the next thing I became aware of was both of us lying in a heap. Patrick attempting to extricate himself, swearing helplessly.

A headache was making me see double but I succeeded in removing the belt from around my waist, unfolding it along its length and assembling the small components it contained. This was the first time I had given anyone an injection of real and not pretend morphine. During training we used vitamins. Uttering nonsensical soothing noises I removed the red check lumberman's coat. Then, dragging my gaze from the flak jacket beneath and thanking heaven for Patrick's prominent veins, I gave him the smallest practical dose. He didn't even notice. I breathed out.

At point blank range a flak jacket, even the latest lightweight one, isn't good enough. I pulled it off over his head and grimly regarded a ruined tee shirt. By now he was on a kind of cloud eight and a half but nevertheless flinched as I rolled the garment up to his armpits and explored for damage.

"Two broken or badly cracked ribs," I announced. "Contusions, and a sinister-looking impacted wound that's probably bleeding inside as well. Bugger Fraser and your stupid theories!"

Eyes closed against the brilliant sunset, and unashamedly relishing not only a respite from pain but other drug-induced sensations, Patrick shook his head. Infuriatingly smugly.

I said, "Say something for God's sake!" my head banging to each and every sibilant.

His eyes snapped open. "A baptism of blood and fire," he whispered. "No—yours, not mine. I had mine years ago when the grenade exploded. This is what you've always wanted, remember? To be treated as part of the team. To be in a man's world. Fraser could have pushed you into a clump of poison ivy back there but instead you got a nicely judged tap on the head with his rifle stock."

He was right but it only made me more angry. I grabbed him by both ears. "What have you done? Did you plan the whole thing between you?"

But, just then, he responded to my anger not to what I was asking.

"It's not easy for me either," he said, moving his head slightly so that I released it. "I too have to forget that we're married and that you're expecting our child. We're just two operatives in a team of three and we depend on each other for our lives sometimes. I had no idea how Fraser would react to my persuading him to tell the truth, but when he had, and when we were discussing how to pull off a plan that would satisfy the people who are leaning on him, the real problem was you. I had to give him the best advice I could on how to incapacitate you without danger. We couldn't shout at you not to shoot him because others were almost certainly watching. What happened is what working for D12 really entails."

I glanced up to where thick smoke billowed in the distance, needing time to think. We were quite safe unless the wind changed.

"I'm not lecturing am I?" Patrick said quietly.

"No," I told him. "You're not lecturing. Please tell me what pressure is being put on Fraser so all this seems worthwhile."

"Rachel."

"His wife?"

"I've no idea. He wouldn't say. He cracked a bit when he started to talk and just kept saying Rachel. I should imagine it's a child rather than a wife or sister. Rachel will be killed unless he co-operates. These people aren't particularly interested in Canadian frigates, just on smashing DARE and its work with Trident, which is a lot more hush-hush and important than I'd realized. Then they dreamed up the last thing he had to do—kill me. Killing two birds with one stone, really. They'd get rid of a troublesome D12 operative, and Fraser would be out of the way on a murder charge. Without him DARE doesn't function. They reckoned if he wasn't arrested here he soon would be at home thus bringing DARE to a standstill once and for all. True, it's naïve and hamfisted—the KGB at their most naïve and hamfisted. Thank God I was able to convince Fraser that if we worked together we could confound them."

I helped him pull down the tee shirt and put on his jacket for he was shivering. "But can they be trusted not to harm Rachel?"

"No, of course not. But knowing their thinking they'll dither, and while they're dithering she's reasonably safe. But it's important that for a while I remain dead."

While he had been speaking my brain had been busy. Patrick saw that I had noticed the gun sticking out of his pocket.

"I aimed for Hurley's shoulder," he said, not particularly contrite. "Did he live?"

"If the fire didn't get him. I suppose it was you who tipped him off, too, so he could be there as official witness."

"Fraser wouldn't risk it," Patrick said in that man's soft Devon accent. "He said he wasn't that good a shot himself. Not in the heat of the moment. That's why he had to get me from really close up or he might have missed the jacket and hit me where it mattered."

"But when did you plan all this?" I burst out.

"Last night. I crept out of bed while you were asleep and surprised Fraser in the same state. I won't tell you what he said when he discovered that I was in his room."

"You're going to come down a hell of a bump when that stuff wears off," I informed him but the patient wasn't listening.

"The element of surprise," Patrick mused. "And you can't yell blue murder in a houseful of friends when another guy's practically in bed with you."

"Have fun soldier," I said, suddenly remembering what Fraser had said. "You'll be seriously ill with an infection in no time at all."

"You should have some antibiotics with you."

I didn't answer even though I had.

"I reckon he'll make it back to UK," Patrick continued, beginning to get sleepy as the drug got into his system. "There'll be a bloody great hoo-ha—extradition proceedings—headlines in *The Times*—and meanwhile DARE'll carry on doing what they were sent out here for. They don't actually need Fraser now Paul has recovered." His eyes were closed again and he was smiling.

"But what about Rachel?" I knew that he wasn't responsible for the euphoria but that didn't prevent me feeling helpless and very angry at seeing the fatuous smile on his face.

"I told you . . . she'll be OK while it looks as though Fraser's done as he's told. We'll sneak back home somehow and find out where she's being held. Must live rough for a few days first . . . disappear."

Patrick only slept for half an hour and when he awoke I removed his jacket and tee shirt again. With a small sharp knife in the survival kit I cut the latter into one long continuous strip, round and round, and bandaged up his chest with it as tightly as I could, using my cotton bra with the straps removed as a pad for the wound. When I had finished and given him a shot of antibiotic it was almost dark.

"You could have let me in on the plan," I said, trying hard not to sound resentful.

"We didn't work it all out until we were driving over."

There seemed no point in pursuing it.

"Give up, eh?" Patrick murmured into the darkness some time later. We were just sitting there, not attempting to go to sleep.

"Afterwards you mean?"

"Afterwards."

"So you can go to theological college?"

I had managed to surprise him at last, he swore softly.

"The truth drug," I said. "Your talking about one day following your father's profession. It was one of the reasons for Le Blek breaking us out of Hurley's Kremlin."

There was an endless silence.

"They wouldn't have me."

"The Archbishop of Canterbury fought in the War."

"Did he?"

"Money wouldn't be a problem," I went on. "We can easily live on my earnings. If it's what you want to do, I think—"

"Why are you talking about this now," he enquired, irritated.

"Because you're now a family man." The pure logic of the answer came right out of the blue.

"You'd hate it."

"Why?"

"Me in a dog collar, for a start."

"They don't all wear one these days."

"Mother's Union. Flower rotas. Bring and buy stalls. Ingrid, you're not even a church person."

What he meant was that I'm not a God person.

"If it's what you want to do," I said again rather lamely.

Some time later I said, "Someone followed me from the pick-up and Hurley swore he'd come on his own. D'you think whoever it is will check up on us?"

Patrick moved, trying to get comfortable, and caught his breath. "The watcher. If he finds us we'll have to kill him."

"But if he disappears . . . ?" I left the rest unsaid.

"They'll assume he took the money and ran when the balloon went up. Shed no tears—it's almost certainly the guy who killed Lanny."

The fire seemed to have died down on its own, probably because the wind had changed and blown the flames towards the flat stony ground. I thought about Leander Hurley and how he had looked at me like a hurt, frightened child.

"If he didn't bring a radio with him he deserves to snuff it," Patrick said savagely when I mentioned what was on my mind.

We kept watches through the darkness, Patrick taking the first while I tried to sleep. The night was fairly warm but I was already regretting leaving my anorak in the pick-up. We sat huddled together with the big jacket around both of our shoulders. Tomorrow, Patrick promised, we would get organised.

Sunrise illuminated our misery. We were soaked in dew, all exposed areas of skin lumpy and mosquito bites, Patrick so cramped and stiff that it wasted precious energy just to get him to his feet. Frankly, we had both been in better shape after a week in the Cairngorms.

"We're going to give this a try," Patrick said in response to a meaningful look from me. "If I start to go downhill, or more importantly, if you do, we'll make for the nearest road and hitch a lift back to town. No doubt Fraser took the pick-up to get him to the airport. We have a compass and even if we move around a bit I reckon—with what I can remember of the map—we can keep the Forty-five Road to Alma within about half an hour's walk."

"Would it be such a risk to contact Terry?"

"The risk would start the moment he left Ravenscliff if he came out here. I don't know, and nor did Fraser, how many watchers there are."

"If we're pronounced dead in the papers at home . . ." There was no need for me to say more. My mother has always prophesied that I will come to a sticky end, but his parents . . . I made myself stop thinking about it.

"Missing should be the worst fear for the present," Patrick murmured, experimenting with walking about. "The papers aren't quite so hysterical in UK. We'll have surfaced before anyone really gets worried."

I looked at our pathetic items of survival gear; compass, fish hooks and line, the knife, two snares and enough morphine to give Patrick very small doses for four days.

"We'll be OK," he said and took the knife, examining its sharpness. Why did any knife, however ordinary, even a blunt table knife, look so deadly in those long sensitive fingers?

"Bodies," I said after a sudden thought. "There won't be any. They'll know we're not dead."

"Fraser's going to say he dragged us off into the forest. Hurley won't know—he won't have been able to see from where he was lying." He cut and sharpened a stick and began to dig with it in the ground. "Worms for bait," he said in answer to my query. "There's a small pool over there where beavers have dammed a stream. I'm only going to use the gun in matters of life and death."

He found some worms but they kept falling off the hook. It had taken us at least an hour to find enough even to think about fishing, and to force our way through the undergrowth to a place where we could drop the weighted line in to a sufficient depth of water. This proved to be the trunk of a fallen tree, precarious and slippery, our combined weight causing it to dip below the surface.

I went digging for more efficient bait and found a disgusting maggot and several more robust-looking worms. Patrick fell upon the maggot with cries of glee and I averted my gaze when he popped the hook through the skin into its fatness. The fish that sacrificed its life to this creature was, if anything, even more revolting in appearance.

"A suicide fish," said the fisherman, taking it off the hook.

I went for a little walk while he took it by the tail, bashed its head on a rock and got busy with the knife. There was no doubt in my mind that we would be eating it raw. Fires draw attention.

"No, thank you," I said after he had called my name. A practically transparent sliver of flesh dangled from a fish guts smeared hand.

The hand wriggled imperatively, as though ringing a tiny bell. "Then said he to Laughing Water, take this cat fish for your supper. Eat up quick with salt and pepper, makem papoose grow up quicker."

"It's breakfast, Hiawatha, or hadn't you noticed?" I went up and took the fish from him. Swallowed like an oyster it didn't taste too bad.

"Breakfast didn't rhyme," he said absently through a mouthful.

We fished for most of the morning, catching two more fish which we ate with some watercress I found growing in the stream. The hot peppery flavour helped it down.

There was an understanding that we wouldn't discuss our prospects or whether we were doing the right thing. Neither would I ask him if his chest hurt nor tell him not to clown around. It was his way of fighting the pain. When he became very quiet I would know he was losing that battle. No, for the moment we would live from one minute to the next. Serious matters could be discussed during the long hours of the night.

The day remained fine, hot in the sun, cool in the shade. We achieved a wash of sorts in the pool and then walked in a northerly direction to test Patrick's theory as to the nearness of the road. We found it, hearing traffic after about twenty minutes.

We crossed a road, taking a game trail that led down very slowly to a waterway which we fervently hoped was the Forty-five river. This and Broad River both joined the Upper

Salmon River which eventually flowed into the sea at Alma. Both the river and the road marked the boundary of the park.

It was very difficult walking. Even though we tried to keep to the trail, the animals which had made it, probably deer, were far smaller than we were and thought nothing of jumping across the many small streams. Thus we continually had to duck beneath low branches or slide down into ditches, cross the water at the bottom and then climb up the other side again. After a while we reached a clearing where Patrick decided to camp.

We made a shelter with broken off branches, and because there were no leaves on the trees yet thatched it with dried ferns. When it was finished I discovered that it was quite invisible from only yards away. Perhaps we had done better at our survival lessons than I thought.

I set the two snares, trying not to think about being famished with hunger, I had no real worries about my health, nor for that matter that of the baby. I was at least half a stone overweight from lack of exercise and good eating since my arrival in Canada. Patrick, on the other hand, had absolutely nothing spare on his frame upon which to live. Right now he was examining some fungi growing on a dead birch tree. They looked like the blackened hands of long dead corpses.

"Not recommended," he observed, pulling a face. "Wonderful things if you're looking for guts ache or the screaming hab-dabs."

"You *can* eat some fungi," I pointed out, purely out of mischief.

"I'll rush out and buy a book about it," he said, and sat down heavily on the trunk of a fallen tree.

"D'you want more morphine?"

He did. This time he gave himself the injection, a rather fragile ploy to discourage over-reliance as he hates sticking needles in himself. Then he slid down and rested his head on the tree. A little while later I heard him singing softly to himself, an Irish tune by the sound of it.

I banished from my mind's eye the precise, delicate movements as he had given himself the injection, and pictures I had seen of drug addicts, and concentrated instead on my surroundings. My mind seemed to open. There is nothing like hunger for sharpening awareness. I smelled strange earthy scents and that of crushed vegetation, and felt the eyes of hidden creatures watching me from branch and stem. The trunks of the budding birch trees shone in the late afternoon light with an almost luminous glow, the same light glimmering on the foliage of the spruces and on Patrick's hair. I loved him, this man of mine, and had a ghastly premonition that Fraser had preyed upon his greatest weakness.

In the morning both snares were empty. There was a small pool near where we had camped but it was stagnant; black fetid water that neither of us even wanted to wash in. We struggled for a short distance to where we could hear more water trickling, hoping to get a drink, but this proved to be the tiny stream that fed the pool and it tasted horribly metallic. Finally, in desperation, we went all the way back to the pool where we had fished. The water was pure in this but the fish weren't biting.

We had by now fallen into the pattern that had been adopted during survival training. It was our own concept, a constant surveillance of each other for exhaustion, bad temper, call it what you will, anything that looked like giving in. This idea worked well for we had different strengths and could feed, as it were, off each other.

One thing upon which we were quite in phase was the importance of retaining a sense of humour. This kind of humour, an absolute requirement of survival, didn't come easily to me as I had never had to live off my wits before. Patrick had started to drum into me the necessity for the right attitude on a previous exercise we had been on together during which I had fallen into a mud-filled ditch. My first reaction to this homily had been to jab him in the ribs with the dummy rifle I was carrying. (They don't trust writers, female, with real ones on assault courses.) He had side-stepped, of course. Even at nearly forty he still has reflexes like a cat.

In a way, participating in training with Patrick was worse than the real thing for there were others present to witness him not carrying my pack for me after I had fallen over for the umpteenth time, or refusing to kill the rabbit that was to be my supper. No one else, needless to say, dared lift a finger. Once, when we had survived to day four and were found, captured and removed to a barn by sundry anonymous servicemen for a little testing of our remaining resilience, Patrick had stared stonily with the rest while all my clothes were removed and I was taken outside and thrown in a river. It was then that I had realised that he was being tested much more severely than I was.

And later, much later, I had laughed.

"You're day-dreaming," Patrick said, rolling up the fishing line.

"I was thinking about—"

"You're supposed to be keeping watch."

"Sorry."

We re-traced our way to the campsite and more than once I caught myself looking at several kinds of fungi growing on tree stumps. Hunger gnawed inwardly like a disease that sapped energy and the will to live.

"A cup of coffee," I said as I slid down into a ditch. "Laura Secord ice cream, hot muffins with butter—"

"Shut up!" he said in the voice that had been one of the reasons for my divorcing him after the first ten years.

Pure bloody-mindedness kept back my tears. Then, on the edge of the glade where we had our shelter, I walked into his outstretched arm, like a band of iron.

"Someone's been here," he hissed through his teeth.

CHAPTER 18

The glade steamed peacefully as the sun evaporated heavy dew. From where I was standing I could not see our shelter, even though I knew where it was. I could see nothing untoward at all, nothing that hinted of human presence.

Patrick pointed to a depression in the ground right in front of us. The soil in the bottom of it was damp and in the dampness was the impression of a shoe. We were both wearing trainers, the kind with wavy patterns on the soles, but this footprint was plain and smooth, probably a size nine, and made by the right foot of man of medium weight.

Patrick went closer and indicated where the left foot had bruised the foliage of a ground-trailing fern. He mimed how the man had crouched down initially then swivelled slightly on his left foot before standing up again. Drawing me down alongside him he showed me a meandering trail of damaged vegetation where the intruder had left the glade, going in the direction of the brook we had tried to drink from that morning.

"I saw shoes like that the other day," Patrick said quietly. "I thought I'd imagined it so didn't say anything to you. He came through the smoke and looked down at us. He was in a hell of a panic—just came and looked and then tore off again."

"So he checked up again."

"At a guess he was ordered to. He might have assumed

that the police took our bodies away—that's if Fraser wasn't
caught and said he'd hidden them. But coming this far, I don't
like that at all . . .''

There was no need for me to ask if running away was the
solution because I knew that it wasn't. Whoever it was might
have detected our shelter, and even if he hadn't he might
have noticed where we had trodden down the undergrowth.

"For Rachel we stay here," Patrick said. "There simply
isn't any choice."

For Rachel, I reminded myself that night. We had rebuilt
the shelter in a strategically better place, tucked into the angle made by two large stones. Beneath it, within my reach,
Patrick tried to sleep. The bruising and swelling of his chest
were quite frightening and the tight bandage caused almost
as much pain as the injury. But without it he could feel his
broken ribs grinding together.

For five hours I sat with the knife clutched in my right
hand. Uppermost in my mind was the worry that the intruder
had guessed we were still alive and had gone away to fetch
reinforcements. Worse, I was not at all convinced of the
existence of Rachel, someone who until the crucial moment
Fraser hadn't even mentioned. There was after all no need
to murder the operatives of D12 if they could be made to
look complete fools by indulging in a self-inflicted incarcer-
ation in the Canadian backwoods. The result of that would
be nearly as bad, character assassination. We would be
thrown out for incompetence.

I knew how to use the knife. The marines sergeant who
had taught me how to kill people had been softly spoken,
built model railways for his son in his spare time and had a
weakness for pink marshmallows. He knew all about the
disadvantages I possessed as a woman and also a few advan-
tages I had over men, some of which had already occurred
to me. Put crudely, to disable a man, a weaker woman went
straight for the most vulnerable region. Men were so sensitive about this area, he had assured me solemnly, that even

male enemies sometimes hesitated before utilising tactics so low. Women, apparently, had no such inhibitions. He had appeared to approve of women's lack of inhibitions generally and had thoroughly enjoyed showing me how to combat rape.

From the way he was breathing I knew Patrick to be asleep. I was almost certain that he was unaware that I knew how to despatch an enemy effectively with a knife. Whilst not actually forbidding me to tell him, Colonel Daws had made it known that certain aspects of my training ought to be deliberately kept vague, even with Patrick. Pistol and rifle practice were one thing, knives quite another. Knives were furtive and slightly kinky, not for women to know about. Strange really, this British thinking. It's amazingly easy to kill with a knife when you know how. Too easy.

An owl hooted nearby. Then it flew across a lighter part of the sky where the moon had risen behind hazy cloud. It was like a large silent butterfly. I watched where I thought it had perched but there was no movement, no sound. Then a twig snapped.

Owls don't snap twigs.

There was only the one patch of light high in the sky. It was as if our glade was a dish filled with night, the tops of the trees the rim. I tried to see into the gloom but my eyes played tricks with me, the blackness shifting and dancing, forming itself into shapes that might or might not be there. Hunger was replaced by a choking sensation.

My blind rush to escape was almost overwhelming—and then the knife passed out of my possession. It was extraordinarily reassuring the way a warm hand slid down my arm to the wrist in a tactile request.

When the powerful flash lamp was switched on we both kept quite still, dazzled by the beam, impaled on it. The man holding it came closer. I could hear his feet brushing through the grass. This must be a person of flesh and blood, I thought wildly, it was only mild starvation that was causing me to picture lights that moved by themselves, an unseen power crushing the vegetation.

"Stand up!"

The voice was harsh, clipped and imbued with an authoritative tone that suggested he was armed.

Patrick grunted with pain as he stood up.

"And you!"

"I've sprained my ankle," I called back. The beam was full on me, Patrick above me in the darkness.

"Get up!"

I made a play of struggling to my feet and then allowed my right foot to give way beneath me so that I fell sprawling. The torch beam followed me down.

There was nothing upon which to congratulate myself afterwards. I went with Patrick to where the flash lamp lay in the grass, picked it up and shone it in the right direction.

For Rachel.

The man was already dying and in the time it took for me to blink slowly the knife was no longer in his neck but somewhere else and then Patrick was wiping it on the grass.

For Rachel.

"Ingrid." He spoke patiently.

I swung the torch beam from Patrick's eyes and sat on the ground. "Sorry."

He took the torch from me and by its light began to turn out the dead man's pockets. I really had the shakes then and sat on my hands to keep them still. We had killed a man without first finding out who he was. Would a court accept a plea of self-defence? Was a small knife thrown with almost surgical precision a more potentially deadly murder weapon than a hunting rifle? That lay in the undergrowth where it had dropped from the intruder's dying hands.

"I feel like filth," I said to the forest. "All my thoughts are concerned with self-justification and saving my own skin."

The body had no identification papers, not even a wallet

containing credit cards. The pockets held ammunition for the rifle, a handkerchief, a photograph of a woman and a flick-knife. Patrick held this out for me to see, springing the blade almost under my chin with a hideous slicing click.

The woman in the photograph was Margaret Howard.

"A Rolls-Royce to a bent pin this was Lanny's rifle," Patrick whispered, examining it. "He couldn't resist stealing it. I'd guess that he was happier with the knife."

For the rest of the night we huddled together for warmth under the thick jacket. Once or twice I dozed and then must have slept heavily for about an hour. When I awoke the sky was getting light and my legs were numb. I sat up, fuddled, and realized that I had been asleep with my head in Patrick's lap. He was leaning back, staring unseeing into space, eyes red-rimmed. The peaceful way he met my gaze told me that he had given himself more morphine.

"We can't stay hidden," I said.

"We must, just for a few more days."

"You'll have a serious infection by then—there isn't any more antibiotic."

"As I said, we'll pull out if either of us becomes ill."

"Do you really trust Fraser?"

"Not altogether. There was a lot he didn't tell me, but I believe Rachel is very important to him."

"Are you *sure* he didn't play on your own yearning to be a father?"

"Yes."

"You're not even thinking about it."

"No—because I'm sure."

"Patrick, your whole career might hinge on this."

But he only smiled at me.

This was the last proper conversation that I can remember. Afterwards, I suppose, we exchanged words, comments, questions and answers, and we might have even talked to ourselves. I know that as far as I was concerned, the difference between pretence and reality—a training exercise, no matter how rigorous, and the real thing—came home to me at this point.

The word reality haunted me. Reality was being in real pain from hunger all the time, feeling disgust at the smell of my own unwashed body, losing my temper when I fell over; the veneer that I liked to call my maturity stripped further away with each passing hour.

That morning also the snares were empty and I know that I sulked. We covered the dead man with stones and branches and started walking, a twisting, turning route to confuse anyone who might follow. After a little while we left what I soon came to realise had been easy to traverse country and entered virgin forest. We were forced to follow more game trails but sometimes it seemed to me that we were going round in circles.

The weather was on our side, the sun warm. There was a light breeze, just enough to keep us cool and the insects from making our life a misery. But as soon as we stopped they buzzed around us in murderous hordes. I think it was at this time that I ceased to see any sense in what we were doing.

Before we became too tired we bivouacked. Patrick set the snares and then we sat by the side of a tiny rivulet, drinking from our cupped hands.

"There's one more shot of morphine," I said.

"Please don't tell me things I already know."

"I wasn't being defeatist—just telling you it's there when you want it."

Silence.

"I've been here before," he said a while later, referring to life after the Falklands War when he had coped by taking small white pills given to him by the doctor. After taking one he had sat around slightly stupefied but free from the relentless torture of his smashed legs. Or he had drunk whisky to the same effect. Or, if circumstances forced him to remain lucid and sober, he had thrown himself into feverish activity.

Once, at home, his mother Elspeth told me how he had emptied his Smith and Wesson into an elm tree in the Rectory garden and killed six rooks which had been clamouring over nest sites in its branches.

There was nowhere to fish so we ate instead the worms we would have used for bait. There was nothing else, even if Patrick had consented to use the gun. Birds sang hidden in the trees during the day, and all night frogs and crickets kept us awake.

For me the days began to merge into one another. We found a place where we stayed for a day and then moved on because Patrick fretted that we were being followed.

Unwelcome, slightly crazed memories still jolt me awake at night. I can remember Patrick seeking warmth, affection perhaps during one of the long nights, and how I pushed him away.

"I've switched off the alarm clock because it's Sunday tomorrow," he said, snuggling even closer. "You've just come to bed smothered in perfume and nothing else."

"A trailer for a forthcoming attraction?" I asked, too tired to concentrate on what I was saying.

"It doesn't have to be."

"I don't fancy you with all those bristles."

"No?" Holding his breath he shifted position, forcing me to rearrange my own limbs.

"You're not serious," I told him.

He presented me with a *fait accompli*, leaned over and kissed me intensely; bristles, unwashed, the foul breath of semi-starvation. I gave him a shove and he desisted, as tense as a steel spring with anger. Time went by.

"That's real love," he said suddenly.

"I do love you," I whispered but he didn't respond.

By the morning he was feverish, shivering, his skin burning hot to the touch. My reaction to this was anger. There was an inevitability, a hopelessness about our plight that in the cold light of day resembled ineptitude. Not for the first time it seemed that the entire assignment in Canada was tainted with failure.

I can remember shouting at him and after a while he agreed to use the compass to take us back to the road. Up until this morning we had guided ourselves by the sun but now it was obscured by clouds.

All day we walked.

We walked all the next day as well with me leading him now because he kept wandering off the narrow trail and bumping into trees. I was looking after the compass too for he kept dropping it. Dazedly, and why I do not know, I checked it when the setting sun emerged from clouds, glowing redly over low hills, all this reflected in a lake, not a road in sight.

"It's faulty!" I gasped, not believing it. "Patrick, this bloody thing's way out!"

"By how much?" he asked dully.

"A lot," I told him and he shrugged, shaking his head.

We drank water from a ditch. The water seemed clean so I unwound the strapping from his chest, bathed the wound and dressed it with moss. The bruising and discolouration were still dreadful to behold but there was no sign of infection. I bedded him down on the same bank of moss and covered him, quite unresisting, as warmly as possible with the jacket. He slept and in the morning his temperature had gone down.

We heard a helicopter at around lunch time, if such an event existed in our lives now. I piled ferns and dead leaves over Patrick where he rested in the shade and then hid myself nearby. It skimmed the lake along the banks of which we had been walking and then flew south. A short while later we heard it again but it came nowhere near us this time.

"I should have tried to attract the pilot's attention," I said, having made the decision that we would be able to go no further that day.

"Why didn't you?"

"I don't know," I replied and went away to set the snares so that I could cry alone.

I'm not sure how many hours later it was, maybe it was the next day, when a horrible high-pitched squealing penetrated my dazed state of mind. I tracked the sound and found a young hare caught in one of the snares. When I laid a hand on it it became still; glorious golden brown fur fading to a rich cream beneath its body, beautiful brown eyes surveying me calmly. The snare had caught it just behind the forelegs. I loosened it, understanding neither its tameness nor why I had caught it in broad daylight.

"Sorry, little one," I said, and then killed it.

With the same knife that had been used to kill the friend of Margaret Howard I cleaned, skinned and jointed the creature. By now I was beyond asking questions, just choked back more tears upon discovering that it had been female and with young. I ate the warm liver and heart right there and then—liver makes Patrick ill. Then I laid the joints in some large leaves and took them over to where he lay.

When you are really hungry it is possible to devour a hare raw, tearing at the flesh, sucking up the blood and gouging out the kidneys with your thumbs. We did all these things then licked our fingers and wiped them on our filthy clothes.

"I hope you offered thanks to your dentist," Patrick said, trying without much success to remove blood from his new beard.

"Of course," I replied. He hadn't been concerned with my good teeth but whether I had thanked God.

I went away for a short distance wondering if God understood whisky and loss of temper in time of trouble but would prefer one to rely on morphine and tears. Neither, came the instant and shockingly alien idea, God preferred prayer.

"Then you're very unreasonable," I said out loud, kicking at a rock. I turned to look at Patrick and found that he was looking at me. "Did you feel cheated when you prayed for the relief of pain only to lose the part of your right leg that hurt the most?''

''No.''

''Do you really believe that we're being looked after even though you've killed a man and I'm pregnant and we're starving and lost, and this is all in the balance with the life of a child called Rachel?''

He didn't blench. ''Yes.''

If this was delirium then my brain was like liquid crystal. ''There's nothing to do with Mother's Union and bring and buy stalls in that,'' I blurted out. ''Nothing to do with flower rotas and dog collars. It's awful—quite awful.''

''Like nailing a man up to a piece of wood and leaving him to die,'' Patrick said. ''Yes—and look what happened afterwards.''

Even more interesting than this exchange was my disappointment when I woke up and realized that I had dreamt it.

Catching and eating the hare however had not been a dream for we both suffered severe stomach pains afterwards. We turned round and retraced our footsteps nearly all the way we had come in the past two days. Whether it took another two days or only one after our meal I do not know, and Patrick is not sure either. He can recollect crossing the stream that fed the lake and then heading over the low hills that I had seen while testing the compass. We came to a logging track that led to a road.

I am told that it was lumberjacks who found us, a team clearing away trees felled the previous winter. Rumour has it that I had to convince Patrick that they were not going to kill us as he had wanted to shoot them all just in case.

They couldn't believe we were British and had survived on our own for over a week.

CHAPTER 19

Colonel Daws was standing with his back to the room looking out of the window when we entered his office. Since we had last met he had moved temporarily to a room in Whitehall while the other premises were refurbished. It was a very small room in comparison with the other and there was no space for the cabinet containing military memorabilia and some of the items from his collection of jade. His grandfather clock and the large wall charts depicting famous battles were also missing. Presumably everything was in store.

I was not sufficiently misguided to imagine for one moment that this was the reason for his anger. Perhaps I am slightly fey but he did not have to turn round to face us for me to know that he was consumed by a choking black fury.

Patrick and I sat down, out of necessity. We had not been invited to.

Daws spun round from the window, his expression confirming my worst fears, and spoke directly to Patrick. "Did you write your report or was it the work of your wife?"

"I dictated it, she took it down in shorthand and then typed it on a borrowed typewriter," Patrick said surprised, too tired, too weak, too downright ill for the warning signals to have reached him.

Daws rested both hands on his desk and leaned on them so that his face was only a matter of a yard from Patrick's. "I prefer hand-written reports."

184

"I know. I'm sorry, sir."

"I asked because it seems to me that it's a clever piece of fiction. Clever, Major, in the sense that it attempts to justify your actions. It fails, of course, because in the real world justification has to be based on facts."

"It's a report," Patrick said, "and thus explains why I took certain steps. I can never remember working with less facts to go on. One of the reasons I was recruited into this department was my ability to use intuition. It was all I had in this case."

The Colonel sat down and opened one of the drawers of his desk. He took out a file that had a photograph fixed to the cover with a paperclip. Even though it was upside down from where I was sitting, I could see that it was of Chris Fraser.

"Fraser hasn't a daughter called Rachel," said Daws. "He hasn't any children at all—legitimate, bastards, wild oats, call them what you will."

He wasn't in the habit of using words like bastard when I was present. I took this to mean that although he was ignoring my presence I was included in his displeasure.

This was the last and undoubtedly to be the worst of the carpetings we had endured since meeting the woodmen. First there had been Terry on hearing that I was pregnant concerning the risks thereto, then Hartland when he had discovered that he would have to spirit us out of Canada and back home, then the medical staff at a London teaching hospital where we had been unceremoniously dumped at two in the morning two days previously, and after this Patrick's parents who had not been mollified when he had threatened never to go home again if they let out that they had heard from us.

Daws warmed to his theme. Margaret Howard's boyfriend, one Karl Melker, had been the eldest son of an East German family who had fled to the West amidst much publicity in a light plane some four years previously. He had been working at Lancaster University as a lecturer in Maths.

"He didn't make us a party to those facts when he came for us in the boondocks armed with a rifle and flick knife," Patrick pointed out sourly.

"Do people go out into the Canadian backwoods without being armed?" Daws enquired.

Patrick groaned under his breath.

"I should imagine that he was in Canada on holiday to be with her and she asked him to look for you when you failed to return," Daws continued relentlessly. "And now you tell me he's in a shallow grave somewhere near the border of a National Park."

"That's if it was him," I said.

"It's still being checked out," Daws said without looking at me. "But we've already discovered that he's not at the University. One other thing . . . who was Fraser's contact? You haven't mentioned who gave him his orders."

"He didn't say."

"But I should imagine you made asking him a priority."

"No. I had to be very careful—I didn't want him to clam up altogether."

"But it was all lies!" Daws shouted. And then more quietly, "It was all a pack of lies. No one was threatening him. He had Quade killed because he thought he was going to steal his ideas and take Rogers off to start a company of their own. The entire threat story was to cover up the murder. We must assume that he also murdered the man he hired to kill Quade. He must have laughed like a drain when Rogers ate those poisoned clams and you sat up all night with him at the hospital in case someone finished *him* off. I've another complaint from that quarter too—that you threatened hospital staff with loaded gun."

"How the hell would they know it was loaded?" I cut in furiously.

"Was it?" Daws barked at Patrick.

"Of course," said Patrick with a look that told me to keep quiet unless I had something intelligent to contribute.

"Furthermore . . ." Daws began and then stopped, resting his temples on steepled fingers as if he had a headache. When he resumed speaking I really feared for us, such was his anger. "I will not be laughed at. Fraser has run us around as though we were a bunch of tinkers hawking chicken shit. I've been informed from a reliable source that David Hartland is responsible for a question being asked in the House as to our efficiency."

We were permitted to digest this for a moment.

"But almost worse than this," Daws went on, "is that you shot and injured a member of the Canadian Security Service. Please don't tell me that he had been drinking—that gem of intelligence has already been made known to me by his superiors. I'm not quite sure why. But they are understandably angry that you put a bullet in one of their operatives in order to . . ." Again he broke off. "Major, what in God's name *did* you shoot him for?"

"At the time," Patrick said on a sigh, "he was waving a rifle around. He might have decided to stop Fraser from getting away."

"He might have decided to stop Fraser from getting away," Daws repeated, and Patrick's Adam's apple bobbed jerkily.

"He was there to see it happen," Patrick explained. "I put it in my report. I wanted someone in an official capacity to witness Fraser apparently doing as he was told."

"Hurley was threatening me with the rifle," I said. "He was drunk enough to have shot me accidentally."

Daws gave me five seconds attention. "Perhaps he thought *you'd* allow Fraser to get away. It doesn't seem to me that Hurley can be regarded as seriously impaired by alcohol—not when one compares his actions with the subsequent behaviour of those I have to believe were perfectly sober."

Patrick said, "Fraser and I had come to an understanding. At the time I couldn't allow anything to risk this child's life—not Hurley, not friendship between nations, nothing."

But Daws was childless. "Would you be prepared to swear on oath that you *were* perfectly sober when these arrangements were being made, and also when you and Fraser carried them out?"

Patrick recoiled as though he'd been slapped across the face. "Yes, sir," he said after a pause.

"But Fraser lied," Daws said as though talking to a mental defective. "All right, suppose for a moment that you haven't made several grave errors of judgement. Where is Fraser? Is he still in Canada and eluding everyone hunting for him or has he succeeded in getting back to this country?"

Patrick said, "The Hartlands' pick-up was found at Saint John airport. It's my guess he flew straight home."

"That wasn't in your report."

"I only found out just now. I rang Meadows. Le Blek's called off the search."

"Isn't that a trifle premature? Canada's a vast country."

"Le Blek must have been thinking along the same lines as I was."

"Major," Daws murmured. "How your enemies must hate you. Do I deduce that the Mounted Police weren't really looking for Fraser, and that with this Le Blek's co-operation you've had the security people over there going round in circles for over a week?"

"You wouldn't understand, sir," Patrick said softly after consideration.

"Then give me a breakdown of your findings from the point of view that Fraser isn't the guilty party," Daws replied, dangerously polite.

There is a vivisector in all of us, I reasoned bleakly. Daws wasn't to be blamed. But Patrick is too old a hand at the game to be reduced to feigning deep thought or jingling the loose change in his pocket. He started talking.

"Up until the moment I pressured him for answers I thought Fraser was heavily involved. But he convinced me that Quade was killed as a warning to him, and that Lanny

Gaspereau was murdered by the same source to prevent him talking. Fraser didn't know where or if Margaret Howard fitted in. Sometimes she'd give him messages which she said had come over the phone—no more than vague threats so he didn't know if they were genuine or if she'd made them up.''

Daws said, "Why should she do such a thing?"

"Because she's a bitch," I retorted before Patrick could answer. "She was engaged at one time to Quade and sleeping with Fraser as well. That nearly broke the company up, too. Paul Rogers gave us the information," I added, seeing the Colonel's scorn. "I can't think of a person less interested in gossip."

"Is Miss Howard still working out there?"

"No," Patrick replied. "She handed in her notice and walked out three days ago. No one's seen her since."

"Did you get that from Meadows as well?"

"Yes."

"Did he have anything else to report?"

"No, sir, nothing of interest."

With an air of finality Daws dropped Fraser's file back in the drawer and closed it. "It goes without saying that your position will have to be reviewed."

Patrick was quite ashen by now. Thirty-six hours in hospital had resulted in the cracked ribs being strapped, a small infection drained—this an unpleasant process involving the insertion of hollow needles—and blinding headaches due to a reaction to one of the drugs he had been given. Sleep and a square meal hadn't quite happened. But he had been recruited to D12 because of his tenacity.

"People don't lie to me," he said, and there was none of his usual deference to the Colonel. "Not comprehensively— just a small fib here and there that shows up when the entire story finally comes out. Fraser might not have a daughter called Rachel but there's someone who means a hell of a lot to him with a gun at their head."

It was as if he hadn't spoken. Daws said, "I ordered you

to take Quade's place and use Meadows in whichever gap needed filling in your estimation. You disobeyed those orders—I suggest that you jeopardised the entire operation by doing so. Your place was in the house, not masquerading as an eccentric gardener. What did you discover? That Emma Hartland was a security risk? That's been known for years. Hartland was sent to Canada for that reason—not much of real importance goes on there.''

I said, "It would have been helpful if we had been briefed on this before we left."

"But the Major wasn't here to be briefed. He flew straight out to Port Charles the same day I gave him his orders, despite a request from me to see me before he went.''

"That's correct," Patrick said. "Someone failed to give me the message.''

"You left without informing official channels where you were and after a period of leave when I had to persuade my superiors that you weren't AWOL. No, there's no need now to explain where you were. I'm no longer interested." He turned to me. "Perhaps you'd be good enough to leave us for a while.''

I left the room as gracefully as possible in such circumstances, responding to Daws' secretary's sardonically raised eyebrow with a shrug and as bright a smile as I was capable of at that moment.

We were in real trouble. I said it again to myself, out loud, standing in the corridor but I was so tired there was no inner reaction at all. I removed myself from the distant sound of the Colonel's raised voice and went to stand by one of the long windows in the corridor, overlooking Horse Guards Parade. I rested my forehead on the glass, deliciously cool, and wished that I was at home in Devon.

I had been more fortunate in hospital in that I had spent just about the entire stay asleep with a little help from sedatives. Tests that had confirmed pregnancy had been conducted without my knowledge. I had been put on a drip feed to consume all sorts of expensive goodies, in the exact words of a nurse, as I had lost a stone in weight and now weighed considerably less than I should. This had surprised me. What I regarded as my normal weight was, in medical eyes, lath-like. But the real shock had been to be referred to by medical staff in the plural. Baby and I. Two of us.

Looked at dispassionately, the Hartlands had been superb. Emma had driven out to the farm where the foreman of the logging gang had taken us to phone and then rushed us back to Ravenscliff for hot baths, several hot meals and head to toe treatment with an insect bite lotion that had relieved the blotchy swelling covering almost very inch of our bodies. David Hartland had delivered his tirade but nevertheless suc-ceeded in arranging a flight on a Canadian Air Force jet that was leaving in a few hours.

For the present Terry was to remain in Port Charles, and until everything was resolved would continue to escort Drew McAlister and Paul Rogers to work. Nasonworth had lent DARE a secretary to replace Margaret Howard until some-one could be flown out from England. The last piece of news that Terry had given Patrick which was unlikely to be of interest to Daws was that Chris Fraser's father, an old man of nearly eighty who had been the founder of the firm, had temporarily taken control.

It was twenty minutes before Patrick appeared. Dazed, unseeing, he came into the corridor and went to the next window to the one where I was standing. Strangely, he cop-ied what I had done, rested his brow on the glass while sup-porting himself with arms high and wide in the window embrasure. Below, a troop of the Blues clattered past.

"I need a drink," he announced from his crucified posi-tion. Then he made one of his rare frightening movements, an explosion of energy that took him several yards further away from me down the corridor.

"You're in uniform," I reminded his rigid shoulder blades.

He turned unexpectedly, for I was sure he had neither

heard nor seen me. When he's driven to it, said an inner warning voice, he's capable of the unspeakable.

"There's a Mess," he observed after a few heart-stopping moments, somehow restored to rationality by my trite remark.

"Where you can have a drink but not get drunk," I pointed out, deliberately utilising my carrying, diva, voice. "Did Six sell us down the river after all?"

It worked. I might as well have thrown my skirts over my head and started to sing *Roll out the Barrel*. Appalled, he glanced left and right to see if anyone had heard, seized my hand and towed me to the nearest lift.

"What has Daws *done*?" I asked when he had rammed a rigid index finger on to several buttons.

He took a deep breath through flared nostrils and let it out again slowly. "I might be court martialled. And that's not all. He's going to split us up. You're to work with Terry."

"Not a chance."

"Say that within these walls and we're finished."

"So we're finished. We fall back on Plan B."

"It's not as easy as that."

Neither of us spoke again until we were outside in chilly British sunshine.

"I sometimes think . . ." Patrick said when we were in a café not a bar, a tiny back street haven I had found when once in London to see my publisher.

"What?"

"That you agonize over your stories, living really deeply with your characters, but when something ghastly happens to us simply trot out a statement like you did just now—'We fall back on Plan B.' "

"Patrick, that's simply not true," I protested. "I was trying to say that I didn't mind. That if you're . . . well . . . disgraced, it won't make any difference to how I feel about you."

The plastic spoon he had been bending in one hand suddenly snapped. "You think Fraser pulled the wool over my eyes too, don't you?"

"I don't know."

"You *do* bloody know," he said in a savage whisper.

"Someone at Ravenscliff, or someone who knew Fraser well and how he dropped the ringpulls back into empty beer cans . . ." I glanced up at him. "That someone is the person who killed Lanny or arranged to have him killed. If it wasn't that man who came after us in the forest—the one who was hired, I mean—then who? Either Fraser did it or he was framed. Nothing's clear in my mind. The man we killed looked like a thug. Not the sort of person Margaret Howard would associate with. But be fair—you yourself were quite sure at one point that Fraser had cut Lanny's throat."

"I said that the night I was on a high from Hurley's bloody truth drug."

"That was the same night you nailed down Fraser for the truth," I said, finding myself thumping the table at every word. "You were stoned on the stuff—that and me having just told you I was pregnant. I said that we ought to have included being taken away for questioning in the report."

"It was an irrelevance."

I bit back what I was about to say, that it would have been an excuse. No, not an excuse, the Army wouldn't countenance excuses. But it might have been a mitigating circumstance, bearing in mind the notes on Patrick's file forbidding the administration of drugs to him during training.

"It isn't a disgrace," I said laying a hand over one of his. "It isn't even carelessness or misjudgement—you'd been nobbled."

But I realized then, looking into his eyes, that he didn't want people to be kind or find reasons. He wanted to be believed.

Patrick said, "That kind of high doesn't impair judgement—it enhances it. That night I felt I could count the stars, see the atoms in the wallpaper. It was as if I had Fraser under a microscope. If I'm wrong it means I'm somehow failing—not that I'd been nobbled. It means that if I get chucked out or severely reprimanded and sent out to the Rhine to organise military band concerts, I shall never feel that I know where I stand again with any mortal being on this planet. Ingrid, does that make sense?''

I nodded slowly. ''And Plan B?''

''It can't be a last resort, can it? I've got to have something to offer, not go cap in hand . . .''

''Your father might say that was spiritual pride.''

''Then I'm proud,'' he replied unhesitatingly, and changed the subject. ''When is this child of ours due to hatch?''

''Just before Christmas. Patrick, you must accept that there's a risk—I am rather old.''

''Old!''

''Positively ancient to have a first baby.''

''But you're as fit as me—come to that, fitter.''

''The risk might be to the baby. There's more chance of its being abnormal when you're older.''

''Down's, you mean?''

''Yes.''

''Better than no child at all.''

''D'you really mean that?''

''I always mean what I say, don't I?''

We returned to Patrick's pied à terre just off Gower Street. I made us more coffee, just for something to do really, found that he had fallen asleep on the sofa, drank it myself and curled up on the bed. When I woke it was nearly dark and a large orange street light just outside the window was shining into my face.

The sofa was still occupied. By a man and a bottle of whisky. No glass. In the lurid orange light I took it away from him, closed the curtains, switched on a couple of table lamps and then went into the bathroom where I had a wash and brushed my hair. When I returned to the living cum bedroom he had re-acquired the bottle and was tilting it to his lips.

"Patrick!"

He grinned and then I noticed that the bottle was full, the seal unbroken.

"Virgo intacta," he said sadly. "I was promised a hideous demise if I touched a drop whilst on these damn pills."

"So you were contemplating suicide?" I enquired lightly, not at all sure of his frame of mind.

"No, I was going to stop taking the pills first."

I threw a cushion at him, on my way to raid the kitchen for food. Expecting to find baked beans, frozen sausages and beer I hummed casually to cover the surprise of discovering game soup and smoked oysters in tins, scampi, strawberries, cream and wholemeal rolls in the freezer, butter and a bottle of champagne in the fridge.

"Found the emergency rations?" he called through the door.

"Pity about the champagne," I said, replacing it in the fridge.

"Pity be blowed. I'm only forbidden spirits."

I took the bottle through to him with two glasses. I love watching Patrick open champagne. "What are we celebrating?"

The cork rocketed into the ceiling. "What would you like to celebrate?" His expression was unreadable.

"How about my believing that Rachel exists?"

"You don't have to," he said, pouring carefully. "I think our relationship can stand a few hiccups now."

"No, I mean really believing it."

"What changed your mind?" He *had* smiled just a little, I told myself. He was not, after all, a man prone to cowboy whoops and bouncing on the furniture.

"Back to basics really," I said. "Thinking about Fraser. If he wasn't doing it because of dreadful threats then it would be for money. And although I should imagine he can be a bit cunning in everyday matters, the thing that really comes over about him is his deep down integrity—he'd rather die than accept money from the Russians. And I remembered just now how he looked when you mentioned to him that I was expecting—his face just froze."

"Cheers," said Patrick, holding up his glass. "To the Oink then."

"Oink?"

"That's what Terry calls small children—Oinks."

We drank to the Oink and after another glass I deemed us sufficiently mellow to talk about the immediate, less pleasant future.

"I made a phone call," Patrick said when I broached the subject. "While you were asleep. If everything goes to plan, our being well and truly alive will be all over the front pages of tomorrow's evening papers."

"Aren't you going to tell me what you're going to do?"

"No—then you'll behave naturally. Don't worry, it's not drastic like last time."

"Does Daws know?"

"I hope not," muttered my spouse grimly.

"I don't think he would court martial you," I said after some thought.

"Perhaps that would be too public. But a ruling of insubordination and emotional instability would probably mean I'd end up in an army mental hospital for a while."

I stared at him dumbly.

"I'm not sure if it's an official accusation," he continued. "That's the worst part. Was Daws just shouting or did he write it all down after I left and staple it on my file?" He drained his glass. "Come to think of it, you accused me of something very similar in Canada."

"Only because of emotional instability of my own," I protested.

"Who's to know? I think I'd rather be court martialled in a way—my blunderbuss and flyswatter lying crossed on the table—better than an ambulance coming for one, don't you think?''

It was an unbearable moment, seeing him smile at me bleakly and the unbounded misery that lay beyond.

CHAPTER 20

Daws rang at eight-thirty the next morning to confirm, using code words with which we were all familiar, that Six's neglect in clearing us with the Canadian Security people had been traced to a certain individual. There was no evidence of deliberate foul play. We were to stay out of sight until ordered otherwise and he would prefer it if we returned to Devon.

"We go tonight," Patrick said to me when he had related what had been said.

"It sounds as though he's washed his hands of the entire business."

"According to him it is now a police matter. Nothing to do with Five. He sprayed that all over me like weedkiller yesterday."

"Then why leave Terry in Port Charles?"

"He's ordered him home on the first available flight."

"But I thought . . . ?"

"Terry asked for a week's leave and Daws had no choice but to grant it."

"I hadn't realized that Terry was so keen," I remarked, baffled.

"He's keen on Drew's new assistant."

"Don't tell me you rang him at three a.m. their time!"

But all I got was an enigmatic smile while he spooned muesli into two bowls.

"I don't really want any breakfast," I told him.

"Feed the Oink,'' he instructed, plonking a bowl in front of me. "Look, I've even been out to get you single cream to have with it.''

Still bemused I sat down. "I do wish you wouldn't make such a mystery of things. Why did you ring Terry again?''

"I didn't. He rang me—at one twenty-six our time, if you must know.'' He chuckled. "I thought you hadn't noticed I slept on the sofa. Terry is exploring a theory of his own. Do you remember a few months ago when all those American diplomats were chucked out of Moscow in retaliation for some Russians being expelled from Washington for spying?''

"Last November,'' I said.

"Right. Well, apparently Canada turned out its cupboards too and got rid of a few odd-balls of its own under cover of supporting Uncle Sam. Terry is getting as many photos of these characters as he can from records and is sending them to Old Bill the gardener, in Vancouver, to see if he recognises any of them.''

"The lad is a genius,'' I breathed. "How come records are co-operating?''

Patrick spoke through a mouthful of muesli. "Leander Hurley's boss trying to make amends. Terry read between the lines that certain folk have been trying to zap our muscle bound hero for some time.''

"So the male visitors weren't Emma's boyfriends—they were there to see her husband.''

"Not so fast. Nothing's proved yet, it's only a theory.''

"And likely to remain so, knowing the Canadian postal service.''

"That's where Le Blek comes in. He's going to Fax them over to the nearest RCMP post to where the gaffer lives with his daughter. Another thing that might interest you is that both the Hartlands left home separately for destinations unknown. Not for Montreal, though, Terry does know that.''

"When?''

"David on the evening of the day we turned up, Emma

the following morning. And if you're going to say that he should have mentioned it before, he said that he hadn't had the idea then and it hadn't seemed all that important.''

"It's a long shot," I said quietly.

"Yes," he agreed. "A bit like shooting an arrow out of a window and asking to be buried where it falls."

I asked no questions when we went out for a walk. All things considered, we weren't in such bad shape as I had thought. A good night's sleep and two square meals had seen to that, and when I stepped out into the fresh air I felt quite invigorated. But I reminded myself that my companion's pallor was concealed by his tan and accordingly walked a little more slowly than I would have done normally.

I also kept my own counsel when Patrick announced that he was going to have his hair cut, successfully guiding him past a grim short back and sides establishment with a betting shop in the basement and a window crammed with faded advertisements for certain articles in rubber. Beaming mutely I bustled him into a unisex salon a short distance away and sat near the door to prevent any change of heart. Soon the unkempt black curls were all around him on the floor and he was undergoing what was probably the first blow-dry of his life.

We took a taxi, the driver being instructed to take a roundabout route, and finished up not far from where we had been the previous day. I still kept quiet although desperate to try to alleviate a condition that had worsened steadily as the morning progressed. Outwardly nothing was amiss. A quick glance from a passer-by, and Patrick collected several for he was again in uniform, would not have elicited that here was a man literally speechless from nerves. As we approached Horse Guards Parade again from Whitehall I reluctantly put a different word to it—fear.

Fear is contagious.

There was the usual crowd of tourists around the gateways, Nikons and Leicas clicking frantically as they photographed the two hapless soldiers of the Household Cavalry. We walked through, attracting a few clicks of our own. Once on to the smooth setts of the parade ground Patrick halted, gazed around as if measuring distances and then went on a little further. I followed, my stomach tying itself in knots.

"If you should see a loose horse," he said over his shoulder, "do keep right out of the way."

I thought about Hyde Park and the riders in Rotten Row, wondering if he had some kind of sixth sense. Then I noticed two men with cameras who were not tourists. Most certainly they were from the Press. They lounged, gimlet-eyed, against an archway.

Several clocks struck but I was too distracted to notice which hour. Behind me there were shouted orders and the sound of hooves ringing on stone. Then from across the parade came a troop of Blues.

"You're kidding," I whispered to myself. "You can't be serious."

The impossible happened. There was a mêlée and a scattering of the approaching horses. I saw no one fall but suddenly a riderless horse broke away. Several of the troopers rode at it to head it off but this seemed to madden the animal and it plunged away from them and headed towards us and the gateway.

The man was crazy if he thought he could stop that half a ton of horseflesh heading towards us at a gallop, and all for a publicity stunt. Its ears laid back, eyes rolling, it clattered pell-mell at him, its harness metalwork glittering in the sunlight.

He stopped it. Any living creature will stop when someone makes the kind of noise that Patrick now uttered. I whipped round to see where the ghastly screaming bark had come from and when I looked back he had hold of the bridle. The horse reared, taking him up with it, and for a moment I thought he would fall beneath the flying hooves. Then it was over and the Press photographers took a few more pictures before disappearing into the crowd.

I decided that it was time a woman was silent no longer

but he forestalled me—not speaking, he couldn't yet—just gestured to an open door in the archway. It opened wider as we approached and closed behind us, the Corporal responsible for this saluting Patrick crisply. He returned the salute and then fainted into the man's arms.

More doorways, a flight of stairs, a large hallway, a long passage. Then into a light, sunny room, the shadows of the glazing bars in the windows making black ladder patterns on a sky blue carpet. Blue and white striped Regency wallpaper, heavy antique furniture, a huge bowl of white lilac and pink tulips on an oval table. It is strange how many powers of observation are heightened at moments like this.

And Daws.

Neither of us spoke, just gazed at the quiet face in the crook of the corporal's elbow. Then the Colonel issued concise instructions and crossed the room to sit in a high-backed chair. I perched on the end of the Chesterfield upon which Patrick had been laid down and placed his hat on a nearby chair, not remembering having picked it up.

"The animal's knee caught him in the chest when it reared," Daws said. "I was watching from the window."

A medical orderly arrived at the double. Patrick's eyes opened when the orderly knelt beside him so he was spared a whiff of sal volatile. There was really not a lot the man could do. The patient was already taking pills for the suppression of pain so an injection was out of the question. After a quick examination to ensure that no further damage had been done the orderly departed, warning against further violent effort.

Daws held out a tumbler into which he had poured a generous measure of whisky. "You appreciate this stuff or I wouldn't waste it on you. Tamnavulin-Glenlivet. Eight years old—eighty per cent proof. Take it slowly and thank me when you feel able."

I became aware of a familiar sound, the homely tick of the Colonel's clock. It stood in a corner to one side of the door behind me, not far from his case of military memorabilia and items from his jade collection.

"I live here when I'm in London," Daws told me upon seeing my interest. "But you're the only two in the department who know so button your lips. It's only two floors from where you saw me yesterday and three from the office of the ragamuffin friend of your husband's who was bullied into this morning's stupidity. With horses at two thousand pounds a head not even chums of Patrick Gillard can allow them to career all over London and risk breaking their legs tripping over tourists without *some* kind of official permission." Like all good raconteurs he paused for effect. "The permission had to come from a rather good friend of *mine*."

But he was smiling.

Patrick gave the glass to me so that I could take a sip, a rare treat. But whisky is not my drink. My experience of single malts is that they are for the educated palate, pleasure coming with time.

"Not to be mucked around with tap water," Daws said severely. "Nor by throwing in sickly stuff out of plastic bottles."

"Thank you, sir," said Patrick.

Daws grunted. "If you want to know why I didn't cheer when that nag belted you in the ribs, I'll tell you. I've had two communications this morning, both intended for you. The first was a telex that had come via Interpol, New Scotland Yard—you name it it had been there—from your Mountie, Le Blek. Tracker dogs have found the grave of that character you knifed. His name was Cody Mullen and he'd been a local hoodlum. There was a cheerfulness in the wording that I found somewhat tasteless. The other was a report over the coded Fax machine from Meadows."

Looking as fragile as spun glass Patrick sat and gazed at him.

"The gist," said Daws, "is that a member of the Russian trade delegation, now expelled from the United States for activities incompatible with his status, was seen at the home of David Hartland some two weeks before he flew out. From the States, you note, not from Canada. He was utterly forbidden to cross borders like that—as you know.''

"The gardener identified him?" I asked.

"Initially. Meadows was given photographs of all the expelled Russians, both from Canada and the States—apparently they were all part of the same espionage cell at home—and these were shown to . . ." Daws consulted a folded sheet of paper he took from his jacket pocket, presumably Terry's report. ". . . William Harper, retired gardener formerly of Ravenscliff. Harper said he thought he recognised three of the men. Upon receipt of this information Meadows then took the photos to the cook who still works for the Hartlands and she positively identified Mikhail Kirov—he walks with a stick apparently, following a car smash last year. She'd returned to the house on her day off to fetch something and saw the man arrive by car and go indoors. She hadn't seen the other two so I'm going to forget them—the old man wasn't that reliable a witness.''

"The Frigate Programme was a gift to Hartland," I said. "Right on his doorstep. How long has he been working for them, do you think?"

Daws said, "I rather think he was recruited with that target in mind. It's been no secret for some time that the Canadians were thinking of bringing their Navy up to date, and also that they haven't built warships for over twenty years. Plenty of ferries and coast guard vessels, of course, but that isn't the same technology. It's really elementary that they would eventually ask for British help—they've bought new submarines from us since the war.''

"But DARE was the real target?"

"Of course. I can't imagine that Canadian frigates are high on Moscow's espionage list." He went over to an old-fashioned bell-pull and gave it a yank. "I hope you aren't going to faint again, Major."

"Margaret Howard was the next victim," said Patrick, who had had his eyes closed. "That was why Mullen had a photo of her in his pocket."

"That had occurred to me," Daws said. "She's probably quite safe now—she rang McAlister yesterday and said she was in California, married that East German of hers. Sorry, I forgot to mention it to you—someone in DARE at Devonport rang my office after you left."

When a steward answered the summons the Colonel asked that a light lunch for three be brought, together with a bottle of Muscadet. Not a lot was said while we waited and I guessed that Daws was hoping, as was I, that food and rest would result in Patrick's feeling stronger. I also had a suspicion that the Colonel was feeling a little guilty, wondering if his savage carpeting was the reason for Patrick's silence. His next remark confirmed this.

"Delayed shock I should think," he said solicitously, "pretty bad to be shot even when you're wearing a flak-jacket."

"That and malnutrition, living on his nerves for weeks, being beaten up and doped," I declared, and then cursed my runaway tongue.

"Oh yes," Daws responded quietly. "He mentioned on the phone to me that he'd omitted it in his report because he'd thought it irrelevant. Doesn't do you any good, of course, but in some individuals can temporarily heighten awareness."

"So you do believe him about Fraser?" I shouted.

"I'm not sulking." Patrick broke in. "And I have forgiven you."

I think it was the first time I had ever heard the Colonel laugh loudly.

CHAPTER 21

Willsworthy, Dartmoor, is an army firing range. The only occasions when its several hundred acres of bog, rough grass and granite are brought to the attention of the general public are when it is actually in use. Prior notice of firing is published in the *Western Morning News* and red flags are flown from various tors. At other times local people tend to forget about it. I know I do. My cottage, two miles from Lydford, lies well within earshot.

Our Gazelle helicopter touched down. A small jolt and the fact that everything in the immediate vicinity became quite level again was the only clue that we had landed, that's if you discounted the lights of a Land-Rover that had guided us in.

"Midnight plus two minutes," said Patrick over his shoulder, shouting above the noise.

I nodded in what I hoped was a business-like fashion and wondered if I was now expected to syncronize my watch and then leave our transport in a forward roll hurling hand grenades. Neither, I saw when he grinned at me. Ye gods, how he loves night flights in helicopters.

I was still very surprised at his secondary reactions to the baby, imagining when the pregnancy was confirmed that I would be confined to barracks with orders to put my feet up. Not a bit of it. He was still overwhelmed of course and I sometimes caught him gazing at me as if I was engaged in great magic. But he had never fussed or been an overprotective person, definitely one to feign deafness, for example, when his spouse was squawking with terror at his side whilst abseiling down a cliff.

We had not discussed what my future rôle was to be but there was an unspoken understanding that I would see this job through. After this, and no longer quite so sylph-like for a while, I could retire to my writing room and try to pick up the threads of *Two for Joy*. Deep down, I had a suspicion that our Canadian frigate assignment might be our last.

"Wakey-wakey." I was offered a hand to help me disembark. Once down a firm grip was kept on my arm until we reached the parked vehicle. Behind us the Gazelle took off again, nearly blowing us over, and was swallowed up by the night and a thin Dartmoor drizzle.

"I get the impression you're dumbfounded that Daws left you with the authority to commandeer transport," I said when we were seated inside the Land-Rover, the driver busy reporting over his radio.

Patrick smiled ruefully. "Officially I'm on sick leave."

"But he is going along with you?"

"That's a perfect way of putting it. He's going along with me. Until I'm proved wrong. If that happens he'll have no choice but to . . ." Patrick shrugged. "That's how it is. It couldn't be any other way. I'm bloody lucky he has so much faith in me."

We bounced off at speed over what appeared to be open moorland, the driver receiving a sharp rebuke from Patrick who reminded him that there were no snipers with night sights on every ridge. The man was therefore slightly startled when we arrived at our destination and he was ordered to proceed with an armed reconnaissance before his passengers left the vehicle.

All having been pronounced safe we entered the cottage. My first, almost automatic, task was to light the Aga, left with kindling, logs and matches ready. The cottage is not quite home without its warmth and constantly simmering kettle, and after the heat of Canada's spring we were both feeling cold.

"My kingdom for a bed," said Patrick, sinking into an armchair. He reached for the phone and was brought up short, wincing.

I passed it to him. "Coffee?"

"Whisky."

"You know you shouldn't."

His glare set me in the direction of the drinks cabinet but he softened it by saying, "I haven't taken any of those damn pills today—they made me feel too sleepy." I glowered myself. "OK. I should have told you. Sorry."

"The medic would have given you a jab," I protested.

"I'm sure he would. But I'd only just come round, hadn't I? And there was Daws large as life in a room God knows where. Right then I didn't altogether trust him not to send me off to somewhere with padded walls and blokes in white coats."

"It was strange how he knew you'd head for that doorway beneath the arch."

"Strange nothing. It's supposed to be one my traits. Something they try to train you out of. An habitual pattern of behaviour that can cost your life. 'Oh yes,' I can hear him saying to his bloody oppo, 'given a spot of bother and none too strong, he'll head for the nearest doorway. Always does, we've been telling him about it for ages.' "

I picked up the crumpled London evening paper I had brought with me. On the front page, below a leading article about a political scandal, was a picture of a man in uniform catching a rearing horse. The headlines read: "Falklands Hero Prevents Carnage."

"Is this the real you?" I asked him. "Or the man with me now who seems to ask for whisky every time life gets a bit rough?" I knew I was being cruel but was only utilising his own methods.

"Neither," he said after a silence. "Perhaps I'll have the coffee."

I gave him a small whisky, sitting on the arm of his chair and kissing his cheek.

"You're coming over all broody," he told me, kissing me back. The next moment the glass and phone had been thrust back into my hands and his gun trained unwaveringly in the direction of the front door.

We both sat quite still in a deathly silence. No, no sound, the ringing noise was in my ears. The front door opened directly into the living room and had a velvet curtain to keep out draughts. Outside it was a small porch, constructed by a previous owner to the same end. From the way the bottom of the curtain was eerily stirring I knew that the outer door was open.

Then, a light knock.

Patrick silently shooed me into the kitchen and stood behind the front door.

"Come in," I called, following a signal from him.

Six months previously Detective Inspector James Hudson had walked blithely into a ruined building in Plymouth and a criminal suspect had leapt at him, armed with a broken bottle. Hudson had survived, saved by a kick in the small of the back that had sent him sprawling at the crucial moment. For reasons unnecessary now to recount the suspect had then died of a broken neck, the man who had saved Hudson being responsible—Patrick. Perhaps this encounter was the reason for Hudson's starting violently when Patrick slammed the door behind him.

"Ye dinna learn," said my husband affably, stowing away the gun.

"Are you allowed to carry that thing when you're off duty?" the Detective Inspector enquired irritably.

"I'm never off duty in the same sense that you are."

Hudson gave him a sour look and sat in the chair he had

just vacated. "I understand that you're looking for a man called Fraser?"

Patrick paused fractionally in moving towards the sofa. "What makes you think so?"

"I was told—by the highest authority. My orders are to make sure you stay right here until I say otherwise." Hudson sat up quickly. "Where are you going?"

"To put the kettle on," Patrick replied from his new course. "Oh heaven be praised—you've been told by the highest authority. Yours or mine, might I ask?"

"Yours. Why are you looking so damned smug?" Hudson was really alarmed now. "I'm warning you, there are two armed men outside."

"I'll make them some tea," Patrick crooned. "Do they take sugar?"

It took a moment for the Detective Inspector to pull himself together and begin to use his brains. Although inclined to be intolerant and over-bearing when dealing with his own staff, he had learned at his first meeting with Patrick that this could be self-defeating with people from outside his circle. In a way I sympathised with him for he loathes the idea of military personnel being permitted to carry weapons on a day-to-day basis. I could imagine him bringing armed men only with extreme reluctance.

"Deny then that Fraser shot you and is responsible for you getting into a lot of trouble," Hudson said, flinging himself back into the chair. "According to my source you've been threatened with court martial if you go after him."

"Most of that is perfectly true," Patrick said, sitting down when I'd intimated that I would provide refreshments. "I know you won't believe it, but I was just going to phone you and ask for your help."

Then he told Hudson everything that had happened in Canada.

Some time later, after several cans of beer, ham sandwiches made with tinned ham and by thawing four slices of bread at a time under the grill, everything had been said.

"How do I know . . . ?" Hudson began, and then threw his arms in the air helplessly. "How can I be expected to know? It's damned complicated and outlandish but has the ring of truth. But you can talk, Major. You'd talk yourself right off the scaffold. If it wasn't the Colonel who spoke to me, then who the hell was it?"

"For a start," Patrick said, "you do know. You know I'm not the kind of guy to go blindly gunning for someone. As to the rest—did he give you a code word of any sort?"

"No—nothing that I can remember."

"Think."

"Something cryptic, you mean?"

"Yes."

"I can't think of anything."

"Then it wasn't Daws. He would have given you his authority code for the day so that you could quote it to anyone who queried what you were doing."

Hudson began to look a bit driven. "Look, I'm a policeman. All this information that you've given me is like news from another planet. On the strength of this phone call during which this character from London spoke to not just me but my superiors, I've been given orders. Those orders are to keep you away from Chris Fraser, a highly respected member of the community in Plymouth. Whether he had a row with you or hatched some plot in Canada is neither here nor there. I'm here to see that nothing happens to him, Rosemary or Rachel."

"No, come to think of it you didn't bat an eyelid just now when I mentioned Rachel," Patrick said shakily. "Please tell me who she is."

"She's Rosemary's young sister. Rosemary is Fraser's fiancée. Their parents were killed in a car crash when Rachel was four years old. Now she's six and Rosemary has to look after her as there's only a brother of eighteen and he's in the Merchant Navy.''

"Rosemary must be a lot younger than Fraser," I said.

"She's in her early twenties."

"Rachel might already be dead," I said to Patrick, but he was shaking his head slowly as I spoke.

"It's a filthy wicked plan," he muttered. "No—they'll all stay alive until I get to wherever they're being held. I assume that's at a safe house somewhere not far from Plymouth. Then they'll be killed and it will be made to look as though I've done it. DARE will be finished—or at least suffer a bad set-back—and D12's name will be dragged through the mud. It'll be the end of Daws for allowing me this much free rein."

"I don't get the reasoning," Hudson said. "I'm here to prevent you doing anything, and even though you're armed and I'm not there are two marksmen covering the only outside door."

Despite everything, Patrick smiled. "One will be on the roof of the barn, the other just behind that handy forsythia opposite the front door. If I climb out of the kitchen window—and I can, I've run this through quite a few times in all sorts of weather—it's possible to knife the man behind the bush before the other one has realized what's afoot. He can't fire at me from there because the angle's all wrong so he'll have to come off the roof. While he's using both hands to come down quietly, I decide whether to finish him off or just hit him on the head with a rock."

"Hypothetical thinking, of course," said Hudson.

"Yes, but only because it won't come to that. You'll allow me to leave here when I want to."

"Now see here, Major—"

"They don't know we've already met," Patrick interrupted in the same reasonable tones. "They can't or they would have contacted someone else. You have a reputation for being tough, that's all. If I'm shot trying to get away from you then so much the better—they fall back on an alternative plan and kill Fraser and the others anyway. Is this safe house in Plymouth?''

''In Devon,'' Hudson replied urbanely.

''Can you contact whoever's looking after them?''

''If I go out to the car. But I'm not going to—I'm going to stay here.'' After a few seconds' silence he said, ''What did you hope to achieve by getting your name in the papers?''

''Mostly to shake my boss rigid—and to force certain peoples' hands.''

''You're really desperate then,'' said Hudson quietly.

''Oh yes—there was nothing phoney about the tears in Fraser's eyes when he told me about Rachel.''

Another silence.

''Come with me,'' Patrick offered. ''I'll give you my gun and you can shoot me if I try to get another.''

''No deal.''

Patrick opened a tin of beer and poured the contents into his tankard with the finesse of a brain surgeon. He then placed the empty can on the table before him, took a sip from the tankard and fixed his gaze on Hudson, frowning slightly.

I have never been able to fathom how this air of brooding menace is achieved. Merely to occupy a room at the same time, even though one knows one is not the person under scrutiny, is uncomfortable. Everyone in the vicinity immediately thinks of small acts of selfishness and bad temper perpetrated over the past few hours and longs to unburden themselves. I am Patrick's wife but suddenly he was too close, too strong and too damn dangerous.

''You interrogate suspected spies,'' Hudson said, his voice sharper than usual. ''What do you do to them?''

''Very little,'' Patrick replied. ''They do it to themselves.''

''Behind locked doors though.''

''No—I always insist on the door being left unlocked when I'm interviewing someone.''

''But there's always a burly redcap on the other side of it.''

"Not necessarily. I always arrange the room so that they have to get past me in order to escape."

Hudson couldn't help it. He smirked. "I seem to be sitting nearest to the door."

"I didn't realize that you were the one wanting to leave," Patrick said coldly.

The pressure went up one inexorable notch and I found myself contemplating begging Hudson to help us. It must be hypnotism, my distracted brain decided when my cat Pirate jumped on to Patrick's lap and his finger gently stroked beneath her chin. She closed her eyes, purring, not party to the conflict but somehow part of the threat. Perhaps it was magic.

"Are the men guarding Fraser armed?" Patrick asked.

"No—it wasn't thought necessary."

"But it was thought that you'd have *me* to contend with!"

"I assure you that everything's in order."

"Go and bloody check that they're OK," Patrick told him in a harsh whisper. "I'll come with you if you like. Handcuff me to the barn door if you'll feel happier."

Hudson's big red hands knotted and I did not have to be psychic to know that he was re-living those moments inside the ruined building. Almost certainly he had been haunted by them ever since he had received his orders. One does not easily forget the flash of broken glass used like a dagger nor the sound that a man's neck makes when it is broken, akin to that of snapping a stick of seaside rock between gloved hands.

"Gut feelings," I said, smiling at him. Not for Rachel nor any other child on this earth could Patrick justify passing Hudson and his men by using violence.

The Detective Inspector climbed slowly to his feet and took a set of handcuffs from his pocket. Then, startling even Patrick, he swore forcibly, threw them on the carpet at Patrick's feet, wrenched open the front door and went outside. He was back very shortly afterwards.

"Nothing." He didn't sound surprised, his voice flat, dead.

I reacted first. "They're not in contact?"

Hudson took a jerky breath. "Perhaps I'm out of my depth. Perhaps I resent taking orders over the phone from some Smart Alec in London. I told them it stank and we were being used."

I noticed that there was a sheen of sweat on Patrick's forehead.

"I can't guarantee your safety," Hudson said. "I haven't said a word. If you follow me I'm not looking in the mirror either."

CHAPTER 22

"I don't believe this," said Patrick.

I wasn't sure that I believed it either. We had driven just over four miles from the cottage along the Coryton road when Hudson's Rover turned into an almost concealed driveway. Two overgrown hedges at least fifteen feet high virtually touched across the entrance.

I drove a little way further along the road and then pulled into the gateway to a field. I switched off the engine and wound down the window a little to listen. It was just possible to hear the other car's wheels crunching on gravel. Then, silence.

Our two back seat passengers prepared to leave, pulling hoods over their faces that left just their eyes visible.

"It's not for me to give you orders or even to say a word," said Patrick, turning in his seat. "But you are not up against armed men of the sort that rob banks or hold up bullion vans. Pretend they're the SAS and you'll get it about right."

"That'll really put the wind up them," I said when they had gone, disappearing silently into the night.

"It was intended to. Hudson should have said it to them."

"He's knowingly walking straight into a trap," I pointed out.

"I realize that. He's a brave bloke with the kind of courage that comes from total lack of imagination. But he still has responsibilities." Patrick opened his door. "Coming?"

"Plan?" I asked, reasonably I thought, when we were standing by the car.

"The usual."

"Is that wise?"

"All right—the unusual. I'll go down the chimney and you drive the car through the living room window."

"Please be serious."

"I can't," Patrick replied. "If they're already dead or I'm wrong on other counts I'm as good as finished. If I think about it too much I'll get the shakes."

With all my strength I slammed him up against the side of the car. "It's a man's world—remember?" I said, somehow keeping my voice to a whisper. "But today's soldier has to contend with subversives and terrorists. Being a hero or getting the shakes under fire doesn't come into it any more. We work in a grey area, with politicians and the police, against dreary small-minded traitors who want Moscow to pay off their mortgages. How dare you become totally duty-shy because a child's been dragged into this assignment."

I'd really hurt him I discerned with a pang when he turned to lean his arms on the roof of the car. The apology was on my lips, anger replaced by shame, when I decided not to utter it.

Even though it was dark I knew that Patrick had turned his head to look at me. But there was nothing else I wanted to say so I walked slowly down the track and on to the road.

The house stood completely on its own. I could remember passing it in the daytime and seeing little more than ornate chimney pots jutting above tall trees. From hazy recollection the drive was semi-circular with two openings on to the road, one of these closed off by rusting wrought iron gates chained together. If my memory was correct, I would reach this one first.

The rain had ceased but the rank grass growing in the disused driveway was soaking wet, instantly drenching the bottoms of the legs of my dark tracksuit. By the gates I stopped, gazing through them up the weed-covered drive, a watery moon illuminating neglect and decay. The detached inner woman who watched, listened and wrote books gave a wry smile at reality's Gothic setting.

I could not see the house from where I stood. There was just the awareness of a dark solid mass in the dense trees and shrubs before me. Then, as I moved slightly, I caught a glimpse of a light. It was not at ground level, perhaps illumination in a first floor room.

Stepping back on to the edge of the road I looked for Patrick. There was no sound, no sign of movement, not even a brief signal from his pencil slim flashlight. I went back to the car but he wasn't there either.

Sixth sense told me that he had climbed over the gate into the field. Carefully avoiding the barbed wire fixed along the top I clambered over and found a lot more wet grass, a patch of stinging nettles and, by one of those crazy shafts of humour that breaks through even murder and mayhem, a ring of about twenty cows all solemnly watching Patrick spending a penny in the middle. They lumbered away as I approached, one lingering animal veering away from me, snorting, after I'd waved my arms at it.

We walked in the lee of the hedge towards the rear of the house. There were no trees hiding it from view here, just overgrown privet and hawthorn, the latter raking us with its thorns as we crawled through.

"Straight in via the weakest door or window," Patrick said in my ear. "A place this size can only be borrowed from time to time so be prepared for outraged residents."

I couldn't stop thinking that this might be the last walk we would take together. There was a clarity in my mind that was recording every detail. Perhaps in the years to come my last memory of Patrick would be this stealthy progress just before dawn in the English countryside.

Dead leaves in the hedge rustled as a breeze wafted through it and my cursed writer's imagination thought of bones and dead things. Patrick was right at my side, I could feel the warmth from his body.

"If anything goes wrong . . ." he whispered.

My heart missed a beat. "Yes?"

"Don't go back through the field. That last one you shooed was a bull."

We went right round the house. It was a rambling two-storey brick dwelling, its brooding Gothic appearance dispelled by the addition of two modern extensions, a kitchen at the rear and a sunroom at the side. The lock on the kitchen door, a cheap alloy device, yielded to Patrick's persistence in about ten seconds flat, causing him to click his tongue disapprovingly.

There was evidence of a meal having been cooked and cleared away afterwards, Tandoori chicken unless my nose deceived me. I shut the door behind me and we both stood motionless, allowing our eyes to adjust to the darkness. After a minute or so Patrick moved carefully to close the slats of the blinds at the two windows. From there he went towards the door, a glass-panelled one through which light shone from a corridor beyond.

In the centre of the kitchen, a large room even by modern standards, was a free-standing breakfast bar and hot plate. This much Patrick's flash lamp had revealed in one quick surveillance. To cross the kitchen one had to go either to the left or right of it, the right being a more direct route. Patrick, being good at his job, went to the left.

I came to the conclusion afterwards that the man hiding behind it refrained from uttering a warning shout to the rest of the household because of supreme confidence he could handle the intruder on his own. Patrick didn't risk a close encounter, just felled him scientifically by a blow to the neck with the edge of one hand. Together we lowered him soundlessly to the floor. There we came upon one of Hudson's men.

"Only knocked out," Patrick reassured me barely audibly. "They must still be using expendable local louts—that lunatic was only armed with a chopper.'' He had caught the weapon before it crashed to the floor, a wicked-looking thing in the glimmer of the flash light, its blade honed sharp.

We went out into the corridor, Patrick seeking and finding the switch that turned off the light. Once again we were in darkness and once again we waited. Murder in the Dark has never been one of my favourite games.

No one came to investigate who had switched off the light. Still we waited. Contrary to some peoples' opinion Patrick does not storm buildings firing from the hip. When engaged in this kind of operation he has the patience of a hunting cat. Over the months I too have learned patience. But I am the fretting sort. I was fretting now.

The corridor in which we stood led into a large, and as far as I could see, rectangular hall. The floor was thickly carpeted and as we moved slowly towards it our feet made no sound. Then I heard muted voices.

I was wondering why no one had been left on guard in the hall when, only feet in front of us, a man crossed from one side of it to the other and went into a room. Light streaming from the door revealed him to be wearing the same kind of clothing as the members of the anti-terrorist branch whom Hudson had brought with him. But this man carried a Russian sub-machine gun.

He came out of the room again and closed the door behind him. His eyes affected by the light in the room he did not see us, but must have heard a faint sound as Patrick stalked him. He began to turn, thus positioning himself for a savage chopping blow to the throat. Within the room the voices murmured on.

Patrick handed me the sub-machine gun and I saw his teeth flash white in the dark as he grinned broadly at me. Oh yes, Ingrid Langley knows how to use one of these too.

We stood one on each side of the door. It wasn't very difficult to picture what was going on inside. A man's voice—no particular accent, ill-educated, amused but tense—was telling Hudson what he would do to Rosemary if the Detec-

tive Inspector's men didn't beat up Fraser. My head swam.
The threat was quite unspeakable.

The voice was not David Hartland's.

"It's only a matter of time before—" Hudson began.

"Your reinforcements arrive?" a woman finished saying
for him. "How predictable you are, Inspector. Are they all
as efficient as the ones who were guarding this house? Or the
man who, for all his training and equipment, succumbed to
being hit over the head with an axe?" She laughed. "I can't
get over what you've just told us—Gillard putting himself
back in hospital over that stupid publicity stunt."

"I earnestly advise you to abandon this dangerous and
stupid undertaking," Hudson said furiously. "There's absolutely no chance of it succeeding."

The woman laughed. "Listen to the man. We *have* succeeded. This is the final stage—the rewards after all the risks
and hard work. Do as my friend says or I'll fetch the brat
myself and pull all her hair out."

"He's taking his time," someone grumbled.

Soundlessly Patrick left my side.

"Rachel's done nothing to hurt you!" cried another
woman, at a guess, Rosemary. "You've got what you want.
You've ruined DARE. Killed all those people. Why does she
have to suffer too? She's only a little—" She shrieked, and
there was the sound of a blow.

"Bastard!" yelled Fraser. "You stinking yellow bastard!"

Then Rosemary began to scream.

"Stop it!" Hudson roared. "All right! Only leave her alone."

All at once I felt so weak my legs nearly gave way. I turned
and was confronted by a dark figure, the head hooded with
just two eye holes. By the time I had controlled a cry of pure
terror I realized that it was Patrick.

He laid a restraining hand on my arm as Hudson was forced
to give orders. The Detective Inspector had to repeat them,
shouting, and there was a protest from Fraser.

"You disobeyed orders," the woman said.

The sickening sounds commenced and it seemed as though hours passed as we stood there having to listen to them. Then the man spoke, harshly, telling the policemen to hit Fraser harder.

Patrick's grip on my arm tightened but I knew that this was involuntary. He was hardly aware of me, concentrating instead on reactions and mood inside the room. The grip became like a vice when one of the policemen swore in protest and then cried out as he himself was struck.

Patrick turned the handle of the door and pushed it wide and they were all so engrossed in what was happening that for a moment or two no one noticed him. Then Rosemary gave a little scream of fright.

"Where is she?" the man said.

"Hiding," said Patrick in his own voice but so coldbloodedly that Rosemary began to cry.

"Isn't the door locked? What the devil do you mean she's hiding?" shouted the woman.

From my position to one side of the door I could see Patrick and now, as he turned to face the speaker, the expression in his eyes was unreadable.

"The door's open. There's no key in the lock," said Patrick. "Perhaps you didn't . . ." He left the rest unsaid, shrugging disinterestedly.

"Go and find her," the woman spat. "If you come back empty-handed consider yourself fired."

Patrick shrugged again and turned on his heel. As he came through the doorway he switched off the light. He dived to one side as the shooting started.

Shoved backwards by my working partner I made myself very inconspicuous in one corner of the hall, the one I had chosen while we were waiting. This was necessary as the individual firing through the doorway was doing so utterly at random. My mind seemed to be full of stabbing jets of flame and the sound of bullets tearing into woodwork and smashing glass.

Silence but for Rosemary's sobs.

The one who had been firing walked into the hall to see who he had killed.

"Get him," Patrick said in a low cold voice.

I thought of Rachel and aimed low, scything the man's legs from under him in a short burst. He crashed down. I ran and picked up the fallen weapon by its webbing strap and was just behind Patrick when he burst into the room and put on the light.

Images crowded into my brain. A beautiful black-haired young woman crouched over Chris Fraser who was lying on the floor. Two men dressed in dark blue sweaters and jeans steadying between them another with blood running down his face, but just about to let him go and tackle the fourth man swinging a gun in Rosemary's direction. And Hudson, already launching himself at the armed man.

Two shots fired simultaneously.

The gun pointing at Rosemary fell, blood-spattered, to the floor. Another, still directed at Patrick, was re-aligned for a second shot.

I hit Emma Hartland on the back of the head with the barrel of the sub-machine gun I was holding and then let go of both weapons, staring at Patrick as he lay on the floor.

"No! No! No!" I heard someone scream. Perhaps it was me.

I got to him first and pulled the hood off his head.

"Where is he hit?" Hudson said, picking himself up.

"Get to the child!" Patrick shouted at him. "There might be others."

We were all stunned, I think, and when a small person presented herself in the doorway, sleep ruffled, her dressing gown on inside out, nobody moved.

"There's a lot of noise," said Rachel.

This observation was quite unanswerable.

"Why are you lying down there?" she said commandingly to Patrick, seemingly oblivious to everyone else.

"I fell over that stool," he told her.

"There's a nice man upstairs who's been telling me stories. He said we could go home soon. Can we? He made me promise to stay in bed when he went away but I wanted to know what was happening. Will he be cross?''

Rosemary went to her and hugged her, controlling her emotion in a way I was quite unable to emulate. Then she took her upstairs to get her dressed.

The storyteller appeared in the hall, giving the man I had shot, who was moaning loudly, a cursory glance. ''I've called in, sir,'' he said to Hudson. And then, with a darting glance in the direction of the stairs, ''Himself's on his way. Can't say he's too pleased.''

Grunting, Patrick got to his feet and slid the stool over which he had tripped beneath a table.

I stepped over Emma Hartland who was not unconscious but pretending she was hurt, and went into the hall. The wounded man when he saw me clutched at his right leg and recovered sufficiently to call me several names. But in the end he saw the folly of kicking in the teeth a potential lady with the lamp and became sullenly co-operative as I bound up the flesh wounds in his legs with clean tea towels from the kitchen.

Whilst thus engaged, and thinking of a small girl with freckles, a snub nose and fiercely spiky plaits, I became aware of a proprietorial presence slowly descending the stairs. He came, monacle screwed into place, sparse white hair standing on end and a vivid blue dressing gown combining to remind me of a variety of crested cockatoo.

''What the deuce is going on down here?'' roared this feast for the eyes. ''Are you in charge here?'' he bellowed to Patrick, glimpsing him through the open door.

Patrick glanced at Hudson who remained tongue-tied. ''It would appear so, Your Grace,'' he murmured, doffing an imaginary hat in a courtly bow.

It was not the first time his phenomenal memory for names and faces has got us out of trouble.

CHAPTER 23

"The Hartland woman's dotty if you ask me," said Colonel Daws. "She said she despises everything her husband's doing—thinks it's a huge joke that she was running her own little counter-network right under his nose."

"Only someone a little mad would have risked everything by coming to this country to finish off the job," I said.

We were in Daws' elegant living room, as before with the sun streaming through the windows, a glass of whisky in Patrick's hand as he lounged on the Chesterfield. But this time he wasn't in uniform nor even wearing a formal suit, he was on holiday and attired accordingly. So was I. We had brought Rachel to London with us for the day.

She sat at Patrick's side, carefully sipping orange juice. I found it absolutely right that so far she had resisted every attempt to remove her from her new best friend's side. When they walked her hand slipped into his; if they sat down then she made sure she was close without actually touching. For Rachel was a lady in the making, not one to romp, fidget, or climb on people.

Patrick was utterly captivated.

"There's a little cat over there," she said suddenly, pointing.

"It's made of jade," Patrick said. "Very old and precious."

"You can go and look at them," Daws told her.

A peremptory hand was held out. "You come."

"I'm tired," Patrick said, yawning. "Count them and tell me how many there are."

"It's actually a tiger," Daws said eagerly, jumping up and acting as escort. "If you look very closely you can see the stripes."

I could not imagine the collection ever having been subjected to such a close scrutiny.

"That's the wonderful thing about jade," said the Colonel, reseating himself. "You don't have to be a collector or even an expert to enjoy it." And then, more quietly, "Has Fraser recovered?"

"He wasn't really hurt," Patrick replied. "Even the nasty bit of work who made them do it knew they were pulling their punches. It was most peculiar how his nose got broken while he was waiting for an ambulance. No one saw it happen."

"I'm sure they didn't," Daws said with a thin smile. "Especially after he'd pistol whipped that constable across the face."

I thought about the various modes of leadership. How Hudson had proffered his handkerchief to staunch the flow of blood to a man too shocked to take it from him, only to have Patrick snatch it and soak it with vodka from a bottle on a nearby trolley. After a mouthful from the same bottle, his face swiftly swabbed and cleaned to reveal a small but deep cut, the patient was laughing at himself with his colleagues because of the way he had yelped when the spirit bit into the wound.

"Exactly who was this character Emma had hired?" I asked.

"An East End racketeer down on his luck," Daws said with disgust. "From what I can gather she just went into a pub somewhere in Bow and recruited her little army. The thugs were his bodyguard and came as a kind of optional extra. Really—this is quite appalling. It'll be the end of Hartland's career.''

''Hatred,'' Patrick said. ''She hates and despises him. He's receiving treatment for impotence yet there was a family scandal not all that long ago concerning his secretary in Montreal.''

Sitting on the floor, clasping her knees, Emma had said to me, ''You amazing creature. You followed him around Canada like a donkey on a piece of string, and yet now you look quite at home with that gun in your hands.''

I hadn't replied.

''She was recruited last year,'' Daws said, reaching for a folder on his desk and opening it. ''There was some kind of embassy party and she was approached by a contact . . .'' He whipped off his glasses and surveyed us in some distress. ''Dear God, when are some of these folk in Six going to dig a little more deeply into the sexual proclivities of the partners of their staff?'' The glasses were slid back on to his nose, long enough a pause for Patrick and I to exchange sideways glances.

''So she wrote two letters to Fraser?'' I asked. ''One to produce to start a panic and the other for his eyes alone, threatening Rachel?''

''Yes,'' Daws said. ''It was made quite clear that if he took both letters to the police the child would be killed. Even if she was placed under police protection she would not be safe. It was a threat for life—if he didn't obey instructions, Rachel's life was forfeit in perpetuity.''

The young lady in question was carrying on a long conversation with the jade animals.

''Quade was killed to give the threats credibility and Emma Hartland an excuse to get all the DARE engineers under her roof,'' Daws continued. ''Incidentally she's volunteered all this information quite readily—there'll be no need for her to be interrogated by a real professional.'' Another thin smile in Patrick's direction. "I can arrange it though. I'd be interested to know her real mental state."

Patrick said, "A shrink would probably say she is a manic-depressive. My conclusions are that she hates men but can't do without them. No, sir, if you don't mind I'd rather never clap eyes on the woman again."

After a short pause Daws said, rather grudgingly I thought, "The case did have its share of red herrings. First of all Rogers ate the clams that almost killed him, and then Margaret Howard was reported to have added something to his coffee."

"She must have given him a sweetener by mistake," I said. "According to the same source she hadn't offered to make the morning coffee before so it was an understandable error. Meanwhile Emma was recruiting the Gaspereau brothers to do her dirty work and one of their arch enemies to murder Lanny after he'd killed Quade. I'm still surprised that David Hartland didn't suspect what she was up to—especially as she was passing notes to Fraser with instructions."

"Too trusting, I expect," Daws commented. "Some of Six's operatives—how shall I put it?—in a career cul-de-sac are true blue and all that, but a trifle blinkered. Haven't moved with the times. Still firmly entrenched in the old boy network way of working."

Somehow I succeeded in concealing my smile.

"He knew that she was carrying on with other men though," Patrick observed quietly. "The picture you've just painted doesn't represent the man that we came to know in Canada. I'm not altogether happy that he hasn't been brought in for questioning, even though I can't see Emma covering up for him."

"There's time yet if it's thought necessary. My guess is that he'll end up as tea boy at the trade legation in Bolivia. Pity really, a woman bringing a man right down like that."

"Do we know who sprayed acid over Fraser's cars?" Patrick asked suddenly. "I'm presuming that Emma only recruited her latest band of thugs since Fraser returned home. And another thing . . . How did she know that the Duke of Bridestowe lent his home to the police for use as a safe house?"

"It's one of M16's safe houses too, must have heard about it from Hartland," Daws explained. "The old boy used to work for them—probably commuted on horseback. As to your first question, I've no idea. You'd need to ask the local police."

Patrick's tendency to frown politely can be more exasperating than downright argument.

"You're on leave, Major," Daws reminded him gently. "Enjoy it."

"I'd like ten minutes alone with that cipher clerk in Six who forgot to clear us with Canadian security," he said, unrepentant.

The Colonel smiled, humouring him. "He's already admitted responsibility and is likely to be demoted. What's the problem?"

"How do they work?" Patrick said. "Would the necessary permission be requested directly from the Canadians or would the message go through the intermediary? Was Hartland that link? Was the clerk bribed to say he'd forgotten?"

"I appreciate your concern for future missions," Daws told him. "But in the meantime there's nothing to worry about." He stood up. "How about lunch? I should imagine that young lady is hungry. My nieces and nephews always are—eat me out of house and home when they come to stay."

I simply couldn't believe it when he gave Rachel the jade tiger.

I was in euphoric mood as we all walked out into the sunshine. It was one of those late spring days when the sky is really blue, the sun hot and only occasionally disappearing behind small fluffy white clouds. All the blossom trees in

London seemed to be in full flower, new leaves on the trees shiny and perfect, as yet untouched by gales and dust. It had rained in the night, washing stone clean so that the buildings glittered in the sunshine.

We had decided to walk to the restaurant where Daws was taking us to lunch, a short journey across St. James' Park. There was a lake with hundreds of water birds, flowers and a man selling balloons. Patrick bought Rachel a silver heart-shaped one and suggested that he look after the tiny jade tiger which she was holding in one hand. She entrusted him with it without hesitating and I wondered, briefly, how old she would be when she realized its value.

Slightly overawed by the Colonel, she chose to hold my hand and the men went in front. Watching them—Daws unmistakably from the military even in a neat pinstriped suit, Patrick strolling with his arms loose at his sides, always careful never to look like a soldier when not in uniform—I was struck by the fact that this was only the second time we had met Daws socially. In actual fact I knew very little about him other than that he was a widower, was in his early fifties, and played squash and swam to keep fit.

From what I could hear of their conversation they were talking about gardening.

The feeling of being out in the open, naked and unprotected, came from nowhere. It was as unwelcome as it seemed to be unwarranted, and to banish it I drew Rachel's attention to a swan stretching its neck to take bread from a child's hand. "You're just pregnant," said my sensible inner voice, "pull yourself together."

Ostensibly looking at the flowers, I gazed around. There was nothing upon which I could hang my nameless fears. Londoners were enjoying the sunshine, lying on the smooth grass, sitting on the seats eating sandwiches and feeding the sparrows and pigeons. Someone was buying a balloon from the balloon man.

We turned on to a patch that led in the direction of Birdcage Walk. A hundred yards further on this merged with a wide road—one of several that are restricted to parks department traffic only—that led to the western entrance. The wrought iron gates were open, no doubt to admit the lorry we had seen carrying grass cutting equipment.

The balloon man was still walking behind us.

My lips were suddenly dry and wouldn't whistle but I achieved the first few bars of Colonel Bogey, our warning signal, swung Rachel up in my arms and then saw a car swerve widely into the park entrance and speed in our direction. I ran, not looking at Patrick but aware of him grabbing for his gun.

I had almost reached the comparative safety of the ladies toilet when I was knocked over. By a miracle Rachel landed on her feet, stumbled and tottered into the arms of a park attendant.

"Hide her!" I yelled at the startled man. "In the gents. Anywhere! Get her away from here!"

I couldn't get up and the sky was full of coloured balloons.

For the first time I became aware of shots being fired. I twisted round, noticed with total disbelief a small pool of blood on the ground, and then my attention was caught by what was happening behind me.

The balloon seller was dead, flung backwards like a starfish, his wares caught in trees or going skywards. The Colonel, flat on his front on the pavement, gun gripped in both hands, seemed to have just shot him. There was blood on one of his sleeves. Patrick was down on one knee, also holding his Smith and Wesson two-handed, aiming at the car which had mounted the pavement and stopped, the driver slumped over the wheel. Getting out of the car, his hands making peculiar snatching movements in the air, was David Hartland.

Coldly, calmly, Patrick put three bullets in him.

Then he came over to me, slowly, and I have never seen such fear on a man's face. I sat up, wondering vaguely how

I could stop the thick rope of blood that was running down from a hole in my calf. I conjured up a smile for him. Behind him Daws was getting to his feet.

"We're a good pair now," I said. "We'll both dot and carry on the right leg."

"Is that the only place you're hurt?" He was so tense he could hardly speak. "When I saw you fall . . ."

"Yes. Perhaps if you tie your hankie round it I won't need a gallon of blood."

He swore, half in tears, half laughing, applying a tourniquet and kissing me all at once.

The police were arriving.

Daws approached, brushing himself down, and then winced as he moved his left arm. "So Hartland *was* in it as well," he said softly.

"He was surrendering," Patrick said, equally quietly. "I murdered him."

A few seconds went by during which I saw Rachel being given into the care of a policewoman. She did not seem to be unduly upset.

"I murdered him," Patrick repeated.

Daws pondered for a moment and then went over to where the balloon man lay sprawled on the pavement. He gazed down at him briefly before stepping into the road and giving David Hartland's body the same scrutiny. On the way back to us he paused to show his ID card and speak to a police sergeant with electric effect.

"I dropped the balloon seller before he had the chance to fire again the Mauser he had pulled from his pocket," he said regarding us both carefully. "Luckily for everyone the pin stayed in the grenade Hartland was holding. Luckily for you Major," he added.

The numbness was wearing off in my leg to be replaced by something quite excrutiating. I began to shiver.

"Otherwise I might have been forced to lie and say that I'd killed him," the Colonel observed, his tone severe.

"Surely I shouldn't have to lecture you of all people on allowing your feelings to take control."

Kneeling beside me on the pavement, Patrick also shivered.

It was another week before I found out where Patrick had been during those two lost weeks at the beginning of April. He had flown to the States and visited the clinic where he had been fitted with his artificial leg for a minor repair. Also, in his other rôle as my agent, he had purloined the rough draft of *A Man Called Celeste* from my desk and sold the film rights.

About the Author

MARGARET DUFFY lives in Ayrshire, Scotland with her family. A MURDER OF CROWS, her first novel featuring Patrick and Ingrid, was also published by Fawcett. She is currently working on a new adventure for the pair.